As noted in the afterword, the foundational premises of this novel are based on documented research.

For we wrestle not against flesh and blood, but against
principalities, against powers, against rulers of darkness
of this world, against spiritual wickedness in high places.
—EPHESIANS 6:12

There are two equal and opposite errors into which
our race can fall about the devils. One is to disbelieve
in their existence. The other is to believe, and to feel
an unhealthy interest in them. They themselves are
equally pleased by both errors and hail a materialist or a
magician with the same delight.
—C. S. LEWIS

The
Canary
List

Sigmund Brouwer

The
Canary
List

A NOVEL

WATERBROOK
PRESS

The Canary List
Published by WaterBrook Press
12265 Oracle Boulevard, Suite 200
Colorado Springs, Colorado 80921

ISBN 978-0-307-44646-6
ISBN 978-0-307-72951-4 (electronic)

Cover design by Mark Ford

Published in the United States by WaterBrook Multnomah, an imprint of the Crown Publishing Group, a division of Random House Inc., New York.

WaterBrook and its deer colophon are registered trademarks of Random House Inc.

Printed in the United States of America
2011—First Edition

10 9 8 7 6 5 4 3 2 1

Prologue

S he knew that they hurt him, because he told her, always, the mornings after he was returned.

She was the only one he trusted. She was five and he was four, and each time, when he would be returned to the house, it seemed he had grown smaller.

Black walls and candles, he said. Hoods and robes, like the scary people in Scooby Doo cartoons. Except it wasn't a cartoon. He couldn't describe what the people in hoods and robes did to him because he would start shaking and sobbing.

He told her it must be something they ate that made them so mean to him. Hales.

She didn't know what hales were and neither did he. But he told her about two pieces of wood crossed, and how they trampled it and kept repeating about the hales they had ate in, but he never knew what they ate the hales in, because they never finished explaining. They just said 'hales ate in' and left it at that.

On the last night she saw the boy, she was in his bedroom. They heard the car drive up and looked out the window and saw it was them again. She had his toy bow and arrow set and she vowed to him that she wouldn't let them take him again.

She was ready when the man in the mask came into the bedroom. She aimed the arrow at the eyes of the tall man and the rubber suction cup of the toy arrow hit him squarely in his left eye and he cursed and lifted the mask and rubbed his eye before he realized that she was the one who had fired the arrow, not the boy. He dropped the mask into place and, with a snort of rage, stepped forward and swept her away with a blow across her face.

"I am The Prince," he said as she struggled to her knees. He moved to stand overtop of her. "Bow to me."

His face. She had seen it before. He was someone she saw at church on Sundays. In a robe at the front, handing out bread to people at the front as they bowed down in front of him.

She did not want to bow.

She rose anyway and on his leg.

He lashed out again. She tried to scream, but the pain was too great.

Another man in another mask stepped into the bedroom and pulled him away. Then they took the boy.

She never saw the boy again. He went to live at another house, the people at the house said.

The man with the mask came back. He wore the mask while he hurt her again. He promised if she told anyone, he could come back and kill her and then kill the people of the house.

So she didn't tell anyone. She tried to believe it was a dream. A very bad dream.

But some nights she would wake up and shiver and cry and wonder where the boy was. And she would wonder too what hales were and what they ate the hales in and how it was that hales could make people so horrible.

Chapter One

E vil was hunting her.

It had driven her toward the beach, where protected by the dark of night, Jaimie Piper crept toward the front window of a small bungalow a few blocks off the ocean in Santa Monica.

It was wrong, sneaking up on her school teacher like this, but she couldn't help herself. She was afraid—really afraid—and she wanted his help. She had to make sure he was alone. If he was with someone else, she wouldn't bother him.

The sound of night bugs was louder than the traffic on the main boulevard that ran crossways to this quiet street. It was June, and the air was warm and had the tangy smelly of ocean. The grass was cool and wet. She felt the dew soaking through her canvas hightop Converse sneakers. Jaimie wasn't one to worry about fashion. She just like the way the sneakers felt and looked. Okay, maybe she liked them too because none of the other kids her age wore them.

Jaimie was twelve. Slender and tall, she had long, fine hair that she tended to wear in a pony tail with a ball cap. If she let it hang loose, it softened her appearance to the point where others viewed her as girlie, something she hated. The alternative was to cut it herself, because her foster parents didn't like wasting money by sending her to a beauty salon, but cutting it herself would just remind her that she was nothing but a foster kid, so she just let it grow. And wore Converse sneakers that looked anything but girlie.

Not only wrong to be sneaking up on her teacher's house, but wrong even to know where he lived. But his wallet had open been on his desk once, with his driver's license showing behind a clear plastic window, and she'd read it upside down while she was talking to him and had memorized his address.

Although this was the first time she'd stopped, she had ridden her bike past his house plenty of times, wondering what it would be like if she lived in the little house near the beach.

It wasn't the house that drew her. It was dreaming about what it would be like to have a family, and it seemed the perfect house for a family with a mom and a dad and a couple of girls.

A real family. A house that they had lived in for years and years, with a yard and a couple of dogs. Beagles. She loved beagles.

Her mom would be a little pudgy but laughed all the time. Jaimie didn't like the moms that she saw who were cool and hip and trying to outdo their daughters in skinniness and tight fitting jeans.

Her dad would not have perfect hair and drive a BMW. Jaimie didn't have friends, because Jaimie wasn't a friend kind of person, but she knew girls at school with dads like that, and those girls didn't seem happy. If Jaimie had a dad, he'd be the kind of guy who went to barbers not stylists, and had hair that was always a couple weeks past needing a barber, who wore jeans and didn't tuck in his shirt and always dropped everything to listen to whatever story his girl wanted to tell him.

A dad like Mr. G, her teacher. He drove an old Jeep, the kind with canvas top and roll bars. Sometimes she'd see a surfboard strapped to the top of it, canvas top gone.. Mr. G had that kind of surfer dude look, with the long hair and a long nose bent a little. Not perfect kind of handsome, but a face you still looked at twice. Some of the girls in her class had a crush on him.

Not Jaimie.

She just wished she could have a dad like him and house like the house that he lived in and sometimes when she was really lonely she would ride her bike in the neighborhood, pretending it was her home and that when she got there, she'd be able to wheel up the sidewalk and drop her bike on the grass and leave it there, because in her family, no one got upset at little things like that.

It wasn't that she just had a good feeling about him.

It was that Jaimie knew Mr. G could be trusted. Jaimie had a sense about people, a sense that sometimes haunted her.

Like tonight, the guy who had gone to her house to talk to her foster parents. She'd watched his eyes as he checked the layout of the house. She'd felt the evil that radiated out from him.

So while he was talking to her foster parents—and this was just as dusk was turning black—she'd snuck out of the house and jumped on her bike and begun the twenty-minute ride from the large old house toward the ocean where she often snuck at night anyway to walk the beach.

But the feeling of evil was so real she couldn't shake it.

She wanted—no needed—to talk to someone about it. Wanted—no needed—to feel safe. Somehow.

She made it to the side of the window. She inched her head to peek through the glass.

There was a single candlelight.

With Mr. G at the couch. Holding a big book open in his lap.

She watched, knowing she shouldn't watch.

It looked like he was talking to the book.

And then he glanced up, and for that split second, it seemed like he was staring right in her eyes.

Chapter Two

Two hours into the one night of the year that Crockett Grey set aside to get as drunk as possible, he felt like someone was watching him and looked up to his long-dead daughter peering inside with, yes, a haunted look of desperation.

Crockett was only a quarter through a bottle of Laphroaig, still able to enjoy the single malt's peaty-smoky flavor roll over his tongue, each sip still giving him a warming finish that deepened the intensity of sadness that came with missing Ashley, a blanket of grief that covered him daily, as he woke or began to sleep.

He would have preferred to get drunk every night, but that would have cheapened his grief and reduced Ashley's memories to a foggy haze. It would have also stopped him from being the best father possible for his son Mickey. So much as he wanted the crutch of alcohol, Crockett allowed himself to get drunk one night a year, an anniversary that marked the horrible night when Ashley slipped away from him into the eternally black chasm. Nanna, the elderly widow next door with whom Crockett had become friends while helping her with yard work and house maintenance, knew Crockett well enough to respect his solitude the day before, the day of, and the day after the anniversary of Ashley's death.

Crockett lived in a two-bedroom cottage he rented from Nanna, on a large lot in Santa Monica a few blocks from the ocean, built just after the second world war. The hardwood floor was not level, but the simplicity of the house suited him, and he had decorated it accordingly. Three times already Nanna had turned down obscene offers from couples who wanted to knock down the house to build a MacMansion among the palms that had been there for half a century; she didn't like change, and she liked having Crockett as a neighbor.

He sat at the corner of a black leather couch, with the bottle of Laphroaig set beside a large flickering candle on the table beside him. The candlelight was girlie; he knew it and didn't care. Couldn't have a vigil without candlelight. In his lap was the photo album.

He sipped at the scotch, testing the sensation on his tongue. He knew from the year before, and from the year before that, when he could no longer detect the smokiness, he'd be one stage closer to passing out.

By the candlelight, he saw one of the rare photos of him with his ex-wife, Julie. Most were of Ashley, or Ashley with Julie. Not Mickey; he hadn't been born yet. Crockett had been designated family photographer, which made him largely invisible in the accumulated years of memories.

It was a beach photo. Crockett remembered the day, when a passerby offered to take the picture. On the beach at Paradise Cove, north of Santa Monica on the Pacific Coast Highway. He was sitting on a towel, in swimming trunks and a hooded sweatshirt. The wind was throwing grains of sand against his skin, tugging at his hair. He had cared enough about vanity then that he was proud to wear his hair long. Julie was on a beach chair beside him. Her hair fine and cinnamon, tanned lean legs and a flat belly, in a bikini, a body that drew second and third glances, even when she held Ashley, who then was just beyond toddler, chasing gulls all day in the cove. Here, some eight years later, the candlelight made it difficult to see any of the photos with precision—that was the point of candlelight—but Crockett knew what brightness of day would reveal in the photo. Both of their faces locked into a timeless moment by the camera lens, faces that showed no awareness that the future held anything but joy.

Then he saw Ashley at the window. Long hair and wide eyes. A shimmering image that forced him to blink.

The face was still there.

At first, there was disbelief.

Then the insanity of hope. Except when he stood to run toward the ghost, he knocked the candle over along with his glass of Laphroaig.

But the time he'd managed recover from this, the image at the window was gone.

Chapter Three

C andlelight cast gargoyle-like shadows that were barely visible on the black painted walls in the small room. The celebrants wore pointed hoods to conceal their faces. Anyplace else and any other time, this would have been a parody of the grotesque.

But this was not playacting.

Ten of them. Breathing and sharing hot humid air, adding to the heightened sense of the forbidden.

The celebrant, the priest, wore over his robe a chasuble with the Sigil of Baphoment—an inverted pentagram. Starting from the lowest point and reading counter-clockwise around the five points of the pentagram were Hebrew letters that translated in Leviathan, the beast of Satan.

Beside him, the thurifer, who carried the metal canister at the end of a chain that burned incense on a hot piece of charcoal. And beside him, the illuminator, who held a single lit candle for the reading of the texts.

The remaining candlelight came from the altar, beside an upside down cross. Near the upside down cross, a chalice of blood, and beside that, a rough loaf of black bread.

The scent of that burning incense added to the swelling sensation of the atmosphere, and the Black Mass began, as a gong sounded, and the celebrant intoned:

In nomine Magni Dei Nostri Satanas. Introibo ad altare Domini Inferi.

Madelyne Mackenzie was among the ten in the congregation at this, the witching hour. With them, she responded:

Ad eum qui laefificat meum.

The celebrant said:

Adjutorium nostrum in nomine Domini Inferi.

Then Madelyne and the others, in the hushed tones of heightened awareness:

Qui regit terram.

Madelyne knew what was coming next, and kept her hooded head bowed as the words filled the room, seeming to swirl with the smoke of the incense.

"Before the mighty and ineffable Prince of Darkness," the priest said, his voice somehow soothing and rumbling and erotic all at once. "And in the presence of all the dread demons of the Pit, and this assembled company, I acknowledge and confess my past error. Renouncing all past allegiances, I proclaim that Satan-Lucifer rules the earth, and I ratify and renew my promise to recognize and honor Him in all things, without reservation, desiring in return His manifold assistance in the successful completion of my endeavors and the fulfillment of my desires. I call upon you, my Brothers, to bear witness and to do likewise."

With incense swirling through the candlelight in ghost-like vapors, the congregants shivered and exhaled in anticipation.

That's when Madelyne felt the vibration.

It could have been interpreted by the others as a shared visceral reaction to the calling of demons to witness how the next moments of worship would unfold at the altar, but Madelyne knew differently.

The vibration was nothing darkly spiritual.

Instead, it was a cell phone. Strictly forbidden. And strapped to the softness of her inner thigh by a wide band, well hidden beneath the robe. Inconceivable that she would answer it.

Each vibration sent a rush of adrenaline through her body. Intellectually, she knew no one in the room would notice. Emotionally, however, she suddenly felt as if she were the woman exposed on the altar.

No one around her shifted or stirred however, and she prepared herself for what held this small congregation in thrall.

The impending ritual of sacrifice.

Chapter Four

Two homeless women found Jaimie Piper at the phone booth, just after midnight, only a half hour after she had ridden her bicycle away from the small bungalow that she knew would never be a home for someone like her

These tattered women were like lepers, undernourished from years of drug abuse .

Jaimie backed away as the two of them tried to crowd her with zombie-like certainty toward the massive pilings of the Santa Monica pier, where she had been killing time while waiting for Dr. Mackenzie to answer her phone. Four attempts she had made already. Dr. Mackenzie had promised Jaimie that she would always answer no matter what. Except now that no-matter-what had arrived, all Jaimie got was voicemail.

And now she had these homeless women to worry about.

They showed no sense of excitement as they closed in on her just beyond the beams of a security light; these creatures were souls in bodies that had long ago given up on the luxury of anticipated pleasure.

They didn't waste energy on the enjoyment of threats either. Hawks in the air shriek to startle their prey; vultures descend in unified slow circles to pluck and tear at their leisure.

One of them cackled and reached for her arm and felt her bracelet at the end of his clawing fingers. She pulled hard, as if expecting a snap. But this bracelet was a band of curled smooth metal. It slipped away from Jaimie so effortlessly, that the momentum of his pull startled the woman, and the bracelet flew from her fingers and bounced across the pavement, clanging into the side of the dumpster.

The bracelet didn't drop, but clung to the metal.

Jamie felt the hunter again, as if Evil had flowed from the man at her foster home into the other homeless woman, who began shaking, like she was having an epileptic fit. She screeched a few words and her hands darted in erratic circles, aimed at Jaimie.

It was like an electrical shock to Jaimie.

"You!" Jaimie said. "You're one of them. I can feel it!"

The homeless woman was one of the people that Dr. Mackenzie had talked about, people who caused Jaimie's horrible feelings of darkness. Jaimie hated those feelings. She hated Evil.

Since her meetings with Dr. Mackenzie, Jaimie had begun to wear a crucifix on a chain around her neck. She held it up in front of her and began a chant, the way that Dr. Mackenzie had taught her to deal with Evil.

Padre nostro, che sei nei cieli, sia santifico il tuo nome...

The homeless woman gave an unearthly snarl and lurched forward to claw at Jaimie's face. But she was old and uncoordinated and probably more than a little drunk. Jaimie ran as hard as she could into the woman's body, catching a whiff of stench, and spun past her, sprinting to safety on the beach.

From a safe distance, she watched. These homeless women were too broken to chase her.

Eventually, they moved on, hyenas scuttling sideways back into the darkness.

She waited until she knew they were clear, then returned to the dumpster. The bracelet clung to it as if glued there. Finally she pulled it loose and snapped it around her wrist.

Evil was continuing to stalk her.

She knew it. She didn't know if she'd be able to make it through the night.

Jaimie was shaking again.

She wanted what she'd felt at the window at the house of the small bungalow.

Calm and peace. And the knowledge that Evil could not touch her there because of how good the man was inside the house.

Chapter Five

When Crockett again saw his dead daughter peering through his window, it came with a rapping of knuckles against the glass.

By then, Crockett had managed to reduce the Laphroaig by another half and he was quietly weeping, engaged in imaginary conversations with Ashley. A few times in this drunken monologue, he'd included Mickey, his five-year-old son, as if Mickey were there too. Introducing Mickey into the imaginary conversation would reduce to Crockett to hiccups of weeping. So amazing to be the dad of a little boy, but why God, couldn't he also still be the daddy of a little girl?

When the knocking on the window sounded, Crockett had already set aside the photo album with reverence, leaving it open on the coffee table. He had a box for it, and in the morning, it would go into the box, and the box would go into the attic. For another year.

On the couch, with the candle's wax spilling onto the floor, he had allowed himself to roam through memories, letting the tears spill without wiping them away, allowing the sensation of bitterness that he tried to keep at bay the rest of the year.

Bitterness.

Crockett had always believed that he was laid back by inclination, but twelve years earlier, becoming the father of a beautiful girl had introduced

him to the unpleasantness of a worry list. Worries that she'd run out on the
street at the wrong time. Worries, for crying out loud, that if he didn't clean
the lint from the dryer screen it might catch on fire and he'd be unable to
rescue her from a burning house. The list was a long one, but well worth the
trade off—it was there because he loved his daughter beyond life.

Nothing dramatic had taken her. Just an on-off switch in a protein in
a cell somewhere in her body, triggering the insidious attack of cancer. All
his worries had consisted of items that if he was vigilant enough, he could
prevent. He was her daddy, but he'd been helpless to protect his little girl
from the real enemy.

A year after she'd died, a sheet of newspaper had blown into Crockett's
face while he was sitting cross-legged on the sand at the beach, head bowed.
Not in prayer. Anything but that. The sun had been bright, and his eyes
needed a break from staring at the ocean water. He was in that out-of-body
state between consciousness and sleep, barely aware of sweat trickling between his shoulder blades.

A gust had thrown the paper into his face with a snap, and naturally
startled him.

A small headline had grabbed his attention as he began to crumple the
page.

"Baby falls from five-story balcony."

That's what the media does, he thought. Draws us in with the misery
of others. Who wouldn't read a story about someone who backed up his
SUV and ran over his own child in his own driveway? Something to cluck
about by the water cooler, a way to feel righteous that you wouldn't be that
careless when it came to something as precious as your children.

Or the media drew us in with that other great mesmerizer. Fear. Threatened us with embedded headline words like *might, could, possible.*

There had been a time in Crockett's life when he dismissed each of those threats with counter phrases. *Might not. Could not. Possibly not.* When he'd point out that the number of good deeds in a single day outnumbered the bad headline deeds by such an incredible percentage that it was only an illusion that the world was a horrible place to live and getting worse every year.

On the beach, snapped out of drowsiness, given his vow not to read again, he would have continued crumpling the paper, except for the smaller headline underneath. "Firefighters express disbelief at baby's survival."

The back of the baby's diaper had first caught on a spike of a high fence that surrounded the building. That slowed the fall enough that when the baby landed on his butt, the diaper, totally full, had literally exploded like an airbag, cushioning his impact.

Others might have found it funny, the image of a shower of baby poop, with a happy baby unscathed in the center of the mess. Others might have found a measure of joy, imagining a relieved mother lifting the baby to gives thanks for divine intervention.

Not Crockett. The article had just made him bitter. What had been the odds? First snagging the spike with the back of the diaper, instead of impaling the poor child. And then the baby landing butt first.

This capriciousness was a result of external actions imposed on the children. How about the capriciousness of a gene programmed from conception to lurk for ten years inside a little girl—his little girl—until it begins a blossom of death? Someone explain that.

Crockett didn't believe in heaven or any of the other platitudes; laughing and crying with Ashley in the altered reality of drunkenness was as close as she could come to accepting any resurrection of his daughter, giving himself a moment where, eyes closed, he saw Ashley outlined against the fireplace in her much-too-small flannel Dora the Explorer pajamas she wouldn't give up. Mournfully drunk and immersed in memories, he was listening to Ashley lisp her way through a Christmas song, during that all too short period between losing her front teeth and growing new ones.

Then, the knocking at the front window which sent Ashley hopelessly out of reach. Crockett's first reaction was drunken fury at the intrusion, driving him to his feet, sending him to the window with the candle in his hand.

What he saw instead in the light of the flame was Ashley, her face framed by long, straight hair that he had once enjoyed watching his wife brush.

The main level of the house was set above a crawlspace, so in the window the girl's shoulders were barely above the bottom of the window frame.

Feeling like he was spinning, Crockett knelt, so that inside the house, his eyes were level with the girl's. Crockett stared, trying to shake off the juxtaposition of this face against the one he'd been clinging to. He took a swig of his scotch, nearly emptying the bottle.

Unlike before, the face didn't vanish.

Instead, the face stared back. Blurry. And he finally realized the long straight hair belonged to someone else.

"Mr. G, it's me, Jaimie."

Jaimie Piper. One of his ABC students, from a classroom of seventeen whom he had prodded and cajoled and defended from the bureaucracy for the previous ten months. Crockett taught the ABC kids in the upper elementary school. Twelve-year-olds. Adaptive Behavior Classroom. A labeled classroom filled with kids with labels. ADD. ADHD, and the rest of the acronyms that were in fashion these days.

No way would he share his evening with Jaimie, Crockett told himself. It was the end of the school year. His responsibilities only went so far.

"I'm scared," Jaimie said, her voice muffled by the glass. She brought her hands up, placed her palms against the window in supplication. "I need you. Just till morning."

Chapter Six

Crockett opened the front door, and Jamie bolted inside and hugged him.

This was a first. Jaimie was not a hugger. She was a loner, someone who shunned others as much as they shunned her.

Crockett knew Jaimie's file. Foster kid. Lived in a home with seven other foster kids. The female foster parent was a tiny middle-aged woman who seemed to vibrate with stress. Crockett had never met the husband who was unemployed, but given the thirty-five bucks per day per foster child payment from the state, Crockett couldn't help but cynically wonder about the numbers, since the yearly revenue for housing the kids was over a hundred grand. Lots of room to skimp on the kids in a situation like this. In an essay on where she lived, Jaimie had described an old, big three story house with narrow hallways, peeling wallpaper and lots of tiny rooms.

The more important part of Jaimie's file, however, was the psychological assessment. Her parents had been killed in a car accident when she was only months old. She had spent her entire life in the system.

Given all that was stacked against her, Jaimie had only been trouble for him once in the classroom. September. On the playground, one of the boys had taken her bracelet, run away with it. She'd chased the boy to the chain link fence where a homeless person had begun howling at Jaimie to taunt her, clinging to the fence to try to get at her. She smashed the homeless man's fingers with a baseball bat.

Crockett's big triumph with Jaimie had been to introduce her to reading. She'd gone from nearly illiterate to bookworm, and Crockett was convinced it happened because of the simple argument that he'd presented to Jaimie. Books are friends; there whenever you are lonely or afraid. Only trouble was that fiction seemed to feed Jaimie's near pathological urge for solitude.

"Jaimie, Jaimie," Crockett said. He was sure his words were slurring. Just thinking that phrase was difficult. *Schlure that he was schlurring.* "You shouldn't be here," he said slowly.

Drunk or not, Crockett was acutely conscious that he was a thirty-five year old man, and a twelve-year-old girl was now alone with him. A student. In his house. At night. Careers of any kind ended because of situations like this.

"I didn't want to come," Jaimie said, still clinging to Crockett. "But I was too afraid to sleep in a park."

Crockett gently disengaged her, tried to draw a deep breath. It only made him queasy.

"Sit," Crockett said. "Sit. Sit. Sit."

Jaimie stepped back and looked up at him quizzically.

Crockett could only guess that he had just schlurred the command to sit.

"On the couch," Crockett said, confused and frustrated. He enunciated the sibilant "s" as carefully as he could. "Sch…. Um, sit on the couch." Why this? Why now? One thing to send Lisa on her way. But a frightened child? Even one who spooked herself with too vivid of an imagination?

Sit, sit, sit, Crockett muttered to himself.

Jaimie moved to the couch, and Crockett walked the short—mercifully short—distance to the kitchen. Advantage of a small house.

A glass of water later, Crockett felt better composed. Not even close to sober, but composed. He returned to the living room. Jaimie was sitting as small as possible on the couch. She was wearing jeans and a dark hoodie, and she was sitting with her knees drawn up, inside the hoodie, stretching it, with her arms inside the front kangaroo pocket of the hood, tight around her knees.

⸺

Jaimie didn't hear Mr. G come back to the couch. He caught her looking at the open photo album. She flipped it closed, the way it was when he'd left her on the couch.

Mr. G sat on the couch with her, but gave her lots of room.

She really liked Mr. G. He was nice but you couldn't fool him. He let you get away with stuff that didn't matter, but didn't let you get away with stuff that did matter. Mr. G had made her start reading books and it turned out he was right. Books were like friends and books were cool. Especially *Black Beauty.* It was one of her favorite books. And *Anne of Green Gables. Black Beauty* because of the horse, and *Anne of Green Gables* because Anne didn't have parents either. It would be cool if Mr. G adopted her, but that would never happen. And all the kids in class knew that Mr. G had a girl who died and it had messed him up. Jaimie had just seen the girl in the photos. Longhair like Jaimie's, but the girl in the photo had a face that seemed like it had never been touched by anything dark; Jaimie knew her own face was different. Jaimie knew a person had to always be on guard. It made her instantly sad for Mr. G, thinking that a girl as nice as the one in the photos was dead. She'd seen the tears on his face when he opened the door. It wasn't hard to guess he'd been looking at the photos and thinking about her.

If Mr. G was mad that she caught him crying or looking at his photos, he didn't say it. He was frowning though. Jaimie guessed it was because Mr. G was drunk and was trying to concentrate on what to say. She knew all about drunk people. But she didn't think Mr. G would hit her. Drunk people, she had decided, just became more of what they really were. Mean people showed more of their meanness. Nice people became happier.

Mr. G? He was mostly sad. So she guessed getting drunk just made him sadder.

She waited for him to speak.

"Tell me what happened," Mr. G said. "Why are you scared? Why aren't you at home?"

She couldn't tell him the truth.. The scary truth. That she could feel Evil stalking her. That always inside was something dark and angry that she pushed down. Like a thundercloud. At the edge of the sky. Getting blacker and blacker and boiling upward. That's what it was like inside her. And that sometimes around certain people the thundercloud mushroomed out of control, dark and scary as she got closer to the person who added to the feeling that she tried to keep pushed down. When a person like that got near, the mushroom started in her chest and went into her head, and it hurt her head and her brain like it was going to explode, maybe like the egg she'd once put into a microwave. It would make her so afraid, like the other person knew she could feel the badness and the person would want to hunt her down. It felt like the darkness was going to pounce on her and suck out her brains.

She couldn't tell him about Evil, the hunter, because he would think she was crazy. And because of Jaimie's deal with Dr. Mackenzie, who had made Jaimie promise to keep everything secret about the stuff they were doing to fight Evil..

"I snuck out of my foster house," Jaimie said. "I do that a lot on weekends because I like to ride my bike to the beach at night. I went out through a window and climbed down a drainpipe. But tonight some home-less people tried chasing me and now I'm too scared to be alone, so I rode my bike here. I didn't go home because after midnight their security systems goes on automatically and stays on till six in the morning. "

Part truth. Part lie. Best way to do it.

"You said you trust me," Mr. G said. "So please listen to me. You need to get back to your foster parents. I'll call them. They'd rather know the truth than have you alone at night."

She shook her head. "You don't know my foster parents. I feel safe around you. I just need a place to stay. One night. In the morning, maybe you can take me to Dr. Mackenzie. That's all I need. Time here, safe, until she answers her phone."

"Dr. Mackenzie."

"She helps me with a lot of things. But I can't find her."

"We're going to call your foster parents," Mr. G said.

Jaimie quivered.

"They'll be worried about you," Mr. G said to enforce his argument. He was blurring his words, and she had to work hard to understand him. "Maybe they've already called the police. They'll need to know you are safe."

"Call them, but let me stay with you." Jaimie wished she could tell Mr. G the truth. But Dr. Mackenzie was right. He probably wouldn't believe her anyway. That sometimes the feeling of darkness was so real. "Just till the sun is up. Please."

"Your foster parents will stay awake with you," Mr. G attempted. "We'll explain to them how you feel. They'll know what to do. Their job is to protect you."

No, Jaimie wanted to say. They can't. Not from this. No one can. The only way is to be out of reach. It was like she swam all alone in a room without walls. Black. With a howling cold wind. And something hunting her, something Evil.

"Mr. G," she said. "They aren't as nice as you. When you break their rules, they get really, really mad."

"Then let me call them to let you know you are here."

"Please don't."

"I'm getting my cell phone," Mr. G said. "I think I left it on the bathroom counter."

It was a small house. Just a living room and a kitchen and three doors she saw from the kitchen. One open, to the bathroom. Two other doors that she guessed were bedrooms. She watched Mr. G walk unsteadily to the bathroom. He left the door open and the house was small enough she could see him throw cold water over his face. A couple of times. He dried off as he swayed in front of the mirror.

She went outside. Jaimie never cried, but maybe now was the time to pretend. No way could she go home. She needed Dr. Mackenzie and a way to stay safe until then. If the darkness could find her on the beach, it could find her anywhere.

She buried her head in her hands and thought about how nice it would be not to feel the scary darkness and how nice it would be to have a family and she allowed herself to feel sorry enough for herself to cry.

Mr. G sat on the steps beside her.

"Don't call them," Jaimie said. "Just let me spend the night. I need to sleep without being afraid. It's been so long since I could. Please. Just one night."

"It won't solve anything," Mr. G said.

"This can't be solved," Jaimie said. It could, if only she was able to reach Dr. Mackenzie. "I just want to feel safe for one night."

"Your foster parents will know what to do," Crockett said. "You just have to tell them."

Jaimie straightened to look at Mr. G. Maybe he knew she was putting it on a bit. She recited her phone number in a monotone.

Mr. G had to ask Jaimie to repeat it. He fumbled as he slowly punched in the numbers. Listened to the ringing. Ten rings, no answer.

She could hear the ringing too.

Mr. G hung up the phone.

"It's not appropriate for you to be here," Mr. G said. "So we are going to go get someone else."

Chapter Seven

Nanna opened her door in a bathrobe—red and fuzzy. With a face like hers she could have modeled for a cake mix box. Apple cheeks, soft white hair. Round eyeglasses. He knew he'd woken her, but nothing about her smile showed it.

"Didn't check the peephole, did you," Crockett said, slightly more sober. He'd installed it in her door himself a month earlier because she refused to spend money on nonsense, which was her word for security technology.

"I most certainly did," she said, grammar correct despite the hour and despite her indignation.

"I had my thumb over it. Nanna, it's midnight. You can't just open your front door without knowing who is on the other side."

"I refuse to live my life in fear either." She frowned. "What are you doing? It's your anniversary night."

"Need help," Crockett said. He pointed at his front step, where the outdoor house light showed Jaimie sitting, hunched over. "Actually, she needs help. She's twelve. Ran away from her foster home."

In her bathrobe, Nanna marched past him without asking who the girl was. She walked across the lawn that separated the two houses. Nanna had a vigorous step for any sixty-year-old, and Crockett knew she was at least eighty.

When Crockett got to the step, Nanna already had her arm around Jaimie, and was leaning in, whispering.

"Leave us be," Nanna told him.

—◦—

Five minutes later, Nanna found Crockett in his refuge, a hammock he had hung in the back yard. Crockett had been staring at the stars, thinking about the illusion of how cold the light looked, when the source was an incomprehensibly hot process of nuclear fusion. Thoughts to take him away from memories of Ashley since his memorial evening had become a train wreck.

"We're going to her house, all of us," Nanna said. "We're going to talk with her foster parents. No child should be as terrified as she is. If her foster parents can't help the poor child feel better, we're taking her back to stay with me for the night."

Crockett rolled out of his hammock, fighting a wave of queasiness and fighting the urge to explain Jaimie's file–and compulsions–to Nanna. He had sobered somewhat, but his digestive system was punishing him for the excess. He was too exhausted to complicate things any further.

"You drive," he said. He didn't have to specify that he meant his Jeep. Nanna only had a motorized scooter but every once in a while, she borrowed his Jeep. Eighty plus, but she loved the stick shift and the wind in her hair.

"Yes, I'll drive," she said. "You can sleep in the back seat. The top is down, right?"

"Right."

"Good. I'm not fond of the smell of scotch."

Crockett tried to doze off as Jaimie gave directions, but the motion of the Jeep made him feel too nauseous. So he sat, head hanging like a dog. He wished he'd thought to bring a bottle of water.

"It will be fine," he told Jaimie as they slowed for a red light, and he could be heard above the wind noise.

"That's an idiotic thing to say," Nanna told Crockett. She was still in her bathrobe. "If it was fine, she wouldn't feel as bad as she does. You and I are going to do our best to help her feel better, but don't make promises you don't know if you can keep."

Crockett swallowed back another wave of nausea with a side of pride. Perhaps it'd be better if he just kept his mouth shut.

Nanna spoke to Jaimie. "You've probably already discovered that men can be well-meaning, but totally clueless."

Crockett didn't mind when the Jeep picked up speed and the sound of their conversation became an unintelligible buzz.

It wasn't until they approached the foster home that Crockett understood why no one there had answered the phone.

Flashing red and blues.

The foster home was almost burned to the ground.

Chapter Eight

Two cruisers blocked the entrance to the street. Five houses down, high arcs of spray from fire truck water cannons were clearly visible, as were the flames shooting from the roof.

It jolted Crockett into a new level of near sobriety.

Crockett glanced at Jaimie, who was now sitting rigidly upright

Nanna downshifted the Jeep and found a place to pull over. Not an upper end neighborhood by any stretch. Best it had going for it were the mature trees in the yards.

"You talk to the police," Nanna said. Up and down the sidewalks, bystanders were clustered in about a dozen groups. Few gave the Jeep any attention, even those so close that Crockett could reach out and touch them from curbside. "I'll wait in the Jeep with Jaimie. But make sure you protect her first. Don't give her up unless you know she's going to be protected. Last thing she needs is a night at the firehouse."

Crockett had to push through a small crowd to reach the cop holding all of them at bay. Neighbors. Easy to guess. Many of them, like Nanna, in bathrobes, strobed by the red and blues, their faces craned as they stared at the burning roof.

"No one past this line." The cop was impassive. Young. Standing straight, taking his command post seriously. A fleeting thought hit Crockett. He was old enough to be in a position where a rookie cop was young to him.

"I'm a teacher of one of the students who lives there," he began as introduction, showing he wasn't just a rubber necker.

"Have you been drinking?" the cop asked.

"Yes," Crockett said. "A lot. But I haven't been driving. I wouldn't be here unless it was important. Trust me, I'd rather still be drinking."

"What do you want?"

"Need to talk to the student's parents."

"Not a chance," the cop said. "Anything you do now will just get in the way. We're not even sure if anyone got out."

"It's a foster home," Crockett said. He swayed slightly.

"Yeah?"

Crockett was about to explain that one of the kids was back in his Jeep. Even in his haze, he realized he'd have to explain she was a runaway. He wasn't worried about himself. Nanna's presence made everything above board. But if he told the cop about Jaimie, given the circumstances, the cop would have to make a call, bring in social services. Which would mean Jaimie would spend the night with strangers, on top of her fear and on top of the stress of knowing that the home was on fire. Nanna had warned him against that; not good, when Nanna got angry.

So he'd allow Jaimie to become Nanna's responsibility for the rest the night.

"Let me give you my name and number," Crockett said. "Have someone call me in the morning when this settles. It's about one of the kids in the foster home."

"Yeah." The cop's expression remained flat. But he took out a pad and wrote down the information.

Nathan Wilby had killed his mother , just after he turned eighteen. He'd put a pillow on her face, as commanded by Abezethibou. Mostly Nathan thought of his demon as Abez, but when Abez knew Nathan was reluctant to do something, the demon seemed to swell with power and invoked his entire name. As in, *I, Abezethibou, command you to follow my instructions.* And on that night just after Nathan turned eighteen, Abezethibou had commanded Nathan to put his full weight on the pillow until his mother stopped moving. Nathan had been surprised by his own indifference to the way his mother flopped until she died, but it made Abez happy, who had cheered him on the entire time.

Ten years of prison after that. It wasn't a bad time. Regular food and exercise, continuous protection by Abez. Since then, in his years outside, managing a trailer park, Nathan sometimes missed the comfort of his prison cell with Abez prowling the confined space.

Now Nathan stood among the gawkers. To see clearly, he needed to be at the front. He was so small that he could have been mistaken for a boy.

Abez roamed up and down the street with a shambling walk like a lop-sided chimpanzee. Abez was missing his left wing, so keeping his balance was difficult. Nathan didn't know any other demons, so he assumed this deformity was the main reason for Abez's irritability. Much as Nathan had appreciated Abez's protection during the years in prison, there were times when Nathan would not have minded a break from his cantankerous and constant conversation.

Now Abez bounded toward Nathan, energized by something.

"Look," Abez said, his head waist high to Nathan and turned upward to speak. It was strange to Nathan. It seemed like he never got a full view of Abez. It was like Nathan's eyes could only focus on one part at a time. When he looked into the hideous face, Abez's stumpy wide body seemed to shimmer into the background. When Nathan gave attention to the one leathery wing that curled around Abez like it belonged to a bat, the potato face would be gone. Nathan had long ago accepted this strangeness as part of a demon's character. He couldn't ask other people about this, because they didn't see anything when he pointed to Abez.

"She's back," Abez croaked. "I told you she escaped the house when you went inside. I told you she didn't die in the fire. We know everything."

Sure enough, one of the street lights showed a Jeep Wrangler had just arrived. Driven by an old woman, with Jaimie in the back seat.

This was good. Very good.

The Prince had been very specific when he told Nathan that tonight was the night to start the fire and get rid of Jaimie. Jaimie had a psychiatrist protector but The Prince knew that tonight, the psychiatrist would be too busy to help.

Usually, Nathan didn't like to think for himself. He preferred instructions and doing exactly as The Prince requested. But if Jaimie had escaped the fire, Nathan needed to take care of this. There wasn't time to arrange to talk to the Prince to ask what to do. Sometimes it took days for him to hear back from the Prince.

The Prince had told him a lot about Jaimie, and he would use the information to his advantage. So now all he needed to do was make sure he didn't lose sight of her.

Chapter Nine

Another knock on Crockett's front door.

This time, just after dawn. He'd fallen asleep on top of his bed, still in jeans and tee. He felt like someone was trying to punch holes through his skull with splinters of wood.

There was no choice but to answer the door. He'd given the cop his name, address and phone number.

He swung his legs over the edge of the bed. From the kitchen, he heard his coffee brewing. Automatic timer, set for 6:45 a.m.. Good. He'd pour a cup, let the thick black coffee travel directly into his veins and jolt him out of his grogginess.

But first, the door.

Where Jaimie darted inside and ran past him, into his bedroom.

So much for the coffee.

He followed, and saw her heels disappear as she slid beneath the bed.

"Jaimie?"

"Don't ask me anything. I just need to hide. Here. He was talking to Nanna and I heard him and felt his evil and ran here because I know he was hunting me. Help me, Mr. G."

That's when the doorbell chimed.

All Crockett wanted was coffee.

Crockett opened the door to a bland man, so little he almost qualified for petite. Maybe Crockett's age, dark hair slicked back, parted in the middle. Grey suit, cheap shiny material, like something bought at Wal-Mart. Shoes to match.

"I'm Nathan Wilby," he said. "I'm from social services. Brad Romans sent me. May I come in?"

Nathan's voice, deep and strong, surprised Crockett. Nathan extended a hand. In reflex, Crockett shook it, discovering a surprisingly powerful grip too.

Over the man's shoulder, Crockett saw a Ford Taurus, a couple years old, parked at the curb. Crockett backed up enough that Nathan Wilby could stand inside the house.

"Horrible thing last night. Just horrible." Nathan dropped his voice to a whisper. "I think it's going to be rough on her. You made the right decision last night, but we'll need to take over from here."

"Last night."

"I saw you there," he said. "With her. I'd been called over by the police. By the time I could get over to you, you'd already left in that Jeep."

Crockett's head throbbed. He really wanted his coffee. He could smell it, freshly brewed, just waiting. Ten minutes, the house would be all his again. Coffee. Newspaper. Time to recuperate, then off to the zoo with Mickey to be a weekend dad. Usually, he picked Mickey up at eight a.m. and they went for breakfast at Denny's, but Crockett knew ahead of time he would be hurting because Crockett knew it would be the morning after the anniversary of Ashley's death and he'd arranged to get Mickey later in the day, with his ex-wife Julie pretending not to know why Crockett would be late when all the other times he was there five minutes before the permitted time to get Mickey.

Nathan must have misinterpreted Crockett's headache frown for an unspoken question.

"It took some time first thing this morning to track you down after that," Nathan said. "You really should have stayed and let the police know she was with you."

"So that someone could take her away?" Crockett said.

Nathan gave Crockett a tight smile. "But there is the unavoidable creaking of bureaucracy. Someone at the top could look dimly at this. After all, she is a minor. You had no authority to make the decision."

The accusation didn't surprise Crockett, but it was nonetheless frustrating. "I didn't have the authority, no. But it's what a decent person would do." He held his ground against the smaller man's stare. "I'm sure someone at the top wouldn't like any bad publicity either. A respected teacher of troubled kids helps out one of his students in need, then gets hassled? And someone at the top might not like a person in the middle of the bureaucracy who forces the issue upon the top."

The bland little man coughed slightly. "Good. Then we see it the same way. I'm not interested in paperwork either. You would be welcome to come downtown with me and Jaimie. She is here, right? I just saw her go into the house. From next door."

"No," Crockett said. "I mean yes. No, I don't need to go downtown with you. Yes, she's here. She spent the night next door with my neighbor, an older woman."

"Of course," Nathan said. "Understandable."

"I'll get her," he said. "Wait here. On the couch, if you like. Help yourself to coffee."

"Certainly." But as Crockett walked the few steps to the bedroom door, the bland dark-haired little man remained where he was, smile plastered as securely across his face as his hair was plastered back against his skull.

Chapter Ten

Crockett knelt beside the bed. When he ducked his head to look underneath, a tsunami of queasiness washed over him.

"Don't send me out there," Jaimie whispered. "Please."

"Jaimie," Crockett said. "We don't have a choice. Where else can you go?"

"Anywhere. But not with him. He is Evil."

"Jaimie," Crockett softened. "Listen to me. You might not like social services, but it's a fact of life. We don't have a choice."

"Send him away," Jaimie said. "Then I promise I'll go. I have some money. I'll find a way to make it on my own. Dr. Mackenzie will help me."

Crockett vaguely remembered Jaimie mentioning the doctor last night. "Who is Dr. Mackenzie?"

"A friend. I know how to get to her. I can go on my own."

"You are twelve. On your own is not going to happen."

Crockett extended a hand beneath the bed. "Come on. I'll help you out from under there, Jaimie."

"Don't try to make me go out there, Mr. G. I'll bite. You can't give me to him."

Crockett sat down, his back against the bed. He heaved a long sigh.

As he was deciding how to handle this, Jaimie wiggled out from under the bed. She looked forlorn and so small in Nanna's spare pajamas.

"He's gone," Jaimie said.

"What? Jaimie, he's…"

"Out the back door."

Crockett pushed himself to his feet. He glanced at the backyard. The gate at the rear fence was just swinging shut.

And the doorbell chimed yet again. He decided then and there that the first thing he would do when all this dust settled was rip out the wiring to the doorbell.

Chapter Eleven

Two people this time. An Asian woman in tan pants and a sweater introducing herself as a homicide detective, Pamela Li, and a tall man, thick dark hair cut short, relaxed smile, jeans and an untucked light blue shirt, telling Crockett he was from social services.

Before Crockett could ask, and that was the first thing he had intended to do this time, they offered identification.

He only glanced at the ID long enough to confirm their names. Pamela Li. Thomas Blearey.

Even with that casual glance, Crockett knew it was like closing the barn door after the horses were gone. He should have asked Nathan Wilber for identification. These two were legit. Why else would Nathan Wilber have bolted? From the living room window, he would have seen the unmarked police cruiser pull up in front of the house. If he was legitimately from social services, he would have stayed. He would have also offered identification.

Concluding Wilber had been posing as social services was one thing. The bigger question was why.

"Hold on," Crockett told them both. It was beginning to feel like the night before. Tossed into waves of events that made no sense, getting rolled by the uncontrollable. He hadn't asked for this. A psychologically troubled kid on his doorstep in the middle of the night. Same kid now under his bed. It briefly occurred to him that Jaimie's resemblance to his dead daughter had clouded his judgment, but he told himself that he would have acted the same despite her appearance. What else could he have done?

Now it seemed like the chain of events was beyond choice. Or maybe he felt like this because he wasn't sober yet. At this point, he needed to cling to one sure thing.

"I'm getting coffee," he told them. "Either of you want one?"

"Black," Thomas said. "Thanks."

"No," Pamela said. Not, *no thanks.* Crockett's acuity was dulled by his aching head, but not so much that he missed the unfriendliness.

He went to the kitchen, knowing it wasn't good that Jaimie was in the house. In the bedroom. Would be stupid to try to hide it. Too bad they hadn't seen her leave Nanna's house on the way to his house.

Crockett returned to the living room with two full mugs, thinking that he should set up some groundwork before telling them where Jaimie was.

Pamela and Thomas were already sitting, a clear indication this was going to be a long conversation. But Thomas rose politely to accept the coffee before joining the detective on the couch.

That left the remaining armchair in the living room for Crockett, his back to the bedroom where Jaimie had insisted on hiding when the doorbell rang.

"Jaimie's a frightened kid," Crockett said. "Frightened kids don't always act rationally."

A frightened kid in his bedroom. Didn't look good, and he knew it.

Pamela didn't give him room to follow up on that opening as an explanation for why Jaimie was in Crockett's bedroom. "Yes, we know you were at the fire with her last night."

Crockett nodded as he took his first sip of coffee. Few things had tasted better. "You see—"

"I presume it was after the party, right?" Pamela pointed at the near empty bottle of scotch. "Hope you took a cab."

"Neighbor drove. Nanna. Where Jaimie spent the night. She—"

"Very responsible. We like citizens like you." Her tight smile suggested otherwise. Why was she so surly? And so insistent on keeping him off balance? He didn't need this. What he did need—with a degree of desperation—was a pair of sunglasses because the light through the front window was going to remain painful until at least a third cup of coffee. Crockett attempted to fix that small problem by drinking more coffee before answering.

"Jaimie was terrified last night," Crockett said. "Maybe I made the wrong decision, taking her away from the fire, but I wasn't thinking very clearly last night and I was trying to do what seemed best. And this morning—"

"Best being a drunk teacher out with a young female student?"

"Not sure why you're ripping me like this," Crockett said. He had no energy to fight. "I know a bit about Jaimie's background. Tough life, being a foster kid. Can't you understand that she when she asked for help, I couldn't just walk away? And this morning—"

"I'm not in a mood to mess around," Pamela snapped. She noisily blew air through her mouth, venting frustration. "Two kids in that house almost died. Smoke inhalation. And the foster dad is dead."

Dead. Crockett hated that word. Never seemed real, until it was far too real. Another one toppling into the eternally deep chasm of silence.

Pamela continued. "Early investigation shows that the fire started in Jaimie's room. We've got social services here for a reason. I've seen her file. No one's going to be surprised if Jaimie's the arsonist."

It began to sink in for Crockett . "When did the fire start?"

Pamela gave him the time.

Crockett slowly did the math. Slowly, because it was all that he was capable of at the moment.

"It wasn't her," Crockett finally said. "She told me she snuck out before the security system at the house was set. She was here already when the fire started."

"The house didn't have a security system," the detective said. "If it did, the foster dad might still be alive."

Crockett was trying to process Jaimie's lie when Pamela gave Crockett a look of scornful pity. "And you don't have to be there to start the fire. Any kid with a computer can Google a dozen ways to delay it. And if she wanted the one place in the house where a timer would wait for half an hour, her bedroom would be it."

"She's a good kid," Crockett said. And at this moment, under his bed. He had to get that out there, but couldn't just blurt it. "When kids are frightened—"

"She lied to you about the security system," Pamela continued. "The fire in her room wasn't an accident and that makes this a homicide investigation. So let's get back to the fact that you're the guy who showed up last night and left in a hurry. A guy who showed up intoxicated."

"I'm the guy who left my name with a cop."

"Intoxicated."

"With nothing to hide. Which is why I admitted to the cop last night I was intoxicated. If you don't believe me, let's go next door and ask my neighbor. She'll tell you that Jaimie spent the entire night with her."

"Funny how last night you didn't mention your neighbor to the cop. Or the fact you had the girl with you. But instead took off in a hurry. That leaves me with questions."

What was frustrating to Crockett was that the detective was so wrong in what she was implying. Crockett wanted to clear this up and have the house to himself. But he was highly aware that Jaimie was in his bedroom right at this moment. How was he going to explain that? Especially with the detective pushing him so hard.

"When Jaimie showed up here last night and this morning," Crockett told the detective, "she told me she was scared and wanted a place to stay. Last night, the first time she came to me, I tried calling the house. No answer. I thought it would be responsible to get her home. We showed up at the fire, and, to repeat, I made a judgment call that it would be best for her to spend the night with my neighbor. Then, just before you got here, for the second time when Jaimie—"

"Makes me wonder about your motives." Pamela cut him off, then turned to Thomas. "Any thoughts on this?"

"It's not a black-and-white world," Thomas answered. "We're here to get the girl now. Maybe it wasn't so bad that she didn't have to spend the night dealing with bureaucracy."

"Why would the girl come to you in the first place?" Pamela asked Crockett.

"I'm her teacher. She trusts me."

"All your students have your address? You give them an invitation to show up at all hours of the night?"

"I don't know how she had my address. Can you stop treating me like the bad guy here?" It was a plea, not a challenge. Crockett should have reacted with anger, but was too exhausted.

"Maybe you are the bad guy here," she said. "I had a look at your employment record."

"Huh?" If his blood wasn't moving through his veins like sludge, maybe he could make sense of what was happening.

"You know what I'm talking about. Sierra Rhimes. Thirteen at the time."

"Huh?" Crockett had felt stupid saying it the first time, and no less stupid the second time. But he knew what the detective was implying. "That has nothing to do with this."

He felt, though, like he was struggling through a swamp. Sierra Rhimes. Four years earlier, the student had been a nightmare for all three of her male teachers. Including Crockett.

"From my perspective it has a lot to do with this," Pamela said. "Think cops don't have access to computer records?"

Crockett needed to dilute the sludge in his veins. He drank more coffee before answering. "It was established that Sierra Rhimes made false accusations. You know as well as I do that this happens a lot. All of the teachers involved were cleared. Completely cleared. She made her claims against us in retaliation for bad grades. You did see that too, on the computer records. Right?"

"It's time to speak to Jaimie," Pamela said. "You said she's next door?"

"You'll remember I said she came over twice. Once last night. And once this morning. She's not next door." He'd wished he'd been more forceful earlier, when he tried to tell the detective about Jaimie's immediate location.

"Where is she?" Pamela said. "Much as we appreciate do gooders who help scared kids, it's called aiding and abetting when the kid is a murder suspect."

Before Crockett could answer, the bedroom door opened.

"I'm here," Jaimie said. "But Mr. G didn't aid and abet me or whatever. And I didn't start the fire."

Chapter Twelve

Pamela Li didn't hide her disgust at Crockett.. "I thought you said she stayed overnight next door."

Although Crockett had done nothing wrong—in fact he had done everything possible since Jaimie's knock on the window to ensure none of his actions could be misinterpreted—he knew he was walking through a minefield. "Yes, she was next door. With Nanna. I was trying to tell you that she came over, but you were cutting me off every time I—"

"What was she doing in your bedroom?" Pamela said.

"See. Again." Crockett said, trying to tame–and mask–his feelings of panic. "You going to give me a chance to talk?"

Pamela gave a rolling forward motion with her hand.

Crockett wanted to lash out at the detective's arrogant presumption of Crockett's guilt, but didn't see that doing any good. Important thing was to establish that he was blameless of anything except being in the wrong place at the wrong time, and of showing compassion to a troubled student.

"Jaimie came here from next door. She said she was afraid. I let her into the house and—"

"He's right," Jaimie said. "I was afraid and—"

"Not talking to you," Pamela told Jaimie. "This is between me and Mr. Grey."

Anger finally overcame his exhaustion and Crockett snapped. "Hey, lady, if you'd step back for a second and quit thinking the worst, I'll have a chance to explain."

"Call me lady again, and your day is going to get a lot more miserable."

"Talk to Jaimie like that again, and I'll welcome the chance to stand up to your bullying."

The social services man finally stepped in. He walked over to Jaimie, knelt, put hand on Jaimie's shoulder, and looked at Pamela and Crockett.

"Whatever happened last night, let's not forget how terrifying it must be for a twelve-year-old. How about we focus on getting through this right now in the best way possible for her?"

Jaimie kept her head tall. "Don't feel sorry for me."

That lack of self-pity perhaps swung the detective away from being a pit-bull.

"Rewind," she told Crockett. With less antagonism. "She—"

"Jaimie," Crockett said. "Not she."

"Don't push me," Pamela said. "Jaimie came here this morning from next door."

Crockett let out a deep breath, hoping his tension wasn't too obvious. He wasn't out of danger yet.

"She came over this morning from next door. She stayed the night with Nanna. Nanna drove us to Jaimie's house last night."

"I was really afraid this morning," Jaimie said. "That guy was there to get me. I had to leave Nanna's house. I knew Mr. G would protect me."

"I understand," Pamela said to her. "Mr. Grey?"

"She ran inside the house when I opened the door, and hid in my bedroom. Then someone else saying he was from social services arrived."

Thomas looked alarmed." We sent no one," he said.

"Did you ask for ID?" said Pamela.

Crockett shook his head. "Things were happening fast. He arrives, I go into the bedroom and Jaimie is hiding under the bed."

"He was a bad man," Jaimie said. "I knew it was danger."

"Who was a bad man?" Pamela said to Jaimie. "Are you saying it's Mr. Grey? You can tell me. You're in safe hands now."

"Give me a break!" Crockett said with more force than he intended. Professionally, he didn't blame the detective. He was familiar with abuse cases. Kids too afraid of their abusers to tell the truth. But he couldn't stay objective here.

"I'm listening to the girl," Pamela said. "Jaimie, who was the bad man? Mr. Grey?"

"No," Jaimie said. "He's the only one I trust. The bad man first went to Nanna's house. Then came here. He was following me. I ran into the bedroom to hide from him when he knocked on the door. But then he went away. And you got here."

"He probably saw your car pull up," Crockett told Pamela. "I didn't know it. I thought he was from social services, and I was in the bedroom, trying to talk Jaimie into going with social services."

"With a man that didn't show ID?"

"I would have gotten around to asking," Crockett said.

"Right. So you're in the bedroom with Jaimie…"

The insinuation was back. Crockett bit off another snapped reply, finally realizing the detective's tactics. Push, push, push. Hoping, if Crockett was lying about anything, for a reaction that would reveal the lie.

"Yes," Crockett said. "Then you made it to the door. I stepped out and you and I began our conversation."

"With the girl still hidden in the bedroom."

"With the girl still *safe* in the bedroom," Crockett said.

The detective gave Crockett a cold stare. The silence kept building, with Crockett deciding he wasn't going to break it. That would show nervousness. Yes, he was nervous, because he wasn't blind to how this entire situation appeared to someone with a skeptical and suspicious eye. But an innocent man would have no need to protest repeatedly.

"How about we talk to your neighbor," the detective finally said.

Crockett nodded.

"I'll stay here with the girl," social services said.

"Good," the detective answered. "Ask her about last night."

Another implied threat to Crockett. With him gone, Jaimie could talk freely. It made Crockett grateful he'd chosen to handle all of it with Nanna involved. Soon enough, it would all be cleared up. Social services would take Jaimie and it would be out of his hands.

This was so overwhelming, that Crockett would try to neutralize by normalizing the rest of the day as much as possible He would have the rest of the pot of coffee, read the paper, shower, and be at his ex-wife's house in plenty of time to pick up his son Mickey for a day at the zoo. He didn't care how cliched it was for a weekend Dad; Mickey liked the zoo and Crockett loved being with Mickey. The zoo gave them plenty of distractions, but the pace was slow enough to give them time to talk too.

It didn't take long however, for Crockett to regret his next several steps, showing his familiarity with Nanna's house and his ease of access to it.

When Nanna didn't answer the door, he lifted a potted plant on the doorstep.

"She keeps the spare key here," Crockett said, then realized he needed to clarify. "I feed her cat when she's away."

He meant it as a way to show the detective that he had a great, trusting relationship with Nanna. Which would have been fine, except after calling loudly and walking through almost all of the house, they discovered why Nanna hadn't answered.

Nanna was gone.

Chapter Thirteen

Six time zones to the east, the mid afternoon Roman air held an oily sensual warmth that American Raymond Leakey was too furious to enjoy as he sat alone at an outside table, cradling his cappuccino.

With the cafe situated just beyond the walls of Vatican City, the diesel rumblings of tour buses and the constant blare of horns was the perfect noise-canceling background to ensure the privacy of his upcoming conversation.

Furious as he was, he'd need to be careful and calculating during that conversation.

Leakey thrived on the calculated and the clandestine. Twice divorced. No children. A past that included a decade in the C.I.A. working in Rome, until, with C.I.A. blessing, he'd agreed to be recruited to work for the present organization inside the Vatican, where his Italian language skills were scorned but serviceable, where all his old contacts were an asset, not a liability.

Leakey was old enough he could see retirement looming, and nothing about his job description promised regular pension checks. Instead, he'd have to leverage his way into a peaceful villa—somewhere in Thailand, he'd decided, where an inexpensive maid could provide more than cleaning services.

That not-so-long-term objective made this meeting crucial.

Leakey had taken a circuitous route to get to this cafe—beginning at the Roma Termini station at the Piazza di Cinquecento in Central Rome, taking the Leonardo Express to the airport, then back to central Rome via taxi, then bus with several transfers to the northwest to mingle with tourists at St. Peter's square, and from there , moving on foot, including a trip through a restaurant kitchen out the back door into an alley and back onto the street. Three hours of circuitousness. Unnecessary precautions, he suspected, but in his business, unnecessary precautions were as natural as scanning the bill in a restaurant to make sure there were no overcharges. He also had in his favor his natural invisibility. His face was thin and he styled his hair in a comb-over, knowing that anyone who looked at him would dismiss him as a mousey albeit vain, average man.

He'd chosen a cassock for further invisibility, for in Rome, a man walking the cobblestone or relaxing in a cafe in priestly garb raised no eyebrows. Scorn, perhaps, from the cynical or those who knew the history of the Holy See's corruption over the last several decades, but never any real attention.

Just as well. This meeting, like all others with the cardinal whose arrival Leakey expected at any moment, needed to be utterly private, with no risk of electronic eavesdropping. And, in an ironic reversal, the cardinal would be dressed in a casual business suit for his own anonymity. The public venue was perfect for their private discussion.

They had agreed that unlike Leakey, the cardinal would make no attempts to hide his route here to the cafe. By pretending there was nothing unusual about meeting an anonymous priest, the cardinal would not draw any suspicion.

⸻

Exactly on time the cardinal appeared—His Eminence Ethan Saxon, the head of the diocese of Los Angeles.

To Leakey, watching carefully, the only attention it seemed that the cardinal drew was from some of the women in the restaurant, even the younger ones. In his elegant brown suit, the cardinal appeared younger and more vigorous than he actually was. His face was remarkably unlined for someone in his sixties, and for a man who had, as Leakey well knew, much on his conscience.

Leakey doubted it was coincidence that the cardinal resembled a famous portrait of Machiavelli, with his short cropped dark hair, emphasizing a high forehead. Rumor had it that the cardinal thought of himself as The Prince. Leakey suspected it was partially in homage to the book of the same title by Niccolo Machiavelli. The other potential reason, well that was much darker, and something Leakey preferred to keep from his own thoughts.

Leakey detested the cardinal, but of course, with a villa and a Thai maid in mind, had his own Machiavellian reasons for association with the cardinal.

—

His Eminence saw Leakey, nodded, and strode toward him.

Both were silent until the waiter had brought another cappuccino.

"Any news?" Leakey asked, tapping his head three times with his forefinger. He needed to add no further reference to his question.

All of the world knew that the pope was in a coma. It had been weeks already, and while the coma had dragged on so long it had stopped making daily headlines, inside the Vatican this situation was without precedence, with the turmoil and uncertainly escalating, something Leakey was determined to use to his advantage.

As for Leakey's tapping gesture, it needed no explanation either.

Although it was said in Rome that *Pietro non muore*—Peter does not die—the mortality of each successive pope made him like any other man. Until abolished by decree by John XXIII a half century earlier, when the pope died, the first duty of *il camerlengo*, the cardinal who managed the properties and revenues of the Holy See, had consisted of a medieval ritual of lightly tapping the pope's forehead thrice with a silver hammer, calling him by his Christian name, asking *dormisne,* are you asleep? If there was no reply, the camerlengo would utter that the pope had truly died, in four solemn words—*vere Papa mortuss est.*

His Eminence leaned slightly forward, dropping his voice, even as a tour bus rumbled by. "It is ugly, the fight for power between the secretary of state and the cardinal vicar. Far uglier than then even hinted by the media. And in this ugliness is much potential for me."

"For us," Leakey said, trying to keep a lid on his fury. Never was he going to let the cardinal forget that once they succeeded, Leakey demanded his payment. Leakey had left the C.I.A. for the Vatican's counterpart—the not-so-secret spy agency called Entity. Always alert for any kind of leverage, when Leakey had been assigned to covertly keep track of an unusual correspondence between the Vatican's chief exorcist and a psychiatrist in Los Angeles, Leakey had approached Cardinal Saxon months earlier to make a bargain. One would become the pope. The other, a retired spy with a new name, new passport, new Swiss account, and most importantly, a new villa with disposable maids.

"Yes, yes, this will benefit *us,* " Although both Americans had a passable knowledge of Italian, their conversation was in English. "But with O'Hare in Los Angeles, the longer it takes for the white smoke to be released, the more potential for complications. The girl is still a problem."

Leakey caught the cardinal's involuntary glance in the direction of the Sistine Chapel, blocked from their view by walls of nearby buildings. Soon enough, the eyes of the world would be watching it for smoke during the conclave to elect a new pope. Black smoke, inconclusive vote. White smoke, a new pope, a man with as much power as a government head, declared divinely infallible, with a billion followers.

"She's a problem because you made her a problem," Leakey said. "No matter what the cops might conclude, I know you are responsible. I need to know why and how before we continue."

"I do not serve you," Saxon said. "You might want to keep that in mind. Especially knowing my future position."

"You won't get to that future position if you interfere with my job. You might want to keep that in mind." Leakey felt the lid bubbling on his fury. Without some sort of venting, he was going to blow. "Any idea how moronic it was for you to step in, let alone step in without discussing it with me first?"

Saxon's face tightened. Maybe Leakey had pushed him too far.

"Were you hoping if it succeeded, you wouldn't need me anymore?" Leakey asked, forestalling whatever reaction Saxon was about to give. "If so, bad idea. You will always need me. And now you're going to need me even more to clean it up."

"We both know O'Hare is there already," Saxon finally said. His face relaxed. Leakey judged the man was containing his usual arrogance because it would serve his purpose better to manipulate Leakey than try to intimidate Leakey. "With that kind of urgency, I believed if I acted without consulting you, it would solve the problem permanently and keep both of us at arm's length. I was wrong. You can fix it."

"Who did you send?"

"Someone who has been convenient to me over the years. Let's leave it at that."

"No," Leakey said. "The girl is our first priority, but we're also going to do something about whoever it was you sent in to mess up the job."

"Trust me, he's not an issue. He believes he lives with a demon, one who ordered him to kill his own mother. I learned this from him in a confessional years ago. He only knows me as The Prince. He's never met me, and even if the authorities catch him, he won't and can't point back to us. Just focus on fixing this."

Interesting, Leakey thought. With this tidbit of knowledge, it wouldn't be difficult to learn who it was that the cardinal had sent in to start the fire. It would be a side project for Leakey. And extra potential leverage for the future.

"Fix the fact that the cops have found the girl at a school teacher's house?" Leakey asked. "My Los Angeles sources tell me there's a detective there right now, interviewing the teacher."

"If you want me to show I'm impressed that you know this already, it won't happen. It's what I expect from you."

"The girl has been alone during the night with the teacher," Leakey said. "Any idea how dangerous that could be? Who knows what she told him about the psychiatrist."

"You've told me all along that they've warned the girl not to say anything."

"She's twelve," Leakey said. "She escaped a fire. She might have even guessed it was meant to kill her. She's terrified. You really think she'd keep everything to herself?"

"Then when you fix it, take care of the teacher too. You have the power."

Leakey wanted to lean back in his chair, hands behind his head, showing the casual disrespect he had for the cardinal. As if Leakey wasn't out way ahead of the cardinal on this.

But if anyone was watching who knew the cardinal, Leakey's body language would be such a shocking display that it might well lead to questions about the identity of a man in a cassock opposite the cardinal.

"I think you're going to need to fatten my Swiss account," Leakey said. "Because I've already started fixing the problem. This teacher has a blot on his record. I've begun to arrange a little computer magic to take advantage of it and make sure if the girl told him anything, no one will believe it anyway. If he ever clears himself, it won't lead to you. And if it did, Entity will protect you, because that would happen long after you've become pope."

Chapter Fourteen

You've got two things to consider here," Attorney Dave Mills told Crockett. "Investigative point of view. Prosecution point of view."

They were finally alone in an interrogation room. With Mills in attendance, two cops—one of them Pamela—had grilled and re-grilled Crockett for the previous four hours. Jaimie was somewhere in the labyrinth of juvenile services.

Thirty seconds earlier, both cops had excused themselves, leaving Crockett alone with Mills, who was in his mid-forties with graying hair, big gut, big smile.

Mills was also a BDFOC, a term Crockett coined for his own wry use. *Before-Divorce Friend of the Couple.* Mills and his wife Cheryl lived down the street from Crockett and Julie. They used to hang out during the idyllic life. Grilled brats and beer. Cut the lawn on weekends. Two cars, two car garage, and two kids.

Lose one kid, and it all changes.

Julie still lived on the street, still clung to the house, still had Ashley's bedroom set up the way it was when she died. Crockett had hated being stuck in a place that reminded him every day of what he'd lost. His discontent clashed with her fear of change and became just one of the cracks in their marriage that had led to unbridgeable chasms.

"Can we take a break?" Crockett asked Mills. "Just tell me—how's

Mickey? We were supposed to go to the zoo." He muttered the last part, feeling bitter over the recent events that kept him seeing his son.

Mickey loved the zoo. Some of the best hours in Crockett's life were at the zoo with his son. Mickey loved the trip to Griffith Park, taking winding roads past the picnic areas where the migrants hung out with their families, then to the zoo itself. Where they should have been right now. They went often enough that they'd begun to recognize when some of the animals had different moods. All of the animals, of course, had names. Given by Mickey. Memorized by Mickey. It may have been a childish tradition, but enjoying the simple things in life with Mickey made Crockett feel less weathered, less adult.

"Mickey's good," Dave said reluctantly. The vague answer didn't satisfy Crockett in any sense, but he wouldn't push.

"I appreciate the help you and Cheryl give our family," Crockett said. He knew that Dave and Cheryl had come alongside Julie when Crockett left, helping her with the little things like lawn maintenance that Crockett used to do.

Dave looked away briefly, then back at Crockett. "Cheryl and I have separated."

"Sorry. I know what that feels like." It was a quick, canned response. Crockett was too emotionally beat up to be empathetic.

"It happens," Dave said. "But what's in front of us is what we need to focus on. We need to get you out of here. Last place you want to be for the weekend is a holding cell. It's like getting thrown into a cage with animals."

"What are my chances?"

"The investigative side doesn't have much," Dave said. "Your neighbor Nanna would have been very helpful. She's the foundation of your story. Hopefully she just went somewhere for the day. Is she cognitive?"

"Cognitive?"

"She's an old lady. Does she have Alzheimer's or anything like that?"

Crockett shook his head. "No, no. She's sharp."

"And her story would match yours?"

"Yes, of course. At this point, though, Jaimie's account also matches mine."

"We'll get to that. As I said, if the cops had talked to Nanna and she corroborated, you'd be at the zoo right now. Instead, from an investigative point of view, they're going to be thorough until they talk to her. They catch a minor in your bedroom—you as a teacher—they have to make sure everything is squeaky clean. Especially with the old allegations on your record."

"Look," Crockett said heavily. "All it's going to take is talking to one of the other teachers Rhimes accused when she was a student of ours. All three of us went through hell, even though we were clearly innocent. Not only did she confess the allegations were false, but we had witnesses placing us in public or with family for about half the times she said we were alone with her. That's on file. Get the principal of my school on the phone. Don Haldane. He'll back it up too."

"Couldn't get hold of him."

"So you tried?"

"Sure, as I drove in. Wasn't calling him about the allegations, just to give him a heads-up."

"And ask him about me?"

"That too," Dave admitted. "This is about as serious as it can get."

It was happening all over again, not only the anger at being accused of something that didn't happen, but the horrible sensation that came with the type of accusation. Teachers and kids.

Dave shifted awkwardly. "Hey, if you're innocent, there are no worries. "

"*If* I'm innocent? What kind of crap is that?" Anger was winning over exhaustion and stress. Or maybe it was losing to exhaustion and stress. "I don't need you of all people having any doubt about this."

Another awkward shift. "Lean on reruns of *Law & Order* here, Crockett. Guilty or innocent is not the issue. I represent you. It's not about truth. It's about the justice system. And that leads me to point two. As far as I can tell, any prosecutor's going to have a real tough time getting anything against you to stick. You're a respected teacher, you dealt with a troubled child with compassion. You identified yourself to a cop at the fire scene, told them to call you. Later, you even let them into the house where the old lady lives. It all adds up and makes sense. Like I said, tough to crack."

Dave was talking slightly louder than demanded by their personal space. Crockett got the sense Dave was talking past him, then realized he was. Crockett was really addressing the one-way mirror, laying things out for the benefit of their hidden observers.

Dave leaned forward, lowering his voice. "They do have a search warrant for your house. They won't find anything, will they?"

Crockett met Dave's stare. "There's nothing to find."

—————

Once again, Crockett was wrong. Ten minutes after he and Dave had finished their discussion, Pamela, followed by Dave, returned to the interrogation room.

She leaned against the wall. Her face was an angular hard slate.

"Tell me about the box in your attic," she said to Crockett. "The one with a hard drive filled with child porn."

Chapter Fifteen

W*hat?*

"Nice bluff," Crockett said. He turned to Dave. "That's a bluff. Trust me. I have no such thing in my attic."

To Dave—whose face registered pure shock—Pamela said, "All that crap of yours about two points of view, investigative and prosecution, all that posing in front of the mirror—pointless. We've got him on both sides."

She barely opened her mouth as she spoke, like she didn't even want to breathe when she was in the same room with Crockett. "And something else. Three other complaints in his teaching record."

"What are you talking about?" Crockett said. "This is crazy."

"I'll explain it to your lawyer," she said. "Because it won't be a surprise to you."

Dave crossed his arms, waiting.

Pamela looked back to Dave. "Students. There are girls, saying he gave them the creeps. It's nothing concrete enough to be followed up by administration at the school, but it's on record."

"Not a chance!" Crockett exploded. "Haldane, school principal. He'll tell you that none of it is true."

"Already tried," Pamela said. "He's on a hiking trip in Alaska. It's going to be a couple days till we reach him."

Dave's shocked expression turned to disgust. He turned to Crockett. "Good luck finding a lawyer,"

"Wait," Crockett asked. "I guess that part about guilty or innocent not being the issue was crap. It's about the justice system, right…"

"I'm a father and a family man, Crockett. I do not represent pedophiles."

"I am not a pedophile." Crockett wasn't sure how he was able to keep his voice from quivering. "Someone must have planted the hard drive. That's the only way it could have gotten there."

Dave snorted. "Of course. Got a list of enemies and motivations to supply me? While you're at it, how about explaining the student complaints?"

"Dave," Crockett said, pleading now. Grasping. "It's got to be linked to the fire." It must be the case. Jaimie, the fire, now this? It couldn't have been a coincidence. "You've got to hang in there with me."

Dave shook his head. "Here's what I'll do for you. I'll lay it out before I leave, so you know what you're up against. So listen carefully."

Blood seemed to fill Crockett's ears. He heard the fast thumping of his heart. And above it, Dave's voice.

"This has tilted the other way," Dave said. "With the hard drive as evidence, no jury will buy your version of last night's events. They will send you to prison based on four things. Previous complaints against you. You collect child porn. A cop found a twelve-year-old girl in your bedroom. That spells pedophile. Not even sure if your neighbor's alibi could help you at this point."

Crockett made it to his feet. "I am not a pedophile!"

Dave shrugged, but Crockett noticed a hint of regret in his eyes.

"If you are innocent," Dave said, "then God help you. He's the only friend you've got."

Chapter Sixteen

Before the orange jumpsuit and general holding, Crockett was allowed his one phone call.

Julie. He needed to convince her to believe in him. Someone had to believe in him.

"Julie," Crockett said into the phone. He told her where he was. "I've got nowhere else to turn right now."

"I heard from Dave." Her voice was ice. "He's in the backyard right now, with Mickey, playing catch. Mickey cried for about an hour, waiting for you to take him to the zoo. At least Dave's here to help him feel better."

It washed over Crockett again. Dave was right. People simply didn't make it back after the pedophile card was played, especially teachers.

Holding the phone so hard that the skin tight against his knuckles hurt, Crockett also realized that he felt worse about Mickey's disappointment than the fact that he was going to be incarcerated indefinitely unless he somehow made bail. Great that his love for the kid was bigger than any other problem that Crockett could face. Not so great that this was one of the few problems that would take Crockett away from Mickey.

"That's why I'm calling," Crockett said. "We've got to fight this. Mickey needs a dad. I need Mickey."

"Dave said you spent the night with a twelve-year-old girl from your class. He said you used a neighbor for an alibi, but she's unreachable. He said the cops found a hard drive with child porn in your attic. Do I have that right? And what about those other complaints on your file? Interesting how you managed to keep that out of custody hearings."

"The twelve-year-old came to me for help and I sent her next door to spend the night with my neighbor, Nanna. I don't know…maybe the same person who planted the hard drive abducted Nanna. I know none of it makes any sense Julie, but I'm innocent. "

"Any idea how weak that sounds?" Nothing in Julie's voice softened.

"You're right. It is weak. Which points to it being true. If I was lying, don't you think I'd come up with something stronger?"

"Dave says the girl probably started the fire as a cry for help. Maybe because you already had a relationship with her and she wanted it exposed. He said maybe she started it and when she came to you, you used her fear to leverage her into staying."

"Tell him the knife in my back is sticking through. What's with you and Dave anyway? Why is he telling you all this? Has he made a move on you or something?"

"At least I'm adult aged."

"Come on, Julie." He ran his hand through his hair. "This is insane. You know me."

"Do I?"

"Look," Crockett said. "Alimony, child support. I've always exceeded the settlement papers. That's because it's best for you and Mickey. Is that kind of person a pedophile?"

"Dave says—"

"Seriously, what's with you and Dave? Something I need to know?"

"My private life is not your business. I'm going to hang up."

"No." Crockett felt like his throat was raspy. "I'm stressed to the break-ing point here. Saying things I shouldn't. Don't go."

"Why did you call, Crockett?"

"I needed you to know that I am innocent. To hear the truth in my voice. But also…" He hesitated, but he had to ask. "I need someone to sign for bail. I gave you the house and—"

"No, Crockett. You didn't give it to me. It was a negotiated settlement."

"Fine, whatever. I just… I don't have much for assets. I give as much of my monthly income to you as possible, so I don't have savings. If—"

"So you're trying to guilt me into giving you something?"

"No! I'm trying to explain why I need to ask you to sign for bail. Something is wrong, someone, for some reason, is out to hurt me, and I can't solve it from inside."

Silence.

"Julie?"

"I've got to go," she said.

"That's it? No help?"

"Gotta go, Crockett."

Crockett knew the tone of her voice. This was the unyielding I-won't-change-my-mind tone.

"Can I talk to Mickey?" Crockett asked.

"Not a good idea," she said, and hung up the phone.

Chapter Seventeen

Instead of being forced to go into juvie, Jaimie had been officially been signed into Dr. Mackenzie's custody. She sat in a bean bag chair in Dr. Mackenzie's library at the Bright Lights Center, out in the Malibu hills with Dr. Mackenzie and some priest guy that she'd just met named O'Hare. He was a big, blocky guy and seemed nice enough. Dr. Mackenzie had told Jaimie that Father O'Hare was from Rome and would be with them for the next couple of days until after Pope Someone Number had died, both of them taking turns to explain how Jaimie needed to help them in Italy. Pope Someone Number, they wanted her to meet, but she didn't really pay attention to the name because what she thought was cool was the number part of the pope's name, which had got her thinking that maybe she could call herself Jaimie Piper One.

Dr. Mackenzie and O'Hare were both looking at her expectantly now, because they wanted her answer if she would help. They wanted to give her way to fight back against Evil.

Jaimie wanted to think about it from all angles. She was dealing with adults, after all, and she had learned when adults offered a deal, it was rarely as simple as they made it sound.

Jaimie looked beyond them, out the window at the view of the hills of the Bright Lights Center. It was a ranch that had once belonged to movie star and had this building with dorm rooms plus some old cabins and a couple barns. And a high chain link fence. Not to keep people out. To keep people in.

Jaimie didn't care how the brochure description and fundraiser blurbs described the Bright Lights Center. She knew it was a place for misfits like her, even more of a misfit now that the house fire made her an official juvenile delinquent.

Not that she minded being there. Dr. Mackenzie had brought her to Bright Lights for a lot of weekends over the last six months.

Most of the time, seeing the hills through the big window at the Bright Lights Center calmed her. Feeding the horses here at Bright Lights made her feel really good. She didn't have to pretend to be tough in front of the horses. Some of the kids hated the quiet, didn't like going on the paths in the hills, but Jaimie loved it. Time slowed down there. She even liked stopping and looking at bugs, although she wondered if other people knew she liked the bugs that they'd tease her about being like a little kid. She found a caterpillar last week, big and black with a tall hook on its tail. That was cool. She'd found a plastic container, filled it with dirt, put some grass on top and made it a mini-zoo for the caterpillar.

Right now, though, Jaimie didn't feel calm. It wasn't that she was currently having the dark feelings that made her afraid of Evil. Dr. Mackenzie was here to protect her, and so was the priest. They were going to help her hunt Evil, so that Evil couldn't hunt her.

Jaimie's lack of calm wasn't from distrust of these two either. Dr. Mackenzie wasn't a pretender. You could see it easily in adults who were pretenders. Some would talk nice to you when other people were around, but when you were alone, would yap or snap or snarl. Other pretenders treated you like toddlers, smirking at you with superior smiles.

Probably what had first convinced Jaimie to relax around Dr. Mackenzie was her clothes. Old stuff. Used stuff. Baggy. No pretending there. Jaimie thought Dr. Mackenzie could probably look smoking hot if she wore make-up and did something with her thick blonde hair, but that wasn't Dr. Mackenzie's style. No pretending. So if Dr. Mackenzie said it was okay to trust this priest from Rome, then it was okay.

The reason that Jaimie was on edge was because she felt bad about Mr. G.

She had seen something on television about him. No way was it true. She knew it was because of the fire and the dark feelings and because she had gone to him for help. It nagged at her like the hangnail on her thumb. She tore it off with her teeth.

Jaimie felt guilty that she didn't feel nearly as bad about her latest foster dad, who had died in the fire. She'd hardly known him anyway. She'd learned not to get too attached to foster parents. They came and went. And this foster dad had been a yeller, so she'd just tuned him out.

Jaimie hadn't done anything to start the fire. She guessed the Evil guy who had visited that night did, but even if she had warned the entire family that the guy was Evil, they wouldn't have listened. It didn't seem real to her anyway, that this foster dad was dead.

What did seem real was Mr G in trouble and it truly was her fault. She should have known better than get near his house when Evil was hunting her, because it naturally drew Evil in Mr. G's life.

"Jaimie?" Dr. Mackenzie prompted her.

They were waiting for her to agree to help with Pope Something Number.

Maybe there was a way to help Mr G and make up for getting him in trouble. Adults weren't the only ones who could make deals.

Instead of answering them about Rome, Jaimie asked a question in return.

"I want to know what we can do about Mr. G," Jamie said, fully aware the man was staring at her, Father O'Hare.

Weird, for Jaimie, thinking that half the world treated an old man like God, even though the old man was in a hospital, living through tubes, somewhere in a country where people didn't speak American. Weirder that Father O'Hare was here because he needed her. And weirder what they were saying to her about the pope. Good thing was they needed her, and she knew it.

Jaimie spit the piece of fingernail on the floor. Dr. Mackenzie winced.

"Sorry," Jaimie said. She kicked at the fingernail. She looked up at Father O'Hare, who was hiding a smile. She figured he must be okay. That was the thing, for Jaimie. She needed to make quick judgments about the adults who stepped in and out of her world. And the quick judgments better be accurate.

"No need to apologize," Dr. Mackenzie said. "I need to be better about letting little things go. Really. What is it you want us to do about your teacher?"

Dr. Mackenzie was decent for someone wound so tight. Dr. Mackenzie, even though she dressed loose and sloppy, had the kind of tightness that a lot of foster kids shared, like tightening your whole body when someone was about to hit you. Jaimie's tightness. Trying to stay wrapped up so no one could get through.

"You have to help Mr. G out of jail," she said. "He didn't do anything wrong."

"We'll help," O'Hare said.

"I hear stuff like that all the time," Jaimie said. "It's like when a president says he's going to help the country. A lot of time he's kinda shy on details, and not much gets done."

Father O'Hare shook his head, smiling. "We learn younger and younger, don't we."

"I'm twelve," Jaimie said. "Old enough. I want to help you guys, but not until I know we're going to get Mr. G out of trouble.."

"Okay, then." Dr. Mackenzie looked at the Father. "Father O'Hare, what are we doing to help?"

Now we're getting somewhere, Jaimie thought. Time and again, in conferences that were 'for her own good', she was like a ping pong ball for adults to bat back and forth, and she'd also learned to figure out who had the power and who didn't. Looked like there was a reason Father O'Hare was here.

"We have considerable resources," Father O'Hare chimed in, speaking directly to Jaimie.

"We?" Jaimie said. "Who's we?"

"The people I represent."

"Nice try," Jaimie said. Her quick judgment was that this guy liked a bit of sass. "And the people I represent," he said with a smile that said she'd guessed right, "really prefer to remain in the background."

"So let me get this straight. You want me on a plane to Italy. To help you out with this voodoo stuff with a nearly dead pope? And 'considerable resources' is all the answer I get? Maybe I don't want to go to Italy after all."

"Jaimie," Dr. Mackenzie began. "Voodoo isn't exactly what we're talking about. You know that."

"I need an answer," Jaimie said. "It's not his fault he's in trouble. It's mine. Because I didn't want to spend a few hours alone on the streets. I should have been able to handle it. Even if Dr. Mackenzie didn't answer her phone like she promised she would, no matter what time I called."

"My battery died," Dr. Mackenzie said. But she was tapping her knee with her fingers, like maybe she wasn't quite telling the truth. "I wish you would understand that."

"I can see why you like this young woman," Father O'Hare said to Dr. Mackenzie. "You know what she's doing, of course. Trying to get a sense of how much power she has in this situation."

Interesting, Jaimie thought. Father O'Hare understood exactly what Jaimie was doing. And he let Jaimie know he knew.

"So what you got?" she asked him. "Nobody can make me get on the plane, right? And even if you did, I could go all stupid on you when I get there."

Jaimie played with the bracelet on her arm, sending a clear signal. She knew it was all about the bracelet.

Father O'Hare gave a theatrical sigh. "Just so I understand, Miss Piper. You're wondering if I can really deliver on a promise to help Mr. Grey. And if I do, that's going to tell you something about the people involved here. And it will tell you how important you are to us."

"I want you to get him a lawyer," Jaimie said. "The best one there is. And I don't get on a plane until Mr. G is out of jail."

"Certainly," O'Hare said.

"I want to see the contract with the lawyer." Not that Jaimie figured she'd understand it, but she wanted to show they couldn't push her around.

"Certainly," O'Hare said.

"And one other thing."

He lifted a dignified eyebrow.

"What can you do about getting me a horse of my own?" Since he didn't seem in a hurry to say no, she continued to push. "And a place to keep it."

In the hallway, as Jaimie headed to feed the horses, Dr. Mackenzie faced Father O'Hare.

"I'm not sure you've been entirely forthcoming with me," Mackenzie told O'Hare.

"Of course not," O'Hare answered. "We're all genetically wired to protect ourselves."

"Classic evasion."

"As was your accusation. I'm very comfortable addressing any questions you may have. "

"Good. I'll be direct. Who is behind what happened to Crockett Grey and why did it happen? Let me go back a little further. Who started the fire and why? You assured me from the beginning that Jaimie would always be safe." Mackenzie knew what was at stake, and that was why this was the time to ask the difficult questions. "She could have died in the fire. Which means she wasn't safe. I don't like the implications. Either you've misjudged the situation from the beginning, or your judgment is fine but you lied to me. Perhaps you gave me this assurance because from the beginning I said that her safety was more important than what you wanted her to accomplish?"

O'Hare's expression narrowed, and it gave Madelyn a slight chill. This affable man, perhaps, had a wolf lurking inside.

"Let's not fool ourselves about what motivates you and me," he said. "Is Jaimie's safety more important to you than dealing with your own past? Is it more important to you than using her to advance your professional reputation?"

"Yes, Jaimie's safety comes first," Madelyn said firmly. But she disliked herself for the slight shiver of hesitation inside.

"Then think of the one motivation you and I do share. Rather, the one man we both know must be exposed with Jaimie's help. And think of what lengths he would go not to be exposed."

"So you're saying that somehow, he knows about Jaimie," she said. "I can't accept the implication."

"I don't want to accept the implication either. But if he does know what we're trying to accomplish, we need to get Jaimie away from here as soon as it is practical."

Chapter Eighteen

Heard you like little girls."

Crockett looked up at a runty kid from where he sat in a corner in a room with about a dozen caged men. The kid was staring at Crockett, chattering with the others. Crockett tried to ignore the smells of urine and vomit. And sweat. The smell of sweat, loaded with fear and anger, filled the cell.

Crockett was terrified, but now was not the time to show it. "You heard wrong," he replied.

Things couldn't possibly get worse. He'd been assigned a public defender, a man who'd shown up half-drunk three hours after Dave had abandoned Crockett, and who had fallen asleep as Crockett tried to explain his story. Crockett knew, no thanks to the public defender, that he would remain in jail over the weekend to await a bail hearing. Of course, he had no chance of coming up with bail money even if there was a bail hearing and even if a judge granted it on Monday morning.

He tried to fight the despair that covered him like the thick air of the cell. Mickey had been all but taken from him. And he would grow older, believing his father was a child molester.

He kept telling himself he'd survived worse.

That, for Crockett, was the moment that Ashley took her last breath, her hand clutching his, the muscles of her hand tight with pain that made her convulse, a pain that he was begging God to take away until her grip relaxed. Then it was just Crockett, weeping, begging God to bring Ashley back, even if it put her back into the pain. Wasn't a morning he woke up without the thought of Ashley's physical pain in the last few minutes, her face contorted as she struggled to breathe out her last words. *Daddy, where's Mommy? I thought you said she would be here.* Crockett, telling a lie, because he didn't know where Julie was. *Her car broke down on the way here. She wants to be with you so bad.* Then Ashley's last words to him. *Daddy, Don't cry. it's okay. I get to go to heaven. I'll see you there. Right? Daddy?* And Crockett lying to her again. *Yes. I'll see you in heaven.*

He'd survived worse. But this looked like it was getting close to the bottom.

"You spend the night with little girls and everything, right?" the runt said, voice rising. He didn't look older than a year into his twenties and wore a black sleeveless t-shirt to show off ropy biceps and crude tattoos.

Good test. Send the smallest guy over to challenge Crockett. Establish Crockett's designation as the new jailhouse squeeze. This was just the holding area. What would it be like after full incarceration?

"Twelve-year-old girls," Runty Kid continued, looking around for encouragement. "My sister is about that age. I'd kill anyone who touched her."

"You heard wrong," Crockett repeated.

The room full of caged men was silent with tension.

This was the hidden face of the justice system. Maybe one of the guards, Crockett guessed, had passed on information to set this up. Same guard or guards who would ignore any screaming from Crockett, pretend not to notice what was happening on the surveillance cameras high in each of the corners of the room.

"You're here, aren't you?" The kid glared, working himself up for action. "That tells me I didn't hear wrong."

Like watching a car skid, slow motion, through a red light in a crowded intersection, Crockett could see it all about to unfold. Runty Kid looking to make himself a bigger man by being the first to bully Crockett. Everyone else looking for a place to unload rage and frustration. Crockett the designated target.

"Maybe you should get a taste of it yourself?" Runty Kid's eyes were wide. A vein had started to bulge on his neck. This was primal. Crockett's blood filled with the chemical cocktail that adrenaline served when all civility was stripped away.

A few of the other men shifted closer. These weren't runts. They were relaxed.

The runt slapped Crockett's face, a short quick snap of the hand that Crockett couldn't dodge. It rocked Crockett's head sideways. The blow stunned him, but also filled him with a roaring sensation of rage.

A cold and calculating part of Crockett began to plan a response, and a detached part of himself was amazed to find the coldness within.

Crockett leaned forward. He clutched his stomach and made noises as if he was going to vomit. From that position, he drove his right fist upward as hard as he could, directly into the runty kid's crotch. Then he rose and pulled the kid upright as the kid went into the instinctive fetal ball.

Crockett wasn't a fighter. He was a teacher. But everyone knew about the most lethal of wrestling moves. Arms under the other guy's armpit, hands locked behind his neck. Crockett spun the kid around and snaked his arms into position. Full nelson.

Crockett outweighed the kid by at least fifty pounds. He didn't feel a second of remorse at taking advantage of it. He shuffled backwards, making sure he got into a corner, Runty Kid in front.

"I'll snap your neck," Crockett threatened. "Yell for a guard."

Runty Kid had retched already from the blow to his groin, and vomit dripped down his shirt front.

Crockett applied pressure. Hopefully his plan would work. He figured a disturbance would bring the guards. A fight might get him into solitary confinement. "Scream. Like a girl," he ordered the kid. He guessed that the guards were already scrambling.

"Scream," Crockett hissed. He was so angry and mentally exhausted he was almost ready to kill. It felt good, lashing out at the hell that had been inflicted upon him. "Scream, kid. Scream!"

Runty Kid let out a bawl, all bravado gone.

That was enough.

His noise checked the advance of the others, who anticipated correctly that the guards would be there in seconds.

When three guards pushed inside the cell, Crockett saw the grin of the first guard, holding a Taser. Like they'd been anticipating this.

Crockett realized the part he hadn't planned for. Yes, the guards would be watching through the surveillance cameras, but they wouldn't turn a blind eye. The caged men around him weren't the only ones who might look for a reason to beat him.

Chapter Nineteen

I s freedom worth a couple million to you?" The woman addressing him looked about Crockett's age. She was attractive with short brunette hair. A tailored gray suit made of a soft material that he could only assume was expensive.

It was Monday morning.

He'd been surprised first to hear from her that a bail hearing had been arranged for shortly after this meeting. Saturday, the sloppy public defender had predicted it would be days. Second surprise was the woman herself. She'd introduced herself as Amy Robertson, the replacement attorney for the public defender, who had replaced Dave. That made her third in a list of lawyers.

Crockett wasn't optimistic Robertson would stay either. The public defender's aura had screamed incompetence. Hers screamed money. Her opening question had confirmed his suspicion.

In answer to her question, Crockett said, no smile, "Be worth it if I had a couple million."

"I know you don't have it," she said. "At least not yet."

"Yet?"

In answer, she pulled a camera from her briefcase, which sat on the table between them. Burnished caramel-colored leather. The shine-of-money leather.

She pointed the camera at him. "These will be the money shots." That word again. She snapped a photo. "Good," she said, at Crockett's dour expression. "Hold that pose."

Crockett had not looked in a mirror since the guards beat him. He didn't need a reflection to tell him how he must have appeared. He'd already seen the bruises on his ribs, dark like plums. The skin on his cheekbones felt ready to burst from swelling. Several teeth were loose.

"Great," she said. "Take these shots too early, and they don't have an impact on a jury. Nice we've had a little time to let things ripen. You look horrible. I love it."

She put the camera back and pulled out sheaves of paper. Gave Crockett a cocky smile. "These notes are just for show. I never forget something once I read it or write it down. It's why I get the big bucks." Money, again.

He remained silent, waiting for her to get the picture. He couldn't pay her.

"What we've got," she said, without referring to the notes, "is a kid named Wiley Jergensen, on record as saying that a prison guard named Alfred Richards pointed you out to him as a child molester and implied that there would be a period of time when the guards had an extended coffee break. Said prison guard has a son who was molested a few years back at a day care and is highly motivated to see punishment inflicted on all molesters. Wiley Jergensen, as you might recall, almost had his neck broken by a certain Crockett Grey."

Crockett was too tired and too depressed to respond.

"What we've also got is a video record of Wiley Jergensen striking said Crockett Grey, which clearly gives Crockett Grey a motivation for self defense. This, combined with an excessive amount of force applied to Crockett Grey by the aforementioned Alfred Richards and fellow guards, puts the city and county in a delicate position should said Crockett Grey file a lawsuit."

At least his plan had worked.

Amy Robertson sat back, smiling. "Word for word, that's my half of the conversation I just had with the prosecutor. It would have been even more effective with photos in my hand." She gave him a sympathetic grimace. "Dang, your face must really hurt."

Crockett ignored her pity. "And the prosecutor's half of the conversation?" he asked.

"Half isn't quite accurate. It's fair to say, as usual, I dominated, so at best he got in ten percent. He did manage to bleat out that with no fingerprints on the hard drive, he'd make the case that you were in the habit of wiping it clean as a precaution before returning it to your hiding place. He said the eyewitness you claim for support is still unavailable, and he said it's obvious that you came up with a lie about a fake social worker showing up for Jaimie to try to throw blame elsewhere. Then there are the complaints against you by adolescent girls on your school record. But you told the public defender it had to be a computer glitch, right?"

"Not my theory. I just said it wasn't me. He suggested a computer glitch. But he sounded sarcastic. I wasn't. Get my principal. He'll tell you those complaints didn't happen. Find out who put the hard drive in my house, you'll find out who messed with my records."

"Why?"

"You have no idea how badly I want to find out," Crockett said. Almost as badly as he wanted to go the other direction. Crawl in a hole and let events bury him. Succumb to the temptation of despair. But Mickey needed him.

"So we'll find out, but it might not be necessary," Robertson said. "I told the prosecutor that anonymous complaints from adolescent girls are viewed with suspicion until corroborated." She leaned forward. "Then he made a big mistake. He tried to make the case that because your daughter died at the same age that Jaimie is now, it won't be difficult to convince a jury that you were looking for substitution in one form or another."

The mention of Ashley once again put Crockett back at the hospital bed on the night of his daughter's death. Just Crockett at the hospital. Julie had gone, because she couldn't handle it, said she needed a break, just for one night. Neither of them knew the end was so near. She left Crockett with their girl, bald from chemo, eyes dark sockets on a face that had shrunk down to bones.

Here, in front of Amy, the memory crushed him again. He wasn't even able to protest. All Crockett could do was close his eyes. With his tongue, he probed his loose teeth, looking for a distraction in the sharpness of jangled nerve endings.

"I told the prosecutor," Amy said, voice soft, "if he did try dragging your daughter into this, I'd arrange for someone to match the damage done to you by the guards. My father passed on six months ago. If you loved your daughter near as much as my Dad loved me, I can't imagine what it was like for you to lose her."

Crockett opened his eyes again. "Thanks," he croaked.

She held eyes with him, then nodded and resumed her fast patter. "As part of my ninety percent of the conversation, I told him that he's up against a respected teacher of troubled kids, Jaimie's testimony in your favor, and no fingerprints on the hard drive. Just as easy to spin it that someone planted it, and made sure it was clean. I told him I have a witness who may have seen someone matching Nanna's description sitting in the front of your Jeep at the fire scene."

"You have someone?" A ray of hope.

"Listen carefully. I told him I did. I'll find a witness, but I just haven't had time. I've only been on this since eight this morning. I'm good, but not a miracle worker." She gave him a grim smile. "Which leads to my original question. Is freedom worth a couple of million to you? Because we've got a deal of sorts on the table. I can get you on the street today, but you're going to have to waive any future shots at a lawsuit."

"For someone who is the best, you don't listen. I don't have it. I can't afford bail or a lawyer."

"I'm covered," she said.

"Covered?"

"As in your bail and my exorbitant fees to represent you have been prepaid."

"Who covered them?"

"Can't answer that."

Crockett tried to sort through this information. An unknown person tries to abduct Jaimie, an unknown person plants a hard drive that dumps Crockett into a sewer, and then an unknown person sends in a rescuer. Bad guy on one side of Crockett and a good guy on the other? He couldn't think of anything in his life important enough or significant enough to earn this kind of attention. Jaimie was the catalyst, but how and why?

Or was there just a bad guy on one side and Julie on the other? Had she come around? That still wouldn't explain though why Crockett had been targeted.

'Just so I have it straight," Crockett said. "You're my new legal help. Someone is covering your tab. And because the guards played drum on my face, I can walk now or sue later, but not both?"

"Exactly," she said. "Want out now? Or are you willing to park your butt in a jail cell at the chance of winning a future lawsuit?"

Chapter Twenty

D ave," Crockett said, working hard to keep his voice neutral.
Dave Mills answered had the door at Julie's house in Van Nuys,
in a t-shirt, shorts, sandals. Holding a barbecue tong and wearing an apron
that said *"Grillin' is chillin'. And chillin' is grillin'."*

There were a lot of implications in the image before him. All of them
stabbed Crockett with knives of jealously and resentment. Irrational, he told
himself. He and Julie had been divorced for at least two years. What Julie
did was her business—even if it was in the house that Crockett had provided for her and Mickey.

"Crockett," Dave said, obviously surprised. Crockett hadn't called
ahead, worried that Julie might tell him to stay away. Crockett just wanted
to drop in and thank Julie and maybe get a hug from Mickey. It hurt how
badly Crockett wanted to squat and look his boy in the eyes and see a gap-
toothed smile in return.

Along with surprise was a distinct look of guilt across Dave's face.

Julie stepped into the doorway. Behind her, everything looked the same.
Furniture, artwork on walls, paint. Except for Dave standing beside her,
it could have been like any other day before, when Crockett would come
home after a day of teaching. And except for the fact that Julie was blocking
him from walking through the doorway. And except for Ashley.

"Your face," Julie said. Her voice held the same chill as it had on Saturday when she'd hung up on him.

"Not as bad as it looks," Crockett said. A lie. He was wearing sunglasses to hide the worst of it.

"You didn't call ahead," she said. "That's part of the agreement."

"I was in the area," Crockett said.

"No excuse," Dave said. "Legally, I mean."

"Shut up," Crockett said.

He waited for Julie to tell him not to talk to Dave like that. When she didn't, it felt like a minor victory.

"Why are you here?" she asked with a regretful expression. Still, she looked so good in jeans and a t-shirt. Simple, the way Crockett always remembered her. A wave of longing washed through him. But all he said was, "I wanted to thank you in person for helping me with Amy Robertson."

Julie's brow creased. "Huh?"

That answered one question for Crockett. He had no idea now who was paying his legal tab.

"Never mind," Crockett said, then forced his tone into something resembling upbeat. "Hey, I was just hoping to say hi to Mickey. I missed seeing him yesterday."

"You missed him because you were in jail," she said.

"I'm out on bail. That's a pretty good indication of my innocence."

"Actually, legally speaking—" Dave began.

"Shut up, I said. You made it clear you didn't want any part of my case."

Again, Julie's silence was gratifying.

Crockett turned his attention back to Julie. "I'm here," he said earnestly. "Can I just spend a few minutes with Mickey? Apologize in person for missing my day at the zoo?"

He hoped it didn't sound like he was begging. Even though he was.

"Crockett," Julie began. "Check your face in a mirror. Do you really want Mickey to see you like this?"

"Yes." Crockett needed to see his son. Tears started to form, but he willed himself to hold them back. Especially in front of Dave.

"Not a good idea," Julie shook her head. "He'll be scared by how beat up you are. And we've got to stick to the schedule. Otherwise every time he hears the doorbell, he'll hope it's you. He doesn't need that kind of disappointment."

His little guy loved him that much. It was so good to hear, the tears continued to pool. Crockett was grateful for his sunglasses.

Mickey loved him. But for how long if Crockett didn't find a way to clear his name?

"Julie…" Crockett's voice broke.

She softened and Dave kept his head down. "Crockett, come back a week from Saturday. He's all yours then. Okay?"

"Mom?" Mickey's voice came from the kitchen. He was so close. All Crockett needed was a hug.

"I've got to go," Julie said. "It's for the best." She shut the door.

Chapter Twenty-One

I've never heard of any complaints against me about inappropriate behavior," Crockett said to Brad Romans, a social worker from the school. They'd worked together for years. "You know that."

Crockett settled back in a chair in Romans' tidy office. His desk was clean of paperwork. walls clean of anything in frames. Brad Romans looked more like a business mogul than a left-wing social worker. Short dark hair, just beginning to gray, and not too much bulk, as if he walked five miles a day on the golf course. Clothes that would not have seemed out of place at a country club. Disarming salesman-like grin. But the illusion vanished once Romans spoke, because it never took long for him to show his liberal, do-gooder leanings.

Brad said, "I told the detective, that woman Pamela Li, the same thing. She didn't want to believe me."

"Something crazy is happening," Crockett said. "How can it not be about Jaimie? It all started with her. That's why I'm here."

"You're here because you can't think of anywhere else to get help."

"Barrel scraping," Crockett agreed.

"What I'm most concerned about is your face," Romans said, clearly trying to keep the mood light. "Ugly. U-G-L-Y." Then his expression sobered. "It's a conspiracy, man. That's what I think. Fascist cops lock you up, throw you to the wolves in there, let them beat the crap out of you. Someone messes with your computer record. You're right. This is insane.

You're one of the good guys."

"So what's the buzz around here?" Crockett asked his friend.

"You're out on bail. You've been charged with possession of child porn, but your lawyer is good. Heard a news clip, her saying the cops needed to focus on who really started the fire, not some kid that came to you for help. She sounded believable."

"My story is true," Crockett said. "The facts support it. Jaimie's testimony supports it too."

"You think there's any chance she started the fire?"

"No," Crockett said. He had seen the fear in Jaimie's eyes as she begged him to let her stay the night. Not guilt. It'd be hard, even for her, to manufacture such intense fear. "And there was someone looking for her. Just before the detective and Thomas came over on Saturday morning, somebody else showed up for Jaimie. A guy named Nathan, said he was from social services, said you sent him."

"Not a chance."

"Didn't think you had, but I needed to ask."

"He knew I was Jaimie's case manager," Romans said. "Strange."

"What would someone want from her? From my point of view, it looks like they wanted her trapped in a burning house, and when that failed, they tried to take her from me. But why?"

"And why make sure you can't protect her now?" Romans asked.

"Protect her?" Crockett said. "I'm just doing my best to keep myself afloat."

"They've got you in deep water. Perfect way to keep you from protecting her."

Crockett had been so wrapped up in his own misery, he'd failed to see this. The ah-ha moment was strangely encouraging.

Romans caught Crockett's shift. "Maybe then you make it backfire."

"Something nuts is happening," Crockett said. "So maybe instead of worrying about me, I switch focus and learn everything I can about her. Find out what it is about Jaimie that caused all this."

"Yeah," Romans said. "That's the way I'd do it."

Crockett tried that out mentally. He liked it. Instead of defending himself, go on the attack against the unknowns who'd done this too him. It made him feel stronger, less helpless, and seemed like a good way to fight the despair, too.

"If I try to meet with her to ask questions, how will that look?" Crockett said. "Me asking for time alone with Jaimie, I mean."

"Not good. Nothing to stop you from visiting previous foster parents, though, like Agnes Murdoch. Jaimie was with her and her husband the longest."

"Right."

"You'd need Jaimie's file," Romans said. "Not the stripped down version teachers get."

"That would be helpful," Crockett said. "It's a lot to ask."

"Giving you that file would be breaking about twenty pages of rules and regs. The easiest way to cover my butt is tell you I need to go to the john, but wink and point at a filing cabinet so that you can sneak a look at it while I'm taking my time. But I'm not interested in covering my butt. I know you're innocent. And when it's proven in the courts, no one will fault me for trying to help clear your name. You want the file, it's yours."

Crockett wondered if Romans had any idea how badly Crockett needed someone to believe in him. No wonder the ABC kids loved Romans. Crockett had to turn his head away to blink away some tears. Seemed like tears were becoming second nature.

"Already had a look," Romans jumped in quickly so both could ignore

Crockett losing it. "First thing that stuck out in the file was that Jaimie's been authorized to visit an exorcist."

An exorcist? "Does the file say why?"

"Nope," Brad said. "It was recommended by her child psychiatrist."

She must be that doctor Jaimie kept mentioning.

"That was the second thing I wanted to ask about," Crockett said. "The psychiatrist. I can't remember her name. I was thinking maybe I could talk to her. "

"Dr. Madelyne Mackenzie," Romans answered. "She's pretty high up the food chain. On the board of directors of the Bright Lights Center. It was what— six months ago?— that Jaimie went nuts on the playground, took a bat to that homeless person? That's when Mackenzie started working with Jaimie."

Silence. A who girl who takes a bat to a homeless person is a girl with serious issues.

"Think she'll talk to me?" Crockett said after that beat. "The doctor, I mean."

"No clue," Romans answered.

"Tell me more about this exorcist."

"I don't know much, just that it's a Roman Catholic priest who performs exorcisms. Apparently he and Dr. Mackenzie are partners. Before the priest will agree to an exorcism, he first consults with Dr. Mackenzie to rule out any mental illnesses. What I heard from the grapevine was that several Saturdays in a row, the shrink took Jaimie Piper out to the priest's church."

"So this psychiatrist believes that Jaimie is demon-possessed?"

"That's one conclusion."

"What other conclusions are there?" Crockett asked.

"None really."

"Nobody in the system thinks this is weird?"

"It's buried information. Have any idea how many case files our system handles? Too many. I didn't even know it was there until I looked. Besides, Jaimie's in treatment. Nobody pays attention to how a certified psychiatrist decides to help her, unless the parents get involved and make a stink. Jaimie doesn't have parents."

Crockett started rubbing his palms against his face to relieve some inner tension. Changed his mind in a hurry when he felt his bruises. "Where would you go with this if you were me?" Crockett said.

"Archimedes," Romans said with a sly smile.

"Archimedes?" Crockett repeated. "The eureka guy?"

"Lever guy too." Romans nodded. "Said give him a big enough lever, he can move the world."

Romans leaned forward and pointed his pencil at Crockett. "You be Archimedes when you talk to the psychiatrist. Velvet gloves, iron fist. Start off asking nice for her help. Tell her you're worried about Jaimie, want to make sure nothing happens to her. If that doesn't work, play a little tougher. It's not very professional or scientific, treating a kid for demonic possession. I'd bet that she won't want that information getting out. If she denies the contact Jaimie's had with the priest has anything to do with demons, you get her the other way. Say she shouldn't be trying to convert the kid, taking her to a priest. You know, separation of church and state. Maybe working it from either angle will give you some leverage."

Chapter Twenty-Two

Crockett was back with Amy Robertson, who sat across from him at a local taco place about a block off the beach. The prices were high, but the fish tacos were unbelievable. Her words. Not Crockett's.

He didn't have much appetite. She'd finished her third taco, washing it down with iced tea. He was willing to bet she exercised a couple hours a day, trim as she was and hungry as she was.

"Unless your silence is admiration of me," she said, "self-pity doesn't look good on you. And thing is, I know that you can look pretty good."

"Right." Crockett touched his face. Winced.

"Really." Amy set some photos on the table.

"These are from your ex-wife," she said. "Her attorney e-mailed them to me, some idiot named Dave. He didn't want to talk until he found out I'm with Vadis and Booth. Then of course he tried sucking up as soon as he found out I was partner. Said he was convinced you were innocent and he'd be glad to take on a role in the defense for such a world-renowned firm, yada yada. I told him the photos would be good for now, thanks."

Crockett said. "Squash him someday, okay?"

"Oh my, I detect viciousness. Intriguing."

"Maybe you'll get around to telling my why you wanted to have lunch."

"It's a legal philosophy. Deliver bad news by telephone, because you can exit the conversation quicker. But deliver good news in person, because it allows you to bill more time, and fawning gratitude kills lots of time. I lap it up like diamonds."

"Then I'm surprised we aren't at the Beverly. Taco lunch doesn't seem like something that fits in your circles."

"You're right," she said. "But neither do you. Better for both of us if I keep you out of that circle."

Crockett laughed. Spontaneous laughter that felt even greater than usual because he hadn't done it in so long. He didn't even care that it made his bruises pulse.

She beamed, clearly happy with herself for jarring him out of his funk for a moment. "Difficult not to like me, huh?"

He smiled. "Difficult. And that's even before you deliver the good news."

Her face lost the brightness.

"You did say good news," Crockett repeated, his smile also fading.

"Yeah." But there was nothing light about her voice. "Let me back up a bit, okay?"

He nodded, sobered by the reminder that this was all a challenge for her. A game. At the end of the day, she went home. End of Crockett's day, he was either a dad to Mickey again, or a punching bag for the general population.

"Our firm took this case because of money, Crockett. Plain and simple." He opened his mouth to ask about his benefactor but she put up her hand. "No. You don't find out who is funding this."

"How am I supposed to send my gratitude if I don't know who's footing the bill? You do realize I have hardly a friend in the world, right?"

She hesitated. "Alright. I'll give you something." She raised an eyebrow. "The reason you don't get to find out is because I'm not sure I'll ever find out."

"You don't know who is paying my bills?"

"The firm has received instructions and payment from an out of town lawyer who has hired us to be part of his team to represent you. Someday, if you find out, you tell me."

"Sure." Crockett couldn't have been more confused. But he was beginning to realize that this was way bigger than him, than his relatively small life.

"Regardless," Amy went on, "there's something about you I like. And because I like you, on a personal level I'm hoping you've been set up. Not sure yet how to prove it, but that is what the retainer is for."

"I'm still waiting for the good news," Crockett said. He reached for a tortilla chip.

"Right. We don't know for sure who paid your retainer, but I don't think there is any mystery in why. Our firm has been representing the Los Angeles diocese in child abuse cases over the last decade."

"As in," Crockett said slowly, "priests and children."

"As in eventual confessed guilt and eventual confessed cover-up."

"What could the Los Angeles diocese possibly have to do with me? I am as far as I could be from one of their…followers."

"Listen carefully. Our firm are known as experts in defending the indefensible. Which means I have also become an expert in separating the professional from the personal. But at a price. I'm not sure how much longer I can adore myself with full satisfaction by making life easy on abusive priests." Her face had lost animation. "So the personal me is cheering for you. It would be great to defend someone who really isn't a pedophile."

Crockett tried to withhold judgment. There was no room for condemnation at this juncture. "It's difficult not to once again try to reassure you of my innocence. You might think I protest too much."

"Inhuman if you didn't. It's a horrible accusation for an innocent man. But I don't need it. So keep your dignity. " Some of her animation returned.

"Anyway, if it wasn't an odd enough coincidence that the anonymous client hired our firm through another lawyer to represent you, this is where it gets deeper. As defending attorneys," she said, then continued after a swig of her ice tea, "we—as in the firm—are able to review all the evidence that will be used against you. We were given a copy of the hard drive they found in your attic. Today we learned that a couple dozen images on your hard drive are identical matches to images on the hard drives of some of our other clients at the diocese. "

Stunned, Crockett had difficulty coming up with an intelligent comment, but tried. "So that could help you prove that I am innocent. That the hard drive was planted."

"That is my full intention. I've got a great connection in the hacker world. You ever want someone who can get past the firewall of a computer in the White House, he's your guy. I'm using him to get some digital analysis done that might help."

"That sounds great," Crockett couldn't help but feel hopeful, even amongst the deeply disturbing news that Los Angeles priests harbored child-pornography. There were some things you could read in the newspaper a hundred times yet still never grew unaffected by them.

She gave a tentative nod. "It wasn't an accident we found the matching images. It was a tip. Sent to me via anonymous email. Someone knew about images on two separate hard drives."

"That alone should show I'm innocent."

"Unless," she said, "you sent the email to make it look that way."

"That seems like a serious stretch in logic," Crockett said, feeling a surge of desperation. "Look, something is obviously going on," he urged. Then remembered his conversation with Brad Romans about the priest. "Do you know about the exorcist?"

Robertson's eyes widened.

"Yeah, exorcist." Crockett passed on what he'd learned from Romans about the psychiatrist treating Jaimie.

Robertson had stopped eating entirely as Crockett explained Jaimie's file. "Interesting," she said when he finished. "The question is, how is the exorcist connected to you? It might further suggest that something is going on here that you got dragged into. And that begs the question, what's the conspiracy, and why?"

"I got nothing," Crockett said. "But it has to be about Jaimie. There's a fire, she stays at Nanna's but the next morning Nanna is gone, and minutes after that, someone tries to take Jaimie away by posing as a social services person. Then, I'm framed into looking like I've hurt Jaimie. As to who did any of this and why, I can't even begin to guess. I've been wondering: wouldn't Jaimie have the answers? If I could just talk with her…she trusts me."

Robertson shook her head. "I don't know if you should go down that road. You need to keep some distance from her. Correction, a lot of distance. That's good legal advice. Take it."

"Doesn't mean I have to stay away from the psychiatrist, right?"

"You could try, but it won't get you anywhere. You think lawyers have client confidentiality? Pediatric psych care is a whole other ballgame." She stood, a clear indication the meeting was over.

"One more thing," Crockett said, not getting up. "Seeing as you have this huge retainer."

"I'm listening."

"Won't it help our defense if we can get Nanna's testimony?"

"Obviously."

"I don't think the police are looking that hard to find her. Can you hire someone to start? I don't know where to begin."

Chapter Twenty-Three

Nathan Wilby's day job was managing a trailer park in Whittier. He was smart enough to work somewhere better, but his prison record made that difficult. Not that he minded. The trailer park took him out of mainstream, and his needs were simple. His own accommodations there, which definitely did not live up to any city codes, was a truck camper. While the truck and camper were parked permanently on a patch of gravel in the remotest corner of the lot, every Sunday, at 10:00 a.m., he'd check the truck's oil, start the engine, let it run for a few minutes, shut it off and check the oil again. After that, the transmission fluid, then the tire pressures, including the spare. It gave him comfort knowing that at any moment he could drive away, taking all his earthly possessions.

Nathan's truck camper had an invisible buffer zone that kids and drunks in the trailer park had long ago learned to respect. This buffer zone matched exactly the geographical area that spanned the reach of the long chains attached to two savage mongrels.

Inside, the camper was an incredible contrast of neatness, as if the owner was OCD, which Nathan was. The old linoleum gleamed, the ancient counter tops were uncracked, and every dish and item of cutlery was put in place to the point where Nathan could have cooked in the dark with confidence.

And cooking was something he revered. In the tiny galley of his camper, he'd consult cookbooks of all ethnic ranges, bickering with Abez as he measured and mixed ingredients, with Abez pretending no interest. Abez was jealous of anything that took Nathan's attention from Abez. Including the friendly old woman who sat at Nathan's small table. She thanked him for the meal he set in front of her: Goat cheese, arugula, and roasted red pepper sandwiches on fresh-baked whole-grain ciabatta rolls.

"I would advise against saying grace," Nathan told the old woman. "You look like the type. Abez won't like it."

She glanced at the door. "I'm glad he's not any closer."

"You can see him?"

"Who else could you have been talking too while you made dinner?"

This put the old woman in an entirely new light for Nathan.

"Why won't Abez like it if I say grace?" she asked.

"Any mention of the J word makes Abez howl."

"The J word?"

"The guy who died on the cross." Abez even hated hearing it spelled out J-E-S-U-S.

"Oh," she said. "I certainly don't want to upset him."

That didn't do much to appease Abez. He whispered to Nathan that he wanted the old woman dead.

"Why should I have to kill her?" Nathan asked Abez. "She can't go anywhere. It's safe to keep her here."

Abez wouldn't be able to argue otherwise. Dog chains on her ankles and wrists made her clank as she nibbled at the sandwiches, and Nathan put a gag on her when he had to leave her alone in the trailer.

The old woman, took a healthy bite from her sandwich and said, "You're like me, you know," she said pleasantly. "I have a friend I can talk to all the time too."

Abez tried to interrupt, but Nathan shook a finger at him to silence him.

"I wouldn't call him a friend," Nathan said to the old woman. "More like someone I haven't been able to get rid of for so long that I finally gave up. I talked to a priest about it. He said that I was lucky. Not many people are given the power to have a demon as a companion, especially one high up like Abez. Well, Abezethibou."

"I think I've heard of him," she said.

"Yeah?" Nathan was starting to like this woman. "Abez is the one who convinced the pharaoh to change his mind and chase the Israelite slaves. You know, with Moses. Abezethibou helped the two magicians who had those contests with Moses and Aaron, like turning sticks into snakes." Nathan shook his finger again at Abez, who was hopping from one foot to another, a sure sign of growing anger. "I told you, hang on."

"Abezethibou," she repeated.

"You can see he's only got one wing, looks like a giant bat wing, but red instead of black. I think that's what makes him so cranky."

"Maybe not," the old woman said. "I'm pretty sure that to be a good demon, you can't be caught in a good mood."

Nathan guessed that sooner or later he'd have to kill the old woman. Abez was too much of a secret to share with anyone who might ever leave the camper. But she was so interesting to talk to, that he didn't want to kill her yet.

"Abez has been with me since I was a kid," Nathan continued. "Showed up when my dad ran out. My mom, she had a friend. And this friend would do things to me—let's just say it wouldn't be proper to discuss the details with you—and I would cry all night because I was so weak. Then Abez showed up and asked if I would like to be strong. Abez helped me get rid of my mom's friend. It must have been Abez because I don't remember getting that knife. I do remember the pillow and what he asked me to do to my mom. But then I had to go to jail. They couldn't keep Abez out of jail though. So I guess he's a true friend."

"It's very nice to have a true friend," the woman said. "I'm glad we're getting to know each other. I hope he'll be okay if you and I are friends too. And thank you so much for this delicious meal."

Abezethibou was screaming for Nathan to cut the old woman's throat, but for the first time in a long time, Nathan wasn't in a hurry to do as commanded.

He'd let the woman live. At least until he found the girl. Even after all the instructions and help The Prince had given him over the telephone, Nathan had not been able to get her yet. But Nathan wouldn't give up. He would have to leave the old woman in the camper while he went back out looking for the girl. He'd make the old woman lie on the bed and then tape her arms and legs together and put something across her mouth so she couldn't make noise. She was a sweet old woman. He would be gentle, and she would understand that Nathan had to tie her so that she wouldn't escape.

"Scream all you want," Nathan told Abez. "I'll do it when I'm ready, not when you tell me to do it."

In the morning, he was going to make rhubarb and strawberry breakfast crostini. There was something about soft cheeses he loved, and he'd spread ricotta over toast before spooning on the warm soft preserves just out of the camper's propane powered oven. The old woman would probably enjoy it too. Looked like her teeth were real, so she wouldn't have a problem with toast.

"What's he telling you now?" the old woman asked, glancing at the door.

"He wants you dead. But I don't. I like you. So we'll fight about it for a while. I'm sorry this place is so small. You'll be hearing us argue all night, I suppose."

"Do you want me to talk to him?" she asked. Her smile had gained more intensity.

"Good luck," Nathan replied. "He only listens to Beelzebub. Or to the priest I was telling you about. His name is The Prince. What's your name again?"

"My name is Nanna."

"Nanna. Hey, Nanna, do you like ricotta cheese?"

Chapter Twenty-Four

Mr. Grey, I'm not sure it's appropriate for us to discuss anything to do with Jaimie," Dr. Mackenzie said as she ushered him into her office. In contrast to Brad Romans' space, her walls were filled with framed photos. Mainly of kids with California hills in the background. Probably the Bright Lights Center Crockett had heard about.

"Call me Crockett," he said. He wished he'd stopped at service station and bought a throwaway toothbrush and spent a couple minutes in front of a sink. He hadn't eaten much during his meeting with Amy, but the spices seemed to stick to his teeth.

"Mr. Grey," she said. "I'm very aware that you are Jaimie's teacher and of the charges against you, so I expect us to have a very short and very professional conversation."

Dr. Mackenzie was about Crockett's age. She had blonde hair and an unlined face that might have been attractive save for her pinched expression, like she was parked on a cactus. She wore her dowager clothes like armor, with arms crossed and stance slightly wide. Crockett doubted Dr. Mackenzie cared whether anyone found her attractive.

"And I'm very aware that Jaimie has been temporarily placed in your professional care because her foster parents believe she started the fire. I may be one of the few people who isn't prepared to believe that. I think she's in danger, and I want to help her."

"Given the accusations against you, I'm not sure it's appropriate for you to be involved in any manner," she said. "Frankly, I was hesitant to even meet with you."

"Someone is trying to get to her," Crockett said. "I don't know why, but what happened to me is because I got in the way."

"Do you have any proof of this?" she asked.

"Someone posed as a social services worker to try to take her the morning after the fire." Crockett's gut was tight. He felt defensive and it angered him.

"This, of course, is a police matter."

"They don't believe me." He tried to keep his voice neutral.

"Because you don't have proof."

"I'm here because I'm looking for something to get me that proof," Crockett said. "Helping me will help Jaimie."

"I don't like you trying to push me around. And it won't work. You should first understand one simple foundation. Everything I do is based on helping each child in my care. I'm not influenced by politics or power games or the position or lack of position of parents or other adults I come into contact each day as I work with the children."

"Laudable," Crockett said. He instantly regretted showing his irritation, and instantly paid the price for it, as the woman became even icier.

"Obviously you're missing my point. I don't care if it's laudable. Nor do I care if you think it's laudable. Or if you don't think it's laudable."

"I'm sorry," Crockett said. "You didn't deserve to get some of the stress backlash here. I'm hoping you might be able to tell me something that will help me figure out what's going on."

"That would entail divulging confidential discussions I've had with a troubled child. I don't think so, Mr. Grey."

"I'm facing total professional and personal ruin because I tried to help Jaimie when she needed it."

"No," Mackenzie said. "You're facing total professional and personal ruin because there was a hard drive filled with child porn in your attic."

Why was this woman being such a pitbull?

"I don't think Jamie started the fire," Crockett asked. "I think it's convenient for someone to have her take the blame. Just like it's convenient for someone if I take the blame for a hard drive that isn't mine. Can't you and I work together on this?"

She put up an open hand to block him into silence. She held it there, looking past him. A long moment later, she dropped her hand, looked at him and spoke.

"I've considered it."

"Thank you."

"And I've concluded that no, working with you is not another way to help her. She's better off at the sanctuary of Bright Lights."

Pretty clear that no amount of velvet would work here.

"Why'd you take her to an exorcist?" he asked.

"She told you that?" Mackenzie asked.

"That would entail divulging confidential discussions I've had with a troubled child. I don't think so, Dr. Mackenzie. Why'd you take her to an exorcist? In your professional opinion, is she demon-possessed? Is that what you want to get out to the media?"

"That's your way of offering to help? Exposing the child to lurid speculation?"

Crockett sighed. "No. I can't even run that bluff past you."

She softened slightly. "My sense is that you are an innocent man. You have my sympathy."

"Nothing else? At least explain the exorcist to me. I notice you didn't deny it. Does that have anything at all to do with any of this?"

"This conversation has gone beyond short."

"Give me something. Help me. Help me help her."

"If you're innocent," she said, "I'm sure the world will find out sooner than later. I'd hold onto that instead of trying to involve yourself with Jaimie."

Was she trying to tell him something?

Crockett stood. If she was, it was obvious he wasn't going to learn more from her right now. He needed more leverage.

"Just so you know," he said. "I'm going to do what it takes to clear myself. I'm going to dig and dig and dig until I find out what's been happening."

"I wish you the best."

Chapter Twenty-Five

Fifteen minutes later, Crockett was on the 405, coming up the hills from the San Fernando valley. He was fighting just enough traffic to make him vow, once again, to sell his five-speed for an automatic. Despite six lanes, vehicle movement was clotted. The slowdowns would occasionally bring him to a complete stop followed by acceleration to forty, fifty miles an hour, this randomness nothing more than the chain reaction from a collective urge to go as fast as possible. What happened in this case, Crockett believed, was the bumper-to-bumper mentality. Some guy—just to vilify him properly, he imagined a toupee-wearing used car salesman in his fifties, driving a black Hummer in a hurry to get to a gentleman's club—filling the rear-view mirror of someone in front of him, has to tap on the brakes, which makes the person behind him do the same. And so on and so on and so on, a long chain of braking that forces the gaps in the road to shrink to nothing. Eventually, Crockett envisions, the Hummer guy gets room again, gooses it, almost nudges the bumper in front again, and all the gaps of the chain widen. Until car sales guy taps the brakes again, restarts the cycle. If, somehow, everyone would simply stay the recommended five car lengths apart, traffic flow would be even. And Crockett wouldn't be stuck in his Jeep, constantly gearing down, then up, then down, then up.

Crockett's cell rang. As he put in his earbuds so he could take the call hands-free, he glanced at the area code. 310. Venice Beach maybe?

He answered, hoping it wasn't a telemarketer.

"There's a four-car pile up at Wilshire," a voice said. "Things are going to jam up real fast for you. You got about two minutes to cross over from the left lane or you'll miss exit 59 to Sepulveda. You've got some zigging and zagging to do to get to the exit. I'm going to hang up so you can concentrate. I'll call back."

Then dead air.

Whoever it was had called it correctly. When possible, Crockett took the far left lane, on the theory that the right lane was too slow and any of the middle lanes put you between two lanes of idiots. Farthest left lane gave you a cushion of the shoulder, or the less heavily travelled commuter lane, in case you had to move for an idiot in the one lane to your right. When possible, Crockett also liked to drive five miles an hour faster than the traffic around him, on the other theory that it was easier to see what was happening when you came up on people, instead of letting people faster come up from behind. He was aware of the hypocrisy, scorning his imaginary toupeed car salesman but engaging in his own traffic games, but nobody drove these roads and remained pure for long.

It told Crockett something too, that the caller also knew Crockett's location, where North Sepulveda paralleled 405, with exit 59 coming up fast.

Crockett didn't have time to be concerned about who was surveying him. He obeyed the caller.

He was glad for the short wheel base of his Jeep. He made it across to the exit, getting on Sepulveda by the big white oil tanks. The left turn took him under the 405, and by the time he was in fourth gear again, the northbound traffic was to his right. And on the far side, southbound, as the voice had predicted, clotted traffic was massing up.

His cell rang again. Crockett reached up and clicked his headset. Sepulveda was a four lane here. Two south. Two north. Relaxed speed, little traffic.

"Smart man," the voice said.

"Not smart enough to know who this is." Crockett tried to ignore the surge of concern that flooded him. He had already felt as though he was being watched. Now he knew he was.

"Catfish. Just call me Fish. Amy Robertson told me I needed to watch your back. Said to give you whatever help you wanted. "

It tumbled into place. The hacker Amy had mentioned.

"Uh, hi there, Fish."

"So, is she hot?" The guy said, as if he was talking to a close friend.

"Yeah, Amy is attractive," Crockett said, going with it. "Trouble is, she knows she's hot."

"I never got too far with Amy, but it was always worth a try," Fish said. Crockett could hear Fish's self-satisfied smile through the phone. "But I was referring to the doctor. She didn't give you much time, did she? I'm not surprised—she's a Burbank girl." It sounded like he was typing on a keyboard. "Let's see. Dr. Madelyne Mackenzie. Completed her undergrad at Pepperdine. Masters and PhD at Berkley. Saw her photo already. No makeup. Hair looks like it's all split ends. Bet she's a vegan, and sometimes vegans are hot. As long as they shave their legs."

Now Crockett knew how long Fish had been tracking him. Since he'd called Amy in the parking lot outside of Mackenzie's office, asking Amy to put her computer wizard in touch with him.

"Not bad," Crockett said.

"So what do you want from me?" Fish said, clearly not needing the compliment. "And give me a big list. Amy's waving a lot of cash in my face."

Crockett was just passing the turn to the Getty Center. It was a great place. Every year he took his class there. He loved watching the kids everyone called misfits lose their too-cool-for-school bravado and gape at the buildings, the view, the art. As he drove, speaking to a hacker who was trying to help clear him of a crime he didn't commit, Crockett passed the Getty Center with an acute sense of nostalgia for simpler times.

"Sounds like you've already started on what I need," Crockett said, ignoring his sentimental feelings. He would gladly use Fish's help on Amy's dime.

This exorcism angle was weird enough that it deserved some attention. And he could think of only one way to get it as fast as possible.

Computer hacking.

"I'd like to know everything I can about Madelyne Mackenzie," Crockett said. "Think you can do some serious digging?"

Chapter Twenty-Six

Jamie carried a handful of carrots. She stood inside the wood railing fence at the retreat center, feeding the carrots to the horse that she called BB, for Black Beauty.

Mr. G had given her the book of the same name during the previous school year. He knew she loved horses, and convinced her to give the story a try. The coolest part for her was that the horse was telling the story, from when he was a colt to pulling cabs in London to his happy retirement in the country. She cried when Rob Roy was killed in a hunting accident, and then cried again later when she found out that Rob Roy was Beauty's half-brother. That was weird, crying over something that was made up. She didn't cry over things that were real.

Maybe part of her crying was that Beauty didn't seem to have family, but was passed from owner to owner. Kind of like her. She hoped someday she would end up happy like Beauty, and she was really glad that Dr. Mackenzie had been helping her. Dr. Mackenzie, and her bracelet.

The first time she had learned about her bracelet, she felt both scared and good at the same time. Scary because of what it meant. Good because it explained so much.

The horse in front of her knew all of this because Jaimie had told him. She wanted to believe that BB could understand, just as if he were a horse who could put his entire story into a book.

Jaimie had her story too.

But Dr. Mackenzie said her story had to stay a secret. If she hadn't been so scared the night of the fire, she wouldn't have said a word to Mr. G about how she felt.

And he wouldn't be in such trouble now.

~~~

Madelyne Mackenzie drove through the gates into the Bright Light Center, and saw Jaimie inside the fence—against the rules—feeding a horse.

Usually, the drive from her Burbank office to Bright Lights refreshed Madelyne Mackenzie. She loved the shift from concrete and pavement and car exhaust and the cacophony of city noise to browned hills against blue sky and dappled tree shadows and the rush of wind through her opened windows.

Not this time, with the pain and confusion so easy to see across Crockett Grey's face, and just as easy to see that he was fighting to hide it and believing he was successfully putting on a brave front.

She told herself she wasn't responsible for what had happened to him, but knew herself too well.

If Mackenzie had been in a position to answer Jaimie's calls for help, Jaimie wouldn't have gone to Crockett Grey's house. That was the first level of guilt for Mackenzie. The second was in not understanding truly what was a stake, and how Jaimie's enemies were determined to stop her.

She could tell herself that it wasn't her fault that O'Hare hadn't done a good enough job of keeping the last six months of correspondence secret. Maybe not even O'Hare's fault. The Vatican was huge labyrinth of the unknowable. What had started as a simple phone call to O'Hare had grown into something so complicated and unbelievable but real, that at no point could she have backed out. The frog in water thing, heating up the water so slowly that the frog allowed itself to be boiled to death.

Maybe that was her. Still, she'd made the choices that got her into the water in the first place.

But Jaimie had been swept into this, little choice on her part.

And Crockett, no choice whatsoever.

That's what was bothering Mackenzie the most. Her own determination to eradicate a childhood bogeyman becoming a campaign that dragged in the innocent.

No turning around. It was all or nothing now.

With some much—everything—riding on Jaimie.

"Hi," Jamie said as Dr. Mackenzie walked up to the fence.

Jaimie slipped underneath the railing and outside the fence, waiting for admonishment from Dr. Mackenzie. Kids weren't supposed to be that close to the horses.

"Good day?" Dr. Mackenzie asked.

"Lots to think about," Jaimie said. Her shadow fell in front of her, melting into Dr. Mackenzie's shadow.

"You afraid?" Dr. Mackenzie asked.

"Not much," Jaimie said. "I think it would be worse, but you've helped me understand a lot."

"I mean are you afraid for the next few days," Dr. Mackenzie said.

"Rome and everything?"

Dr. Mackenzie nodded.

Jaimie could have given an evasive answer. She was good at that. But after all that she and Dr. Mackenzie had been through, it was better to talk about stuff.

"Not afraid of Rome," Jaimie said. "But it's weird. I've been feeling sad. I hardly ever feel sad. Maybe it's because of Nanna, you know, Mr. G's neighbor. You know, she and I stayed up a long time after he brought us back from the fire. Talking."

Jaimie caught the look on Dr. Mackenzie's face. Brief alarm.

"Not about Evil," Jaimie said quickly. "I made a promise to you that it would be our secret. It is. I don't want people thinking I'm crazy."

"Jaimie, you're not crazy. If you're feeling sad about it, we can talk more."

"We've been through that, so don't worry. Thing is, she really was a sweet old lady. It's like, two in the morning, and she made me hot chocolate and sat and talked with me like she was my grandmother. It's not like I want my own grandmother or anything, because that would be like wishing for the moon, but it got me to thinking that I'd sure like to be that kind of grandmother someday. You know, someone who would be nice to kids and have a house with cats and family photos and be able to look back on a whole lifetime of snapshots that didn't have Evil waiting nearby. Kind of makes me sad, wondering if I can ever have that."

"It's what we both want for you," Dr. Mackenzie said.

"I notice you're not promising it will happen."

"I'm doing my best to make it happen. It's why Father O'Hare is here."

"What about the guy who burned down the foster house?" Jaimie said. She'd been waiting a while to ask this question. Now seemed like as good as time as ever. "What does Father O'Hare say about that?"

"He says we are safe here at Bright Lights. And that once you help him in Rome, you'll always be safe."

"You believe him?"

"I do," Dr. Mackenzie said.

"Good," Jaimie said. "When all of this is over, I'd like to go back to Nanna's house. She said I could stop over anytime I wanted. Every day, even. She wants me to help her with computer stuff because she says it's too hard to see things on the screen and it would be nice to have my help. I think she knows I'd like to pretend she's my grandmother and was just using an excuse to make me feel better about visiting. But you know what I think? I think she wouldn't mind having someone like me stop by a lot. Maybe she wants to pretend I can be like a granddaughter."

Something strange about Dr. Mackenzie's face.

"I promise," Jaimie said. "I'll never tell her our secret. Or anything about Rome. Evil won't hunt me at Nanna's place, right?"

Chapter Twenty-Seven

Crockett parked near a two story building out at the Santa Monica airport. He was shutting the door to his Jeep on his way to see Fish when his cell rang. It was Julie.

As usual, his heart jumped as if a high school crush was calling.

"Hey," he said, keeping his cool. She held so much that he wanted for himself.

"Hey," she said back, voice softer than her usual neutral. "Look, I feel bad about this morning."

He leaned against the car door. "Me too. But not about telling Dave I'd kick his butt. Look, if you guys are going to be an item, he's got to know that—"

"Let's not start this again," she said. "It's obvious how you feel about him."

"Actually, what I was going to say is that he's got to know that his job number one better be to take care of you and Mickey. And if he doesn't, then he deals with me.."

Long silence. Then a strange sound. It took him a moment to understand. She was crying.

"Julie…"

"I'm okay," she said. "Anyway, I called because Mickey misses you. Hang on."

A shorter silence.

Then came Crockett's favorite word.

"Daddy!"

He choked back the tears. "Mick. Hey buddy! You doing good?"

"I'm doing well," Mickey said, his voice full of innocence that Crockett envied. "Mommy doesn't like it when I say I'm doing good. I'm supposed to say 'doing well.' Anyway, I missed you, Daddy. Where were you? I thought we were going to the zoo."

"We still are," Crockett said. "Some grownup stuff got in the way. But we'll go very soon, okay?"

"You never let grown-up stuff get in the way before."

"I know, buddy. But it shows you that this grownup stuff was something too big for me to push aside. 'Cause you know if I could have been with you, I would have. You are the most important person."

"I know, Daddy. That's okay. But let's go soon, okay? I think the kangaroo is going to have a baby. Won't that be cool?"

Crockett found himself nodding to nobody. "Very, very cool."

"See you later, alligator," Mickey said. Crockett had to chuckle at the abrupt conversation ending. Mickey wasn't much for phone conversations—he liked Skype.

"After a while, crocodile," Crockett answered, his mood markedly lifted.

Crockett was hoping Julie would get back on the phone too. But nothing.

He slipped the phone into his pocket. Thinking. Whatever it took, he would keep his promises to Mickey. They were going to the zoo.

⁂

The Fishloft, as Catfish called it, was on the top floor. The center piece of his loft was a black leather couch where Crockett now sat. He faced the de rigueur, 3D flatscreen television, hooked up to video controls.

There was an L-shaped computer desk in a corner with a rolling chair, where Catfish sat in front of his three computer monitors. There were a couple of cheap floor lamps in the room too. Not much else. No paintings or posters on the walls.

From the computer desk, Catfish leaned back in his chair, hands clasped behind his head.

Catfish was big, like football big. Brush cut, earnest face. Could have stepped out of a set of *Leave It to Beaver.* When he had met Crockett at the door, he'd crushed Crockett's fingers in a handshake and grinned while doing it, then headed to the computer setup with almost a jolly gait.

"There's a reason I wanted you on the couch," Catfish said from where he now sat at his computer screens. He looked studious in his black, horn-rimmed glasses. "You have to check out the video. Grab the remote and hit play."

Crockett clicked once, and the screen slowly became luminescent, showing the side of his own head in a close up. It took a couple of seconds for him to realize what it was.

It was Crockett in Fish's doorway. Crockett's bruised face filled the screen. Then came his wince that Crockett had not well hid when Catfish crushed his hand.

The video kept running, and Crockett saw the side of his face, saw the couch from a sideways view.

Without turning his head, Crockett raised his hand closest to Catfish and that too, appeared on the flatscreen. Although the television was high-def, the image wasn't, so it came from a camera that didn't have megapixels to play with. A small, simple camera.

Crockett clicked off the television. He examined Catfish's grinning face.

The angle of the footage was coming from Catfish's direction. Crockett scanned the area around Fish for a camera. Then it hit him. Low-def camera, had to fit in a tiny place.

"Your eyeglasses," Crockett said.

"Not bad." Fish pulled off the horn-rimmed glasses tossed them to Crockett. The light in the room was dim, and Crockett ran his fingers over the frame to confirm. In the center of the rim, there was a small circular depression. A camera lens.

"Got them from a private eye," Fish said. "Cool, huh? Been using them in client meetings. Or sometimes I leave them on the desk and walk out, record what clients say behind my back. Valuable. Really valuable."

"Yeah," Crockett said. "Valuable."

Fish was studying Crockett. "You don't look like I expected."

"You mean the bruises? Never thought I'd say this, but I got hammered pretty good by a prison guard."

"Yeah, you've got some nice raspberries. But that's not what I mean. I was expecting some accountant-looking guy. Your bank accounts, bill payments, all of that stuff. They're meticulous. Conservative. I was going to write you off as boring, till I found the surfing stuff about you. It looks good on your resume, that whole story about how you singlehandedly pulled a guy out of the water after a shark attack. I don't know if I would have done it. Surfboard's not the safest escape strategy in blood-filled waters."

"That was a long time ago," Crockett said, simultaneously impressed and disturbed at the access Fish had gained into his life.

"Show me the scar?"

"Um, no." The shark had taken a chunk out of Crockett's left calf muscle. "So why do you bring this up? Just showing off?"

"Yup. Cracked your home computer in under ten minutes. You need to set up a firewall. Really. And set your web browser so it deletes your history once a day. Got to say, though, you're one of the few clients I've had who doesn't surf adult sites."

Tell that to the authorities.

Crockett was ready to cut to the chase. "You left me a voice mail that said you found something about Madelyne Mackenzie?"

"Yep. Crazy stuff. She's running a genome test on your student. As in analyzing her genetic code." He began clicking away at his keyboard then turned back to Crockett. "After you asked me to find out what I could earlier today, I did a little bit of spear phishing. The genome thing is one of the strangest bits I discovered about her."

Fishing by Fish? What? "How did spear fishing help you discover Madelyne's genome project?"

"P-h-i-s-h-i-n-g," Fish spelled it out as if he was talking to a six-year-old. "Basically, spear phishing is a more sophisticated version of regular phishing, when someone creates a junk email that tricks the person into clicking a link and thereby delivering personal information. It's clumsy. Spear phishing on the other hand is much more elegant. Targeted specifically to the victim. In this case, Mackenzie. She clicked the link and I was then able to access everything in all her e-mail accounts."

"You've already gone through her emails?"

"Scanned, read, and transferred. I put them on another server. I'll give you the URL and a password so you can access them anytime. Mostly boring crap. But this genome thing. It's specific to Jaimie Piper."

"Genome. As in DNA." This guy was as good as Amy had said.

"Exactly. Mackenzie sent a blood sample from Jaimie Piper to a geneticist at the University of Tennessee. Asked for a complete analysis."

"Weird," Crockett said. How this information was going to help him he didn't know, but somehow he sensed it was part of the bigger picture of his arrest. "How long ago did she send the emails?"

"On-going for the last six months."

"Did the emails give any reason why Dr. Mackenzie is looking into Jaimie's DNA?"

"Nope. But for whatever reason, Mackenzie was posing as a guy named Greg Biette, a divorce attorney. She set up an alias email account under that name to feed to her real account. Obviously, she's trying to keep this secret for some reason."

Crockett let out a breath, starting to feel more comfortable with this Catfish guy. His calm and forthcoming demeanor made Crockett want to trust him. "Strange, looking into Jaimie's DNA. That alone should mean something. Right?"

"It should, yeah. Given that your doctor friend also hired a genealogist to put together a family history on Jaimie, going back three centuries. Maternal side only."

"Three centuries? Anything in the emails that indicates why?"

"Here's where it gets really weird. Mackenzie specified for the genealogist to look for witches." Catfish grinned at Crockett. "Turns out it was a dud. No witches in the girl's past. But you got to wonder why such an odd and specific request. And there's more."

"Spill it…"

"I'm not the only person tracking in her cyberspace."

Crockett felt himself gaping.

Catfish kept his self-impressed grin in place. "Someone else is tracking Madelyne's digital activity. A keystroke logger. It's a new technique, from Europe. Not many standard virus detectors will find it. But it's not quite good enough to operate without hogging a bunch of her CPU."

"Let me get this straight," Crockett said. "Keyboard logging. As in knowing everything she types."

"Yes. Someone records every keystroke she makes," Catfish said, his face staying so earnest it contributed well to his manufactured aura of innocence. "Emails. Passwords. Web surfing. But it wasn't done to rip her off. I checked her credit rating. There's no identify theft. No strange withdrawals or transfers from her bank accounts. "

Crockett said. "You went all those places? You can do those things?"

Fish waved it away, like it was nothing. "Easy. Even better, I can remove those pesky anonymous complaints about you from the school system computers. Oh wait, already did that. Do you think that will mess with the cops? And the people who put them there in the first place?"

Crockett's mouth was still hanging open as Catfish continued. "I went ahead and set up a backdoor Trojan, which will help me find out the other guy who's tracking her. But in the meantime, you should find this interesting. She's got a reservation at a hotel in Rome in the next few days. But I can't find anything showing how she's going to get there. No airline tickets. Nothing either to show what she plans to do there, or if she's meeting someone.."

Crockett leaned back against the couch, processing all of this. Italy. Genealogy. DNA. It seemed disconnected, but he knew it wasn't. A thought cropped up. "What about the results of the genome testing? Has Mackenzie gotten them back?"

"Yup."

"And?"

"There was an e-mail but I couldn't find the attachment; she must have printed it and deleted it. But there's a way to work around that. A little thing I like to call social engineering. You're going to have to do it yourself, so let me explain."

Chapter Twenty-Eight

On Tuesday morning, early, the sun just up, Crockett swung in his hammock in the backyard of his bungalow, alone except for a ruby-throat hummingbird hovering in front of his feeder. Seconds later, he had true solitude. Hummingbirds didn't stick around too long. He wondered if that was a metaphor for something.

Normally, he treasured his solitude. The acreage of his backyard was tiny, but there was a palm tree. A charcoal barbecue. The hummingbird feeder. His hammock.

Until the events since Friday night, Crockett had made himself as content as possible considering the circumstances. He had a decent job that made him feel good about himself. He had an amiable enough relationship with his ex-wife with his continual hope they might reconcile, and he had a son he loved as much as life. And a neighbor he enjoyed visiting with on occasion.

Now solitude was troubling. First, it reminded him that Nanna was missing. And that reminder led to a domino effect. He couldn't escape that all the rest of what he had structured his life upon had collapsed. With little likelihood of resurrection.

Deliberately, he rubbed the scar at the back of his calf on his left leg. He was wearing a workout shirt and sweat pants, cut off at the thighs. Normal early morning clothes, ready for a run once he put on some shoes.

Crockett didn't think much about that morning, out in the swells, when some guy, maybe twenty yards away, had gone down, flailing and screaming. Everyone else bailed out of the water, Crockett too. Except bailing felt wrong. Not that he'd analyzed it in the moment, but later, he'd realized that what turned him back to save the guy was knowing that no matter how much he rationalized it, not turning back would have been an act of cowardice so grave it would have haunted him always.

There'd been the brief flurry of news reports, but then it was gone. He never talked about it because there was nothing really to talk about. You live and die. Not too exciting. It wasn't that Crockett minded simplicity. He really just wanted to be a good dad and a good husband and a good teacher.

Still, he rubbed his leg to remind himself of his moment of bravery. That bright piercing moment of timelessness, pulling this guy out of the water, the shark bearing down on his board, Crockett reaching out with his fist to punch the rough skin of the shark's nose. The pain that wasn't pain thanks to adrenaline, realizing the shark and the gaping mouth had veered and the teeth had come down on Crockett's leg. Then nothing to think about expect for the hard, hard swim back into safer waters, wondering if the shark would return. Crockett recalled thinking the strangest thing: that the guy he'd rescued had horrible halitosis.

There'd been other occasions when Crockett drew on his survival from the shark attack, reasoning that if he could take on a shark, he could take on anything.

Then Ashley had died.

He'd finally run into something that he was powerless to fight, something worse than a shark attack, something that had weakened and drained him to the point he could barely get out of bed for months.

He rubbed his scar one last time, fighting the urge to get back into bed and lose himself in the enveloping depression that threatened.

Mickey deserved more than that, though. So did Nanna.

So it was time for more bravery, in the form of Catfish's social engineering.

—⊸

Crockett had his cell phone in hand. It was a three-hour time zone difference, but he still wasn't in a hurry to dial the number. He mentally rehearsed the way the conversation might go, based on advice from Catfish. Finally, he punched the numbers. Only took two rings for an answer.

"Dr. McFarlane here."

Crockett tried to imagine the man on the other end, in Knoxville, at the University of Tennessee. Lab coat? Round spectacles? What exactly did a genetic scientist look like?

"Dr. McFarlane," Crockett said with an air of total confidence. "It's Greg Biette calling. I hope this isn't too much of an intrusion on your time."

"Not at all. What can I do for you Mr. Biette?"

"I trust you recall the DNA analysis project I sent you?"

"Yes. I was hoping to hear back from you."

"Right. The thing is, I was clickjacked," Crockett said.

"Clickjacked?"

"Sounds ridiculous, doesn't it. Essentially, someone stole control of my computer. It could happen to anyone. And trust me, you don't want it to happen to you. Had to wipe it clean. Lost all my data."

"That's a shame."

"Indeed." Crockett hoped he wasn't overplaying the academic-guy shtick. "I'm not a computer geek, so I might have some wrong terms here. But what happens is that Web pages will have a concealed link. There will be a set of dummy buttons, and when you click on the visible buttons, you are really clicking on buttons on a hidden page. The short of it is, some malicious hacker installed a bunch of viruses and caused my computer to wipe itself clean."

"Shocking," Dr. McFarlane said, clearly buying it. "What do they say? The internet is the wild, wild west all over again.

Crockett forced a chuckle into his voice. "Good one. Wild, wild west. WWW. Never heard that before."

The guy chuckled too.

It was working like Fish had promised. Social engineering. Access the computer through a person, not a firewall. Get a conversation going, unite the person on the other end against a common foe, make a good emotional connection., and then ask for what you wanted.

"As you can imagine," Crockett said, "I'm in the process of rebuilding my computer and files. And I'm a little gun shy about work emails right now. If I give you a brand new email address, would you mind resending the report to me?"

Crockett expected some difficult questions now, expected he'd have to prove he was Greg Biette. He was armed with all the background info that Catfish had scoured from Madelyne's emails.

"No problem," Dr. McFarlane said. "Happy to email it again."

Crockett gave him the hotmail address that Catfish had set up.

"Mr. Biette," Dr. McFarlane said when Crockett was finished. "I know you mentioned that you weren't interested in sharing where you got Ms. Piper's DNA sample, but now that we're on the phone, I feel it's important to try again to learn more. The genetic aberration might seem minor, but it doesn't take much to make a difference. Nothing about the gene sequence gives any hint of what actions the code dictates. Can you at least let me know if it's disease related? I'd really, really like to know how the DNA change is manifested."

"Manifested?"

"Yes. In other words, which actions and physical changes result from the code difference. I mean, something like this could be huge from a research point of view."

Huge? Crockett wanted to ask how huge, but didn't know whether the fictional Greg Biette should already know.

"Here's my promise," Crockett said, choosing the cryptic route. "When it's alright to share the information, you'll be the first to know."

McFarlane seemed satisfied, and after they said their goodbyes, Crockett hung up the phone, floored by the conversation.

Huge? What in Jaimie's genetic makeup had marked her in such a way that a genetic scientist would declare it as *huge*? She'd always seemed like an average messed-up girl to Crockett. Was it something about this darkness?

Maybe he'd learn it from Agnes Murdoch, the foster parent Brad told him about, the woman who'd had Jaimie the longest. But first things first. Now that he'd done all he could at the moment to learn more about Dr. Mackenzie and Jaimie's mystery genes, he had to do what he could to take care of Nanna.

Chapter Twenty-Nine

C rockett had been to plenty of police stations before. Aside from his recent adventure with the Santa Monica police force, he'd spent time at police stations because of his ABC kids. Typically, he was meeting parents there because the kid had done something wrong. Or worse, and tragically more often, he was meeting kids there because their parents had done something wrong.

He especially recognized the smell. To Crockett, it was like old cheese. Too many hormones and pheromones and the rest of the catalogue of "mones" emitted through sweat of predators and prey, hookers and johns, victims and victimizers, emitted through the sweat of the cops themselves, who were sometimes predators and johns and victimizers themselves, decades of a stew of sweat in confined quarters with not enough ventilation.

He also knew to expect the tired cynicism on the other side of the counter. He wouldn't have taken it personally if the guards hadn't made it personal during his most recent visit. So when he approached the woman behind the counter, he didn't hold back his attitude in trying to get what he wanted.

"Let me get this straight," said the irritated receptionist. She was young, black, in uniform, and probably felt like she was twenty hours into an eight-hour shift. She was doing her best not to stare at the mess of Crockett's face. "You want to check if a missing person report is on file, but you need a homicide detective to help you."

"Not any homicide detective. Pamela Li. Just get her already. And tell her it's Crockett Grey."

"Your face," she said, blatantly ignoring Crockett's request. "I got money you deserved it."

Crockett couldn't help a snort of laughter. "Deserve is a complicated word. Look, I'm not trying to push you around. The lady missing is my neighbor. She's old. She makes me cookies. I cut her lawn. I'm afraid for her. And I want the best for her."

"I liked pushy better. Easier to say no to." She gave a theatrical sigh and picked up the phone. "You're going to want to hope Li likes you. 'Cause when she gets it into her head she doesn't like you, it's no fun. Trust me."

"I'm not impressed with this little game you're playing," Pamela said, refusing to come around the counter as she faced Crockett. "And no, I'm not discussing this with you."

"Just tell me you're looking for Nanna" Crockett said, trying to keep his cool.

Young And Black And Tired leaned on her elbows on the counter. "Detective, the missing lady is his neighbor. Old lady. Makes him cookies. He cuts her lawn. Can't we... you... help him out?"

"The guy in front of you is also an accused pedophile," Pamela snapped. "He's out on bail. With an order not to get within a hundred yards of a playground. His little game is that he's here to pretend he wants his neighbor found."

Young And Black And Tired lost her smile. "Sorry I called you down. How about I deal with this?"

"No," Pamela told her subordinate. "You made the right decision calling me. Gives me an insight into this creep."

Pamela turned to Crockett, who realized he was rolling his eyes. This was exasperating.

"Is this some kind of bluff?" Pamela said.

"Nanna's gone, Detective. I've been feeding her cats. She never leaves unless she's arranged that, either with me or a pet service."

Pamela let out a sardonic laugh. "I know what you're trying to do, Grey. Set up some sort of conspiracy thing. You're innocent. Somebody is doing all this to you."

"I *was* set up. Look a little farther than the dish someone served up on a tray for you."

"I don't do missing persons anyway. What I do is try to find out why people died in a fire. And your face is dead center on the whodunit dartboard."

"See?" Crockett said. "That's why you're the person to find Nanna. You're a bulldog."

"You're right about that," Pamela said. She turned on her heel to leave.

"Please," Crockett begged, turning his tone soft. "I get it. You think I'm scum but please don't punish Nanna for it. Tell me at least if there's anyone out there looking for her?"

"She's a person of interest."

"That's it? No missing person search? She's in her eighties."

"And, from what her son in St. Louis said, she's very spry and independent and prone to going on short trips without telling him. And if she was as close a friend to you as you say, and if she really was as helpful with Ms. Piper as you claim, seems she'd have saved one of her random jaunts for another time. When there wasn't the possibility of a scandal at your door."

That was one way to look at it. He had to keep trying. "Can you at least check to see if her credit card has been used?"

"I'm done discussing this with you, Mr. Grey."

"Then I'll file a report. I can do that. I'm her neighbor."

Pamela Li turned to the receptionist.

"He's all yours. File it for him."

"Your name," Young And Black And Tired said even before Pamela was gone, a hard flatness to her eyes. "Address and relationship to the missing person."

Crockett wasn't a detective. But it didn't take a detective to conclude that filing the report was going to be less than pleasant. It was just another reminder of how life would be for a man accused of abusing children

Chapter Thirty

C rockett didn't know if he'd be able to learn a lot from Agnes Murdoch, but he was going to be alert for anything that remotely hinted at the need for DNA testing or a genealogy report.

It was why he'd driven to Anaheim, almost within the shadows of Disneyland. The place was bleak to him now, as it baked in sunshine white through smog. Crockett pushed away memories of his time with Ashley there, not needing the weakness and where it could lead.

Now he sat in a house that had been built before Disneyland, breathing through his mouth.

"Talking when you should have been listening?" Agnes Murdoch said in a raspy voice. She pointed at Crockett's face.

No problem deciding how it had become so raspy. As she finished speaking, she reached across the armrest of her green couch, crushed the remnants of her cigarette into a nearby ashtray, and immediately lit another.

"Wish I had a better answer," he said, "but yeah."

"Other guy look worse than you?"

"Wish I had a better answer," he said, "but no."

Crockett turned his head to the side and stifled a cough. Cigarette smoke. Agnes' ashtray—a statue of a cherub holding a plate above his head—looked suspiciously like it had been co-opted from a garden, that it was supposed to hold water for birds. Filled with twisted cigarette butts, it was the perfect height to stand at the edge of her couch. Reaching it took her no effort.

"So, Crockett Grey, tell me why you're here," Agnes said with what looked like an unintentional scowl.

Crockett sat forward. "I'm doing a little research, and Brad Romans mentioned you've had lots of foster kids over the years."

"Research?"

"Well, I'm specifically asking about one child. You had Jaimie Piper until about three years ago, right? Until your husband died?"

"You get down to business, don't you? Yes, George died. He was a good man. Hard worker. He died of lung cancer, bless his soul."

From information in the case file, Romans had told Crockett that Agnes was in her mid-fifties. Obviously she had not received the memo that linked smoking to cancer. Or the one that warned of the damage cigarettes did to skin. Blonde wig notwithstanding, she looked two decades older. In the saggy springs of an armchair across from her, Crockett was amazed at the depth of the wrinkles in her face, getting a visual of what might happen if Agnes stepped outside in a good rainstorm. He imagined those wrinkles filling with water, imagined Agnes stepping back inside her trailer, giving her head a shake, like a dog throwing water off fur, imagined the rainwater splattering in all directions.

"Was Jaimie an easy child to live with?" Crockett began.

Agnes' eyes narrowed with calculation. "Why should I talk to you about Jaimie Piper?"

Crockett was surprised. "Didn't Brad Romans call ahead?" he said. "To let you know it would be okay to discuss her with me."

"Yeah, he called. Okay's one thing. Lots of things are okay to do. But I still need a reason to do it."

"Fair enough," Crockett said. "Well—"

"I'll take Cowboy killers," she said. "That's a good reason."

Crockett felt what he'd call justifiable confusion.

"Marlboro Reds," she said. "A carton of cowboy killers would be a great reason. I'll even buy them myself and save you the errand."

Ah. She wanted cash. "A carton. That'd be what, fifty bucks?"

She sneered. "Non-smoker, aren't you?"

"Not at this moment," he said, eyeing the smoke-filled room but avoiding the temptation to wave the fog away.

"Hundred bucks gets you close," she said. "The lousy government taxes people to death on cigarettes. How about a fat tax? Stuff burgers and fries down your gullet all day, kills you just as quickly as cigarettes. Except you're fat and ugly when you die."

Instead of wrinkled and ugly? "Hundred bucks for a carton," Crockett conceded, keeping his thoughts to himself. He'd be willing to pay for whatever information he could collect about Jaimie. Although he cared about her, his investigation wasn't as much about helping as it was about looking for answers, any answers that might open the door a crack to exoneration. He wanted Jaimie to be safe, of course, but helping her had already gotten him into enough trouble. He needed to understand why someone seemed to be after her, and why somebody was also after him. "Sure. I'll pay it."

"Costs me gas and time to get to the store too."

"Twenty for that?"

"Hundred. I'm not cheap."

"Fine." Crockett clenched his jaw. "Two hundred for a carton of cowboy killers." He'd see if Amy Robertson's legal fund covered it. If not, still didn't matter. Wasn't like he'd be able to spend money if he went to prison.

"That's right."

"Tell me anything you remember about Jaimie Piper."

"Just a minute," she said, enjoying the game of testing his patience. "It's a little early in the day, but it's 5 o'clock somewhere. You like vodka?"

"No, thanks." Crockett pulled out his wallet. He put two fifties on the coffee table. "Two more of these when I leave. Now please, tell me, you had Jaimie as a foster child when she was just a baby, right? What was she like?"

"Jaimie," Agnes said. "Easy one to remember. Social services people said she'd be a lot to handle. Said the first family that had her just gave up trying to keep her. Said she cried and howled all the time, no matter what they did. First night with us, same thing. Until I gave her to George. She calmed right down. Didn't take us long to figure out it was his golf bracelet."

"Golf bracelet?" Crockett felt like he'd stepped into a black and white television episode, spliced between *The Twilight Zone* and Abbot and Costello, where he was playing the part of the man to set up the punch lines. He couldn't imagine that anyone who lived in this house was a golf enthusiast. It didn't fit the profile.

"George couldn't hit a ball out of his shadow, but he loved the game. Bought every gadget in the world to try to fix his swing. He wore a copper golf bracelet on his left wrist. It was some kind of magnet meant to help circulation, make you less tired, all that stuff."

Crockett nodded like this made sense.

"See, he's holding Jaimie in his left arm and she went quiet right away. Remember now, she was hardly more than a baby. That arm'd get tired, so he'd switch to his right arm, she'd start howling. He'd switch back, she went quiet. Took a while to figure it out, but it was the bracelet. She loved it. If we put her in the crib without it, she'd howl. Give her the bracelet, she'd settle right down. It was some kind of soother for her."

"Interesting," Crockett said. "Make you think maybe she was demon-possessed?"

"Are you messing with me?" Another suspicious scowl.

"You're right. Bad joke."

"I promise you, the thing never failed. Even when she got older. We ended up buying her a smaller one as a bracelet. She wore it like jewelry. Probably still does, for all I know."

This wasn't exactly helpful.

"Did she act out a lot otherwise?"

Agnes looked offended. "We were good parents, George and me. We kept a good eye on all our kids. We didn't do it for money. We were foster parents for love. I've gotten letters from some of them, grownups now, thanking us for giving them a home." She took a puff of her cigarette and Crockett detected a hint of sadness in her eyes. "And just so you know, we never smoked in front of them. Took it outside when the kids were around. Back when George was around."

Crockett was surprised by this woman's genuine affection for her foster kids. He'd pigeonholed her immediately, based only on appearance. Okay, and on her bribery. But humans were complex.

"I don't doubt you were a good parent," Crockett said, and meant it. He had no real idea what he was looking for, or even how to best phrase the question. But there had to be something in the mystery that seemed to surround Jaimie's family tree that led to someone framing him. Something that Dr. Madelyne Mackenzie wanted to find out too, as evidenced by her secret research.

Or maybe there was no connection at all. But Crockett didn't know what else to do, except flail around. The alternative was to stay at home, crawl back into bed, and wait for a trial that in all likelihood would end with a court-ordered separation from Mickey.

"Anything weird about her family background?" Crockett asked.

"Well, it's funny you should say," Agnes said after a long pause. "There was a doctor's appointment. We had all the records. We had them on Jaimie's birth mom too. The doctor said that their blood types didn't match, said that maybe we should look into it. What I said was that this was a foster parents thing, that social services made mistakes all the time, maybe the original paperwork was wrong. The doctor was busy, moved right on, didn't push us to find out. But I always wondered."

"Wondered?"

"Sure. Was there a mix-up at the hospital? You know, like you hear it on that Maury Povich—wrong baby going home with wrong parents. But I never did track that down. Never thought it would matter that much, one way or another."

Chapter Thirty-One

Your face is looking slightly better," Amy Robertson told Crockett from behind her desk. "But you still need a little help on the cover-up front."

She reached into her purse and came up with a small round disc. Snapping open the disc, she pulled out a buffer pad. Crockett realized it was some kind of makeup. The flaky light brown stuff.

"Don't move," she said. "Tilt your head back and close your eyes."

She leaned over him and gently applied the makeup, first to his neck, then to his face. Crockett gripped his armrests hard, like he was flying through turbulence.

She must have noticed.

"Relax," she said.

Crockett tried. It never made sense to him either, the gripping of the armrests during turbulence. Like that would help if the plane went down.

It took her a few moments to finish patting his face. Meanwhile, Crockett enjoyed the smell of her perfume.

She stepped back. "See for yourself."

Crockett opened his eyes to a small circular mirror. "Uh, thanks," he said. Most of his bruising was hidden.

"You won't draw frightened stares now. Use the makeup often."

She snapped the clamshell container shut, dropped it in his lap, then returned to sit behind her desk. "Now, down to business. Tell me about this email attachment which my secretary had to kill a few trees in order to print out for us. "

She nodded at a stack of paper on her otherwise empty desk. Her large, burnished, and predictably expensive desk.

"Explain client confidentiality to me," Crockett said before he divulged his recent foray into Fish's... questionable methods. Fish may have been her guy, but Crockett had eagerly participated. "For example, hypothetically, if you knew that a hypothetical client committed hypothetical computer crime, are you obliged to keep this hypothetical information confidential to protect your hypothetical client, or are you obliged to take this hypothetical information to the police?"

"Tell you what," she answered with an amused smile. "Lay out this hypothetical situation. Tell it in first person, hypothetically of course. Just stop using the word hypothetical twenty times per sentence for goodness sakes."

"So, uh, hypothetically... I made a call this morning," Crockett said, "to a genetic scientist. I asked him to email me this information."

"Genetic scientist. This, I'm sure will be interesting. I love good stories."

Crockett told the story, starting with how he and Catfish had discovered that Madelyne had posed as a man named Greg Biette in email correspondence with a geneticist at UT, the fact that Madelyne Mackenzie had sent out a sample of blood from Jaimie Piper for DNA analysis about six months earlier, the fact that Mackenzie had hired a genealogist to look into Jaimie's family history. And that her computer had a keystroke logging program on it. For good measure, he told Amy about his meeting with Agnes that morning—during which Amy interrupted and confirmed her client would be happy to reimburse Crockett for the money Agnes had gouged from him. He concluded by telling her about the bracelet and the doctor's claim of mismatched blood types.

When Crockett finished, both he and Amy eyed the printed-out email attachment as if it were the last unwrapped item under the tree on Christmas morning.

Chapter Thirty-Two

Raymond Leakey had a huge headache.

Not literally. He could deal with those. He knew he was verging on alcoholism, and was fine with that. Pills could help him deal with headaches, and he had yet to let his drinking habits affect his work.

His huge headache was right in front him, on a bus bench just off a busy street, almost within the shadows of the Vatican walls.

His Eminence Ethan Saxon, the head of the diocese of Los Angeles. Legs crossed, arms crossed.

Leakey sat on the bench, holding a folded newspaper. He had not had time to take the usual precautions. Saxon hadn't given him the time. Maybe the newspaper and the bus bench would convince any observers that it was coincidence that they were waiting for the same bus. Not likely. Cardinals did not use public transit in Rome. Saxon was too easily identified.

"The man is not in jail," Saxon said. Actually, hissed. "I thought you said you would take care of the problem."

"Maybe there wasn't a problem in the first place." Leakey was weary of coddling the cardinal, but there were orders from above. "There's been no indication that the girl told him anything."

"Either that, or his lawyer is playing it smart and is hiding it until it will have the most impact. You do know who represents him, don't you? Where does he get that kind of clout?"

"I know who represents him," Leakey said. "Still trying to find out how it happened."

Saxon uncrossed his arms and his legs and leaned forward. "If I have to take the next step, I will."

Leakey asked the logical question. "What step?"

"His neighbor. The old woman. It won't be difficult to make it look like the teacher killed her."

"That would be very, very stupid," Leakey said. "It's under control. You don't have to wait long for what you want."

"To me, it doesn't appear to be under control. Plant some evidence that makes it look like the teacher tried to start the fire."

"Impossible. The investigation is already complete."

"Then get rid of the teacher. Completely. If the girl told him anything, there is too much danger if he gets his lawyer looking into it. It's a danger that will always hang over my head, no matter what position I have in the church."

Saxon was making it too easy on Leakey. Until now, there'd been a question of whether to come down on O'Hare's side or Saxon's side. What mattered to Leakey was who's name would be announced to the world when the white smoke was released. For Leakey to get his villa, he needed to be certain he chose the winner. Ahead of time.

And Saxon was quickly becoming a man who needed to be cut loose.

Chapter Thirty-Three

I'm an audio," Amy said after she'd handed Crockett the stack of paper. "Read it to me."

The report was twenty pages long. At Amy's instructions, Crockett had skipped straight to the geneticist's overview.

"Audio?" Crockett echoed.

"Some people learn better by seeing. Some through tactile, hands on. I learn best by listening."

"Ah, learning styles," he said. "I am in the educational field, remember? Seven styles. The correct term for audio learning is aural. There's also verbal, logical, social—"

"Whatever," she said. "Read the summary."

She leaned back in her chair and closed her eyes to concentrate, assuming Crockett would do as commanded.

He did.

In general terms, this analysis involves human DNA and the comparison of more than 32,000 genes and the inherent three billion or so nucleotides within those genes. (Nucleotides are strings of molecules that compose the structural units of DNA.)

"Please," she said. "Tell me this is going to get interesting. I'd rather sandpaper my eyeballs than listen to this."

He kept reading.

In specific terms, the analysis of Jaimie Piper's blood sample was based on a two step process. The first was to have the sample sent to an independent lab for high-throughput sequencing to decode the genome of Miss Piper.

The second step involved searching for differences between Miss Piper's genomes and the map provided by the HGP (The Human Genome Project). The map includes both the genes and non-coding sequences of Miss Piper's DNA.)

"Crockett," Amy groaned. "Shoot me. Please."
Crockett read on, obviously more interested in science than Amy. He was already captivated.

The difficulty in searching for anomalies between Miss Piper's genomes and HGP's map was the sheer volume of data. With 32,000 gene sequences, it was like looking for a needle in a haystack made of needles.

However, through lengthy and painstaking analysis of data generated by computer software, a striking and obvious anomaly for Miss Piper was found near the FOXP2 gene, in the region of chromosome seven.

Miss Piper's anomaly is unknown and/or unreported in any and all fields of human genetic research. But this is what we do know: it is a genetic difference that may manifest itself in any number of diseases or behaviors. The FoxP2 gene, which for example, was identified by studying a severe speech disorder that affects 50 percent of a family in England, caused those with the disorder to be unable to coordinate the fine tongue movements required for speech.

Unfortunately, that a unique anomaly exists in Miss Piper's genetic sample is all that can be stated at this point. Without any information about the individual's health, history, and/or behaviors, it is impossible to speculate as to how the gene sequence manifests itself in development or function.

As previously requested, information on the source of this sample would likely advance this analysis.

Crockett set the paper down.

"Done."

"That's it?" Her eyes were open again. "In short, Jaimie's blood sample contains a genetic difference that has never been charted but he can't guess what it does."

Crockett shrugged, as underwhelmed by McFarlane's conclusion as Amy. "That's it for the overview, and yeah, sounds like that's what he's saying." He paused for a moment, recalling his phone conversation with the geneticist. "Here's something else, based on our earlier conversation…"

"Make it interesting, please."

"McFarlane says the minor code change could result in something 'huge'. He wants to know if there is anything unusual about Jaimie."

"And?"

"I've been thinking about that. The only thing I can come up with is that magnetic bracelet Agnes mentioned."

"Wow," Amy said, without any wow in her voice.

"I know. Not much. But maybe it's something."

Amy idly nodded while flipping through the report. "This is interesting. The last page is an invoice. The analysis cost more than $50,000. Hard to believe that Madelyne Mackenzie cares so much about Jaimie's wellbeing that she'd spend that kind of money. So it begs the question: what does she get out of it?"

Chapter Thirty-Four

Sunlight through the windows of her Bright Lights office. Not exactly an office, though. More like an informal library. The main building at Bright Lights was a long, low structure, meant to blend with the hills behind it, with dorm rooms in both directions forming a kitchen and administrative area in the center.

Weekends were busy, kids and group leaders up and down the hallways in a constant but monitored flow. Middle of the week, like now, quiet. But even at the busiest, Madelyne Mackenzie's room reflected serenity. Comfy couch, bean bag chairs, thick throw rug in the center, book shelves.

She'd hold group sessions in here, or individual counseling. It needed to be relaxed, to get the kids to open up to her.

She wasn't relaxed at this point, even with a mug of tea in her hand.

O'Hare was in a chair opposite, satchel on his lap. Ten minutes earlier, standing outside under an oak tree, Mackenzie had suggested maybe it wasn't the right time to take Jaimie out of the country. He'd requested a quick meeting, but needed to get something first.

The satchel in his lap.

"I understand your concerns about Jaimie," he began. "It's a difficult situation."

"It wasn't easy, either, looking a man in the face who has been dragged into something he doesn't understand." Mackenzie had given a lot of thought to the few minutes Crockett had spent in her office in Burbank earlier in the day.

Poor man. Face swollen from a beating in prison. but shoulders square. An aura of exhaustion and sadness, but somehow resolute. She'd taken the meeting for a couple reasons. One, curiosity. Jaimie spoke so highly of Mr. G, and it was so unusual for Jaimie to have that kind of respect and affection for an adult, that Mackenzie wanted to get a sense of the man. She'd liked him, even to the point of checking the school website and looking for his photo in the 'staff' section to check his appearance without the hideous bruises, enjoying what she saw, the longish hair and the set of his face.

Two, she'd wondered if not taking an appointment might make him too curious. She'd decided ahead of time for the short and impenetrably polite professional approach, responding to his request to meet as if she had nothing to hide.

Three, she did have something to hide. Although Jaimie had insisted she'd said nothing to Mr G about the issue at hand, after consulting with O'Hare, they'd realized it would be wise to see if what Mr. G might know about why Jaimie had been on the run when she knocked on his door.

Good thing. Crockett's question about the exorcist had thrown her. If he hadn't learned it from Jaimie, it must have come from Brad Romans, the social worker, who had access to Jaimie's detailed file.

Mackenzie thought she'd handled the meeting reasonably well. Maybe she'd been a little too cold in places, but that was a reaction to her natural sympathy for the man, overcompensating for it. On the other hand, she didn't know if it had been smart to try to give Crockett some hope. Mackenzie knew that it wouldn't be long until everything in Rome had been resolved. At that point, as O'Hare had promised, levers would be pulled. Crockett would be out of this, life back to normal. Nothing she could tell Crockett though, much as she wanted to help end his nightmare.

"Dragged into something he doesn't understand," O'Hare said. "You mean the teacher."

"Crockett," Mackenzie said.

"I've promised you and Jaimie that in less than a week, it will be over. Trust me, I'm not too happy at what happened. Nobody innocent should suffer here. That's why he's getting the legal help we found him. I'm not an ends-justifies-the-means type of person. Second, it wasn't a practical solution. Effort from one part of the organization to implicate him in something as horrible as child porn, and now me, on the other side, spending resources to negate that. I'm not doing it just because Jaimie insisted. I'm doing this to make it right. Putting the hard drive in his house was stupid. We needed a solution to move him out of the way. Instead, he's getting more involved. But you need to realize that's not the issue here. It's Jaimie."

He patted his satchel on his lap, as if he understood how curious Mackenzie was about it. "Yes, ideally we should reconsider Jaimie's involvement. But you'll see in practical terms, how urgently we need her at this point." He opened the satchel, and pulled out sheaves of paper. "Genealogy reports."

"You have more on Jaimie's family?" Mackenzie had taken the comfortable chair beside the couch, turning it to be able to face O'Hare. "I thought her genealogy chart was a dead end."

"I'm not talking about Jaimie's family tree," O'Hare said. He was usually so confident in his conversations, but now he hesitated. "But others. As it turns out, Jaimie is not the only one."

"What?" Mackenzie stood. "Why did you wait until now to tell me?"

O'Hare pinched the bridge of his nose, like he had headache. "Can you sit? It's not that I waited. This was never supposed to reach you. Understand that even telling it to you now is something that some back in Rome would find unacceptable. But if you're threatening to keep Jaimie here, I don't see that I have a choice."

Mackenzie paced to her door and back. She was angry, of course, but her curiosity and the implications were a bigger factor. Much bigger. She'd deal with the anger later, but right now, she wanted more information. "Others. Like Jaimie. This changes everything."

"Does it?"

"Of course it does. It's staggering. Think of what how this helps me present my case in scientific terms. Other girls like Jaimie! Nobody could continue to deny the conclusions of my research."

"I'm aware of the report's significance," O'Hare said dryly. "Yes, girls that share Jaimie's genetic anomaly, but there are two differences. The first, you will find extremely encouraging for your research. The second difference, however, is what applies now."

"I'll take the good news first."

"I have now confirmed six family pools with the same genetic anomaly These genealogy charts map those six families, ranging from a span of two hundred years to five hundred years, and while we have genealogists still trying to fill those charts completely, already we see that an inordinately high percentage of the women in these families—high enough to make it statistically impossible to discount—are women who were condemned and/ or executed for witchcraft across Europe and North America. In short, it bears out your speculation."

Mackenzie stood again. This time not from anger, but because she couldn't contain the excitement of the discovery. "I knew it. I knew it. I knew it."

First there had come the revelation about the magnetic bracelet and Mackenzie's first inklings this might a genetic factor. Listening to the audio tape of the first session in which Jaimie had opened up under hypnotherapy, Mackenzie had been struck by Jaimie's confusion over her feelings of 'darkness', and her struggles to understand why it overwhelmed her when it did.

The real revelation for Mackenzie had been listening to Jaimie wonder if she was a witch, if people would have burned her in olden times, as Jaimie had said. If it was genetic, Mackenzie had realized, maybe there were girls and women who had suffered in the past for sharing those feelings of darkness. O'Hare had agreed to Mackenzie's suggestion of a genealogy trace of Jaimie's family tree. Both had been disappointed at the lack of results.

"Yes," O'Hare said. "You deserve the credit for suggesting the genealogy trace. What you didn't know, of course was that I applied the same suggestion more broadly."

"Where? How?"

"Where? The most logical place to look. Vatican archives. How? My own research. Dozens of hours, privately. If a person didn't know what to look for, it wouldn't have been found, but you pointed me in the right direction."

"Six family trees!"

"So far. I'm doing my best to untangle all this, but I have to move slowly, making sure no one else connects the different pieces of research and understands what we're trying to learn."

"Six families," she repeated it like a lottery winner might do in the first few hours after the ticket was drawn. "Other girls like Jaimie. Same genetic anomaly."

"Now. And, confirmed by DNA, in the past."

She lowered herself again onto the chair, leaning forward. "DNA? Not just a pattern of witches on the maternal side of a family."

O'Hare gave a discretionary cough. "I arranged for, um, some graves desecrated for the purpose of our research."

Mackenzie didn't care about the impropriety. Or illegality. Or whatever it was. This brought the revelation to a new level. "You're telling me that you ran DNA tests on some of the women who had been executed as witches?"

"Let's just say the church has a long reach, and a lot of cemetery real estate."

"And the genetic correlation was also confirmed?"

"Yes, although you'd never be able to claim that every woman accused of witchcraft carried the anomaly, because witch hunts were unpredictable political beasts. And, let's face it, sometimes all it took was insanity—or even a misdirected grimace—for a woman to be deemed a witch."

"Insanity," Mackenzie said softly, "If some of those women were like Jaimie and didn't know why they felt how they did, that could have *led* them to insanity."

O'Hare nodded, his lips tight. "Poor women. None of them understood their power."

"This just makes it even stranger that my theory about Jaimie's family tree was incorrect. Everything else seems so connected."

"I think it's the DNA analysis that really matters. There is no doubt Jaimie *is* one of them. We'll worry about her family tree later. For now, we really need her in Rome. Soon. If and when the pope dies, everything goes into motion, and if we don't stop it now, you'll never have permission to publish your papers."

He put the papers back into the satchel. "Please forgive me for this, but the stakes are simply too high, and in this specific instance, yes, I have to be an ends-justifies-the-means type of person. If Jaimie doesn't go to Rome, you won't get any of this. All you'll have is Jaimie. And no family tree."

"You're threatening me."

"I have no choice. It doesn't change our agreement. You are only to publish the findings after we've deemed it suitable. Obviously, if we make it through the death of the pope, we will have passed the crisis. Within a year, you can use all of this as research material. But first we need Jaimie's help. Isn't that enough motivation for you?"

"What I want is secondary to what's right for Jaimie."

"Then find a way to convince yourself it's right for Jaimie. Like the scholarship funding that will ensure any education she wants."

He leaned forward, clutching the satchel. "Jaimie is the only one who can help us. The other girls? Our last medical reports give the pope, at best, another two days to live. We don't have enough time to recruit them. They have families. Jaimie doesn't. At this point, as a foster child in your care, she's the perfect candidate."

"We can't put her on an airplane. Aside from the fact that she's a juvenile suspected of arson and her passport will be flagged, we know that she is being hunted. If he knew enough to send someone to burn her house, he's going to know she's on the way. "

"Who says it needs to be a commercial flight?"

Mackenzie blinked a few times, then smiled a tight smile. "So easy to forget exactly how much reach you do have."

"Crockett's out of jail," O'Hare said. "I thought that alone would have been a good indication of my intentions toward helping him. And a better indication of the levers I can pull."

"But not before someone nearly killed him in there."

"Of course," O'Hare answered.

"Of course?"

"We arranged for a guard to beat him up. To work on his face the most. It was Crockett's best chance of getting out. And his attorney played it perfectly. Our organization can get a lot of things done." He shook his head with a wry grin. "On the other hand, I could use suggestions on where to keep a horse for Jaimie."

Chapter Thirty-Five

The setup of Dr. Lorna Moller's office differed from Madelyne Mackenzie's office in a few fundamentals, but the overall effect, at least to Crockett, was profound and calming. Romans had recommended Moller as another psychiatrist who might provide some more information on Jaimie. Romans occasionally sent children or parents to her.

The browns and tans of her office added a subtle warmth, and the large oil paintings blended with the comfortable autumn feel. Moller's potted plants were real, or maybe good fakes. Short of plucking leaves, Crockett couldn't decide. He found it strange that his thoughts wandered in that direction. Here to talk to a psychiatrist about demon possession, and he had the urge to slide over and tug on a plant. Just another reminder of how surreal all of this was, like the shark attack had been.

"Couch or chair, Mr. Grey?"

He was here because he was metaphorically flailing, grasping at straws, or maybe more accurately, trying to unravel a massive ball of yarn with no idea what strings were important. He knew so little, and he was hoping anything would help. But you started with the weird and unusual, and pulled and tried to find out where it led.

Genetics. Genealogy. And exorcism.

Weird enough.

So find out what another psychiatrist might say about exorcism, and hope that might give him something to take back to Mackenzie and push harder.

Slim as the odds were that it might work, what else could he do? He wanted to be a father to Mickey. No way was he going to take Dr. Mackenzie's advice and trust that his innocence was enough so that when a little time passed, he'd be free of this situation.

"Chair would be good," Crockett said. "And I appreciate an appointment on short notice."

He noticed that she was studying his face but trying not to get caught. She said nothing about his bruises.

"Happy to help," she answered. She had a radio voice and a television face. A decade or so older than Crockett, Moller had light auburn hair, cut in a bob that added fullness to her slender features.

She sat in a chair opposite Crockett, crossing her legs and smoothing a long black skirt. "How may I help you, Mr. Grey?"

Crockett settled in as well, not feeling nearly as relaxed as she looked. His appointment was only a half hour. He didn't want to waste it.

"I'm a teacher and I have come into some information about one of my students that is a little…unorthodox. How much credibility would you give to the possibility that one of my students could be demon-possessed?"

"Oh, my," she said. "Interesting."

Crockett nodded, letting it sink in for Dr. Moller.

"If you're serious about this question," Dr. Moller answered, keeping a diplomatic tone, "and nothing about you suggests otherwise, then I'm happy to answer in generalities, but not specifics. And I'm not willing to make any kind of diagnosis based on your description of how this student acts out."

"Sure. Would that apply to a discussion of a colleague as well?"

"You're going to suggest that another psychiatrist is also demon-possessed?"

"No," Crockett said. "Definitely not. I'm asking about a psychiatrist who works with an exorcist."

To his surprise, Moller stood. Like a cat moving in sunlight.

"I think I'll get a coffee," she said. "It sounds like this conversation is not going to be about assessing any personal problem, and I'm happy to discuss it like we're colleagues, which in a sense we are. Two professionals, trying to help a student."

He'd noticed the stainless steel exterior of a sleek one-cup coffee maker on a desk in the corner.

"Black would be great."

When she came back, she extended the cup as if it were a handshake.

"Gave me time to think," she said. "I don't want to cross any ethical boundaries in discussing another doctor, but I think I can safely tell you a couple of things based on my experience."

Crockett nodded. The coffee tasted as good as it smelled.

"I'm aware of exorcism as a rite in the Catholic church," she said. "And I'm also aware that priests who are exorcists are instructed to eliminate every other cause or diagnosis before finally concluding—in their view—whether a person is possessed by a demon. Enter psychiatry. If a priest asked me to help understand someone's underlying problem, I would do so no differently that if it were a patient seeking treatment."

She held up a finger when Crockett was about to speak. "With one difference. I wouldn't be open to any diagnosis that suggested demonism as a cause. In general, then, I would not make any judgment on a colleague who works with a priest under that condition. On the other hand, if a colleague was prepared to blame symptoms on a demon, I would find that professionally unacceptable, and in essence could not help that element of criticism."

"That's why you stressed 'in their view' when speaking of the priests."

"Obviously, they hold to a worldview that allows for the existence of spiritual creatures. It's not something that strays into my office, however. Mental illnesses need to be treated as mental illnesses, not sprinkled with holy water."

"But, as you said, you're aware of exorcism as a rite. Does your professional awareness extend to symptoms of demon possession?"

"Alleged demon possession. Yes. So I'm also comfortable talking about a student who may believe, or worse, may have been told she is demon-possessed. While, again, I can't comment on specifics, in general, I think that's a very damaging approach."

Crockett sipped more coffee. This would be an enjoyable abstract conversation, if it weren't for the fact that he was embroiled in this.

"Let's start with the exorcism itself," she said. "It's a form of hypnotism, riddled with autosuggestion."

Dr. Mackenzie had taken Jaimie to a hypnotherapist.

"The rhythmic incantations of a priest, combined with the patient's inward focus, encourages dissociation and, for someone predisposed to believe, the sense of demonic possession. Let's face it, a good priest can make someone bark like a dog. It's not a far stretch to say a priest can make someone talk like the devil in a situation like this." She sighed. "It gives the patient a chance to deny his illness and put the blame for anxiety or depression or schizophrenia on a so-called demon. Ironically, in many families, there is less stigma attached to demon possession than there is to mental illness."

"What about reports of superhuman strength?" he asked. Crockett had done some quick on-line research about demon possession and learned some of the characteristics that exorcists attributed to it.

"Adrenaline," she answered. "You've heard of people lifting cars to save a child. Same thing."

"Speaking foreign languages?"

She shrugged. "Somebody babbles a few words during an exorcism, and everyone else assumes it's a foreign language, without anyone around who's qualified to confirm or deny. Give me a little time, and I'd point you to research that backs this up specifically in regards to demon possession."

"Okay, what about aversion to sacred symbols?"

"Classic manifestation of obsessive-compulsive behavior. Let me ask you, isn't it most likely a Catholic who would believe in demonic possession and a Catholic who would be brought before a priest?"

"Yes," Crockett said.

"It's unthinkable for a Catholic to blaspheme the Church. So an exorcism, in the patient's eyes, becomes proof that a demon does exist inside them. The exorcism then is a placebo and appears to work."

She shook her head, continuing in the same tone. "Mr. Grey, demons do not exist. They don't prey upon people. If you're looking to help one of your students, I'd suggest this: those who insist on demons and those who exorcise them are the predators. Have I made myself clear enough?"

"Like your name is crystal," he said. He thought of Dr. Mackenzie's secretiveness, and realized this perspective was very helpful. "It's exactly what I needed to hear."

Chapter Thirty-Six

F ather O'Hare loved Skype for the anonymity it provided. Not the
video calls, of course, but computer to land line calls. His hotel had
great wireless—sometimes you got a room that only picked up a few bars—
and the computer's sound quality was as good as any cell phone. He listened
to Muzak while he was on hold, waiting for Amy Robertson.

After decades of surviving and thriving in Vatican politics, Father
O'Hare also loved the massive web he'd created over the last six months
since meeting Dr. Madelyne Mackenzie. Like a patient spider in the center
of all that he'd spun, O'Hare waited for vibrations on the various strands to
alert him when he finally had his prey totally enmeshed and helpless.

The main strand—none more crucial—led to Jaimie and Madelyne
Mackenzie. Around it, he'd woven another strand between him and the
Entity, anchoring this second filament with a cynical ex-C.I.A. American
who had no idea how neatly O'Hare had suckered him.

Three other strands each led to three of the highest profile cardinals in
the Vatican. Yet more strands led to genetic experts and genealogists.

While the arrest of Crockett had at first threatened to punch a hole
in all that he had woven, O'Hare was beginning to get an idea of how to
bring Crockett Grey into the web—the man was a problem, but with careful planning and manipulation could become another main strand, his role
in O'Hare's ultimate goal almost as crucial as the contribution from Jaimie
and Mackenzie.

And there was this strand, a recent addition too, forced upon O'Hare by the stupid actions that had been taken against Crockett—the strand that trailed from Amy Robertson back to O'Hare at the center of everything.

Her voice broke in halfway through a cheesy saxophone riff. "Mr. Atholl, I'm sorry to have kept you waiting."

"No worries." O'Hare played up a fake Australian accent. He'd been provided with seamless credentials as an Australian criminal lawyer. "Just looking for an update on our client's welfare."

The criminal lawyer pose was necessary to convince Robertson that she was part of a team engaged to clear Crockett Grey. Given what he knew about her track record, O'Hare doubted Robertson would breach client confidentiality; with O'Hare as the supposed lead lawyer, she would report to him as team leader.

"Seems to be going smoothly," she said. "I'm sure you received my email update about successful bail."

"Yes. Well done. I'm hoping that some progress has been made in re-gards to the hard drive and clearing him of that."

"Not sure if we can call it progress yet," Amy said. "But Crockett is persistent and he's learned some interesting information. Trouble is, I don't know if we can use it to defend him, as it was obtained in a way that the court would frown upon."

"What kind of way?"

"First, although I set him up to meet a hacker that the firm sometimes uses for legitimate purposes, I want to be clear it was Crockett's initiative. This is your case, and you don't need to worry that any of this will ever hurt you."

"Of course."

"He's hacked into the computer of the girl's psychiatrist. He found a lot of information about the girl, plus the fact that a third party has plant-ed a key-logging program. Crockett's not the only one who has learned a lot."

"Astounding." O'Hare didn't have to act much to put surprise in his voice. Crockett was turning out to be a remarkable man for someone who'd spent his adult life as a school teacher. But then, maybe O'Hare shouldn't have been surprised. With a degree of fascination, he'd read the report on Crockett surviving a shark attack.

O'Hare pretended he was flipping through some case notes. "What's the doctor's name? Mac something, right?"

"Madelyne Mackenzie," Amy answered.

"Yes," O'Hare said, rolling the single syllable off his tongue with a per-fect Australian emphasis. "Dr. Mackenzie. Why don't you tell me what Mr. Grey has learned?"

Raymond Leakey sat on the edge of his chair in his kitchen, sucking on an ice cube. He groaned when his cell phone rang. The dehydration of hangover was so ridiculously predictable, as was the aversion to sudden loud noises. When would a man learn to avoid rum, especially when Pyrat was so expensive to import?

Rhetorical question of course. Humans had been succumbing to the tipping point every since humans learned to ferment liquids—you get half-way through the bottle of rum and you're too far gone to let the future hangover stop you from the present consumption.

He glanced at the incoming ID. ANONYMOUS.

In his business, that was a good sign.

He looked out his Roman terrace as he answered. With no preamble, Father O'Hare began. "You have no idea how angry I am."

"And the top of the mornin' to you, too," Leakey said, imitating Father O'Hare's Irish brogue.

"Let me repeat part of our earlier conversation. You were an idiot to try to frame Crockett Grey. He's started asking questions, which was easy to see coming. We're lucky the cops aren't buying his story and asking even more questions. You could have let him walk away, and we would be hours from getting that girl into the hospital in Rome. Instead, I'm forced to clean up here when I should be on an airplane."

"Then let *me* repeat," Leakey said. "It was a chain reaction. Your cardinal was the one who sent a lunatic after the girl."

"He is not my cardinal."

"I'm babysitting him for you," Leakey said. "That makes him yours. There was no time to plan. I did what I thought was best, which meant reducing whatever risks were there if the girl had talked to the teacher, and also making sure your cardinal didn't do anything else idiotic. Remember, it was your idea to let him know about the girl. So do you want to keep fighting about the past, or look ahead to what needs to be done. Trust me, it's going to be easy to take care of him."

"I want to believe that." A pause. "You said your computer people were untouchable."

"And?" Leakey fought another groan that came with his sudden queasiness. From the hangover. He wasn't especially worried about O'Hare's anger. Even blind, or stumbling drunk, Leakey could swat O'Hare into oblivion. The priest had stepped into unfamiliar territory when he made a bargain with Leakey.

"And Crockett knows about it. Including the keylogging program on Mackenzie's computer."

Leakey nearly choked on his ice cube. "Say that again."

"Crockett knows about the keylogging program you had installed. He knows about the genetic research and about the genealogy tree she requested."

"How?"

"His computer people must be better than yours," O'Hare replied in an acid voice. "It's time to take this to the next level."

Chapter Thirty-Seven

It later afternoon. when Crockett finally arrived at the Fishloft, cranky about traffic, stress, and his lack of progress. Julie wasn't returning calls. He was tired, but doubted he'd be able to sleep.

"Hey," Catfish greeted him.

"Did you find out who else is tracking Mackenzie in cyberspace?" Crockett asked.

"Chill, surfer dude," Catfish said.

"Sorry, it's been a long day. I'm tired. We could have had this conversation by telephone, but y wanted me to drive here. Here I am."

"We shouldn't use your cell phone for conversation about this." Catfish pulled a cheap-looking cell phone from a lower desk drawer, and tossed it to Crockett.

Crockett gave Catfish a questioning look.

"This one's prepaid," Catfish said. "Start using it. In case they are tracking you via your phone."

"They?"

"We're swimming in the deep end. For all I know, someone's put a bug on you. I'm thinking some kind of spook organization is behind this."

Crockett looked at the pre-paid phone, back at Catfish. "Spook organization?"

"Do I look like the kinda guy who could successfully torch a house?" Catfish said. "The kind of guy with the skills to kidnap someone?"

"That's a rhetorical question, right? Especially coming out of nowhere like this. It's not like I'm accusing you of starting the fire."

"Crockett, you're not listening. I'm a hacker. A good one. Takes years to develop these skills and it needs a certain mindset."

"Your point?"

"Even if I had the mindset to physically hurt people, learning how to hack means I wouldn't have the time to learn how to hurt. Or vice versa. More like it's an organization, not one person."

Crockett understood. "Already we've seen two kinds of attacks. Fire and attempted kidnapping of Jaimie. Computer hack on Mackenzie, and computer stuff on me, planting the fake complaints."

"Two kinds of attacks that required opposite sets of skills. What we're seeing is slick and needs resources. Plenty of resources. Like the C.I.A.."

"I'll go with you on the organizational part," Crockett said. "But why would the C.I.A. get involved? This is crazy."

"I didn't say C.I.A.. I said *like* C.I.A. Doesn't every country have its own spook thing happening. Even Vatican City. It's a country. Maybe it's got a spook organization too. Why bring up the Vatican you ask? You asked if I found out who else is in Mackenzie's cyberspace. Short answer, yes. I was able to get a trace in through her computer. Tracked it down to Popesville."

"You're telling me that somebody in Vatican City planted spyware on Mackenzie's computer."

Amy Robertson, representing the Los Angeles diocese. Dr. Madelyne Mackenzie, working with an exorcist. Graphic images on the hard drive planted in Crockett's attic matching images found on a priest's hard drive. Now this. Even Maxwell Smart would see a common denominator here. But could Max Smart figure out why there was a link? And why it involved Jaimie? And what was at stake for the Catholic church that led them to arrange all of this?

"Or maybe just someone in Vatican City," Catfish said. "It could be a proxy server. Someone cracked the server there, has a sick sense of humor, wants people to believe the pope is now Big Brother."

It hit Crockett again, how surreal this was. He was just a teacher. This really wasn't happening to him—except it was. Taking this information to the authorities seemed out of the question. They didn't appear to be taking Nanna's absence too seriously, unless they really believed Crockett had murdered the old woman and were hiding an investigation from him. They didn't want to believe someone had planted a hard drive and complaints on his employment files. They'd laugh him out the door if he said it was a Vatican conspiracy.

"So we've got a child psychiatrist who runs a DNA analysis on a kid, orders up a genealogy report that looks for witches generations deep, and takes her to a priest who does exorcisms. And this somehow matter enough to someone or some organization enough to try to kill the kid by torching the house she's in?"

"How's this for outside the box?" Fish answered. "Say the girl is actually possessed by a demon. Explains the lies. Explains beating up a homeless person on the playground. Explains the arson. For all you know, Jaimie's the one who planted the hard drive at your house. She knew your address. So she sets the fire, pretends to need your help, makes sure you take the real heat. So it's not an organization, but a demon girl!"

Then he grinned.

"What about Nanna?" Crockett asked, still thinking about how surreal this was. "Same organization takes her somewhere. Why?"

He hadn't received a useful report from the private detective that Amy Robertson had hired to look for Nanna. Every passing hour squeezed Crockett more. He didn't want to give up hope on her.

"All I have is what you know," Catfish said. "Tracked down the source to Vatican City. Scares me enough that I don't want to talk over the phone anymore. Unless you use the pre-paid."

Chapter Thirty-Eight

Jaimie didn't cry often. She couldn't even remember the last time she cried. To avoid it, she'd learned to divide herself into Inside Jaimie and Outside Jaimie.

Whenever Inside Jaimie was sad or scared or lonely, she would make Outside Jaimie squash those feelings into a dense little ball.

Squashing Inside Jaimie wasn't working tonight, though.

She was in bed—a bunk bed in one of the dorm rooms—half thinking about trying to run away. But Bright Lights had impressive security that included sensors if doors or windows were opened in the dorm rooms, cameras everywhere, and the security was one reason she wasn't in juvie.

She knew running away wouldn't change anything about herself, how messed up she was. How she knew when Evil was around and how Evil knew what she knew.

Evil could find her anywhere, no running from it.

She turned her head on her pillow, thinking she heard the hooting of an owl.

Most times, she liked the sounds of the outdoors, especially coyotes, with their high-pitched chorus of yipping. She liked hearing owls, too, which happened a lot less frequently.

Except tonight, burrowed beneath the covers, trying to feel warm and secure, she was trying to squash Inside Jaimie because Outside Jaimie had to deal with going to Rome and making sure she helped Dr. Mackenzie. And Outside Jaimie had to make sure to help Mr. G, but Inside Jaimie was worried about what might happen in Rome and thinking about how it had felt in Nanna's kitchen talking to Nanna like she was a real grandmother. Feeling all of this, the lonesome sound of the owl had formed into a little rock, rolling down a hill and kicking loose bigger rocks that kicked loose bigger rocks until suddenly everything felt out of control.

And she found herself crying.

Worse, she was feeling sorry for herself. That had not happened in forever.

Was it too much just to hope for a family to belong to? Just about every other kid in the world had that.

And why, of all the kids in the world, was she the one who could feel the Evil?

She knew for sure she'd never have her own family, and that was bad enough, but she was also getting the feeling that she'd never grow into a calm, peaceful old woman, content in her little house.

Really, she thought as she buried her face in her pillow to let it soak up the tears, what kind of future did a kid like her have?

For all she knew, the owl hooted at the Evil waiting for her right outside the chain-linked fence, ready to pounce at the first opportunity.

Nathan Wilby sat in his Ford Taurus, deep in the shadows of trees, overlooking the gate to the Bright Lights Center.

Wondering if it would be worthwhile to make a move tonight.

The girl was behind the fence.

He felt a vibration in his front pocket. Only one person he expected to call at this time, well past the witching hour.

He dug it out and snapped it open, aware that Abez was in the back seat, hunched forward in his miserable way. Abez had not talked much tonight. Abez was sulking, because Nathan would not get rid of Nanna.

"I'm here," Nathan said to The Prince. "Watching the place where they are keeping the girl."

"Don't worry about the girl. You need to take care of the old woman. You have your instructions. What's the delay?"

"There's nothing she can do to hurt us."

"You have your instructions. Do I need to say more?"

"No," Nathan said. "You are The Prince."

The phone went dead.

Nathan sat in the darkness for a long time, staring ahead, not thinking about the girl anymore.

Chapter Thirty-Nine

Nine a.m. the next morning, and halfway across the valley after an hour of fighting traffic, Crockett faced an RN wearing an ID tag that read Richard Jerome.

"If you're not interesting in talking to me," Crockett told Jerome, "I'll find out other ways. Human Resources next. There's a department that would hate any kind of media exposure on this."

In his fifties, Jerome was not a typical candy-striping nurse. He looked more like Harley Davidson guy. A real Harley Davidson guy, not a wannabe weekend rider. Shaved skull, surprisingly elegant facial structures for someone so big. He was easily four inches taller than Crockett's six feet, and easily forty pounds heavier. His short-sleeved green uniform strained against the man's bulk. Not what Crockett had expected after his arrival the neonatal intensive care unit at the Methodist Medical Center, nor what you'd expect for a man in his fifties.

"That's a threat, isn't it," Jerome said. "Not hard to guess why your face looks so bad, if you operate like that."

He pushed Crockett up against the wall, placing his hands on Crockett's shoulders. Hands capable of holding preemies in one palm. The guy could probably crack walnuts between his knuckles.

"Archimedes," Crockett said.

"The fulcrum guy." Proving Jerome was well-read.

"Yeah, leverage," Crockett said. Weird, looking upward at a man. Weird, seeing the gap in the guy's teeth and thinking about Shrek in this situation. "Look, there's not much you can do to scare me, so don't make this worse on yourself."

Jerome backed away, panting slightly. Probably not from exertion, but from restrained anger.

"I've got nothing to say about this," Jerome told Crockett.

"That tells me a lot," Crockett said. "I ask you about your name on a birth record twelve years ago, and you decide you have nothing to say. Must have been memorable, if you can remember it that far back and not even ask me for more details. Or maybe you've been wondering all this time when it would catch up to you."

"Who are you? And why you asking?"

"How about," Crockett said, "You find time for a ten-minute break, and I buy you a coffee. "

Crockett waited in the hospital cafeteria, ebb and flow of doctors and nurses and visitors no different than during the hours and hours of hell he'd spent in a similar setting during the final months of Ashley's life.

It had taken willpower just to park at the Methodist Medical Center, let alone step through the doors to the corridor smells and sounds that had stained him permanently during his vigils. He'd only been in a hospital again for Mickey's birth. It should have been a completely joyful event, something to scrub away some of the stains, but he'd known then that the marriage was gone, so even holding his new son had been tinged with sorrow. And cutting regret that Ashley wasn't there to hold her baby brother.

Crockett thought about death a lot. Sometimes he envied those who believed there was life after death.

Ashley's words. *Daddy, it's okay. I get to go to heaven. I'll see you there. Right? Daddy?*

No such belief for Crockett.

Ashley was gone. No longer in existence. He knew that questioning *why* was a cliché, but he couldn't help it. Why had *she* been taken?

Jerome had glared at him and asked who he was and why he was asking.

Crockett, at least, knew the answers to those questions.

He was a father. And he was asking because Brad Romans had given him Jaimie Piper's birth records, and Crockett was still grasping at any straw to fight for the right to be a father to his other child. With Ashley, much as he had refused to buckle until her final breath, it was a fight that he never had any chance of winning. Maybe the odds were the same now, trying to stay out of prison so that he wouldn't lose Mickey too, but he was going to fight in the same desperate way.

Richard Jerome stepped into the cafeteria. A difficult man to miss. Conversation muted briefly, then picked up again.

Crockett mentally shifted gears away from Ashley and Mickey and the weight inside him that every parent who loved their children understood was always there, the weight of the fear of loss.

One thing at a time.

⚬⚬⚬

"Right up front," Crockett said, "I'm not interested in taking this conversation past our table. I just want to know who was Jaimie Piper's real mother."

"Why?" Jerome's voice was rumbly deep.

"I'm hoping that answer will lead me to other answers that will keep me from going to prison."

Jerome leaned back, arms crossed. "Maybe that gives me a chance to threaten you. I'm sorry… I mean, apply leverage."

"It's why I gave you that."

"Not tracking."

"Obvious you're a straight up guy. You don't like games, I'm guessing. I don't want to leverage you into something. I just want your help. Easier to tell you this over a Styrofoam cup of acid coffee than with you pushing me against a wall."

"You wired? "

"This isn't television."

"You didn't answer."

"Okay," Crockett said. "I'm wired."

"Really?" It obviously wasn't the answer Jerome expected.

"It's a stupid question. If I'm wired, I'm going to deny it. I say no, then you have to chose to believe me or frisk me. Only nurse I'll let frisk me is female. So why not say yes and get that game over with."

"How you'd find out?"

"Jaimie's blood type didn't match the birth mother's."

Another long pause. "This is what happened. Two women come into the natal unit at the same time. One's from a good family, has money. She'd been coming in every week, getting check-ups, reading up on being a mother, telling me about the nursery she put together for the baby, her husband, he's so in love it's beautiful. The other one is a homeless woman. Has no idea who the father was. She was just a kid, really, but she looked a couple decades older. It's easy enough for you to guess what happens next."

"I'll just listen."

"And I'll tell it, no meat on the bones. The good woman, ready to love her baby, has complications. Homeless woman, pops out a healthy girl. Happened so fast. It's three in the morning, all this stuff happening. They take away the good woman's baby, and you can tell this one's not going to make it. Homeless woman, she's screaming, trying to push away her healthy baby, shrieking about demons. Both babies are girls, about the same size, same hair color. There's one way to make both women happy, and make sure the baby gets a decent home. What would *you* do?"

Crockett nodded. "Hope someone never came back asking questions."

"Like now." Jerome shook his head. "Then I hear six months later, after what I did to help that little baby, that her parents get killed in a car accident. Baby girl is homeless anyway. Tell you what, sometimes life is bleak."

"Bleak," Crockett said. He wanted to get away from the smell of the hospital. Too much of Ashley in it. Strange, his daughter didn't exist anymore, but still filled him and his thoughts. "This won't come back on you. The only other thing I need is the name of the homeless woman."

Chapter Forty

Next stop for Crockett was an attempt to catch up to Madelyne Mackenzie during her morning time at the office. Forty-five minutes after that hospital conversation and glad that freeway traffic had been relatively, Crockett didn't know if what he'd learned about Jaimie would help.

Crockett didn't know if anything he had learned would help, her or him. He was just flailing, grasping, paddling. The alternative was to stay in bed all day, blinds closed.

Maybe increasing the pressure on Mackenzie might result in something. Especially since he could read her emails, and she didn't know it. Provoke her as much as possible, see what came out of it.

She was behind her desk, and he'd been forced to bully his way in past Mackenzie's secretary, a tiny elderly woman, shorter than the potted palm in the austere front office of the practice. Not a comfortable sensation for Crockett, playing the bully. Hadn't been fun at the hospital and it had not been fun with the secretary. Crockett had been as gentle as possible with the assistant, delivering his threat to go to the media. Still, the woman had scurried into the doctor's office like Crockett was trying to share bed bugs.

"Overly dramatic, wouldn't you say?" Mackenzie asked. "That message of yours? Heard that saying, catch more flies with honey?"

"Didn't work for me yesterday," Crockett said.

"This new approach is even less efficient. I'm not interested in hearing you bluster about the media. Instead, I allowed you inside my office so you could hear it from me. Go away. If you come back, I will call the police and have you charged with trespassing and harassment. Goodbye, Mr. Grey."

"Goodbye, Dr. Mackenzie."

Crockett didn't move, however. He studied the woman behind the desk. Somewhere, a Goodwill store was missing an entire clothing collection donated from a senior citizen's home, with Mackenzie obviously determined to model it day by day .

"I said goodbye, Mr. Grey."

"So did I. " He grinned. It was fun, getting her to react. Despite her efforts to be unlikable, he liked her. He couldn't explain why, not even to himself. "It's a very polite word."

"Ten seconds, then I lift this phone to call the police. "

"Excellent. I'll do my best to time their arrival with the journalist I'll call. The more publicity the better. I can see the headlines now: 'Bloodsucking psychiatrist pairs with exorcist to abuse young girl.' Try to picture it in bold. All caps. Above the fold."

"Picture this one," Mackenzie said undaunted. "Desperate pedophile thrown back in prison for harassment."

She picked up the phone as she studied Crockett. Crockett heard the phone ring outside in the reception area.

"Marge," she said, "what time does your watch say?" Dr. Mackenzie listened to the answer. "Thank you. Wait precisely three minutes. If you don't see Mr. Grey leave by then, can you call the police? Tell them there is a man in my office making threats."

She hung up. She reached for a pen, and started working on some papers on her desk.

"I guess the clock is ticking," Crockett said. "Why take blood from Jamie Piper?" Crockett asked. "Why pay so much for a DNA analysis?"

She continued to focus on her paperwork. He'd expected her to flinch, at least.

"You see," Crockett said, beginning the story he had mentally rehearsed. "About a week before school ended, I received a phone call from a scientist at the University of Tennessee. Named McFarlane. He wanted to ask me a lot of questions about a student of mine, based on enquiries from a medical person working with this student. Apparently he found something interesting."

It was a bad lie. Hopefully with enough diversion to keep Mackenzie from guessing where Crockett might have learned about the blood samples. And with enough truth to provoke her into something. Anything. He had no doubt that Mackenzie knew enough about all of this to help him make sense of it. Crockett was struggling, through, with finding a way to motivate her to share.

So much riding on this, and he didn't have much time. The longer this went on, the further he went as an accused pedophile and the longer he went without reuniting with his son. Not to mention Jaimie. The girl was clearly in danger and needed to be rescued before it was too late. Then there was Nanna. If she was still alive, and that was a big *if,* how much longer would she remain alive?

There was the other time pressure. He was very conscious that he needed to be gone in less than three minutes. Mackenzie did not appear like someone who bluffed.

Nor did she appear interested in Crockett's wonderful obscuration.

"I suggested to this scientist that he'd be better served by perhaps getting a genealogy report on said student," Crockett said to the top of Mackenzie's head. "Jaimie's talked a lot about witches in class. I wondered if that had anything to do with it."

Still nothing except for scratching of pen on paper. Crockett felt grudging admiration for Mackenzie. He'd just exposed two secrets that should have staggered her, forced her to demand how he learned them. This woman could play poker.

"After that," Crockett said. "I found some tiny goldfish and sucked them up through my nose before swallowing them alive."

Finally, she looked up.

"Just checking to see if you were listening," Crockett said.

"You need help," she said.

"Then help me," Crockett said.

She looked at her watch. "You have less than a minute to leave."

"Do you think she's demon possessed?" Crockett asked, wondering if this would finally get a reaction. "Is that why you took her to an exorcist?"

Slight flinch. So her poker wasn't perfect.

"Thirty seconds," she said.

"What about the hypnotherapy?"

"Tick. Tock."

"I'm going to keep digging." A lie. He didn't know where else to dig. If he couldn't get anything from Mackenzie, he was out of options.

"Wonderful," she said. "Are we finished here?"

"Not quite."

Crockett moved to the wall thermostat and made an adjustment.

"What are you doing, Mr. Grey?"

"Raising the temperature, Dr. Mackenzie." Game over, and he'd lost. Badly. He should have left with dignity. Instead, he succumbed to a petty impulse. "You're a cold, cold person, and I have no idea what it would take to thaw you out. Maybe this will help instead."

Chapter Forty-One

Headed back to the Fishloft, Crockett had decided against taking freeways out of the San Fernando Valley. He was trying to live in the moment, instead of worrying about the future or letting longings about the past drag him too far down. Living in the moment meant top down on the Jeep, taking Laurel Canyon up the hills, across on Mulholland, then down to Bel Air, across on Sunset. As he reached Mulholland and caught a glimpse of the wide valley below, tinged with yellow from smog, he was listening to the Eagles, getting lost in the great mixture of rock and roll and melancholy.

Then came the first cords of *I Can't Tell You Why*— his theme song for how the mirage of his marriage to Julie had slowly shimmered into nothingness in the aftermath of Ashley's death. Up all those nights in the hollowness of defeat, letting their love tear them apart. Two people, living through years in the dark.

That definitely wasn't a song for living in the moment.

Crockett turned down the volume and, stuck behind an elderly couple in a black Lexus, mentally ran through the conversation in Dr. Mackenzie's office, trying to decide if there was had been anything but defeat as he'd made a fool of himself.

His phone rang briefly. No caller ID; it was the prepaid Catfish had given him. The ringing stopped before he could answer. Cell coverage was sketchy along Mulholland.

The distraction bumped his thoughts away from Mackenzie, and on to McFarlane. The geneticist had asked if Crockett could tell him anything unusual about Jaimie. Was what he'd learned from Agnes Murdoch something worth passing along ?

Back and forth, in his mind, Crockett went between making a quick call or not, until finally the impatience of following the elderly couple goaded him into some kind of action. He waited for a stretch of road that showed a few bars of signal strength on his cell .

Crockett was grateful that McFarlane didn't answer.

"Greg Biette here," Crockett said, staying in character. "Thought I'd tell you the only strange thing I can think of about Ms. Piper's DNA. Wearing a magnetic bracelet seems to positively affect her emotional wellbeing. I have no idea if that helps you, but I thought you should know."

The elderly couple turned off to a gated mansion, letting Crockett pick up the pace. He glanced at his phone. There was a voicemail waiting.

He put the phone to his ear and he heard Fish speaking: *Got more spy stuff to talk to you about. In person. Soon as you can.*

Wind blew across his face. It felt good. He didn't want to think about spy stuff. Just enjoy the wind and the drive and try to lose the feeling of defeat and sadness and worry about where life might go if he couldn't be the father to Mickey because he ended up in a prison cell.

Too quiet though. Back to the Eagles, bumping to a new song.

Welcome to the Hotel California...

The iconic song about the dark underbelly of the American dream. Crockett drove past the mansions of Mulholland, listening to the potent lyrics, wondering about the master's chambers and the steely knives that couldn't kill the beast.

He decided the images of the song were too much for him to handle—*we are just prisoners of our own device*—and Crockett turned down the volume again before he heard the night man say that he could check out any time he liked, but he could never leave.

Chapter Forty-Two

O'Hare watched Mackenzie pace the library room at Bright Lights. Day before, she'd managed to sit, holding a cup of tea. Now, two hours after Crockett had been in her office in Burbank, she was a totally different person.

"I'm a little freaked here," Mackenzie told O'Hare. Not that he needed her to explain. "Okay, a lot freaked. He's in my office, talking about the DNA analysis and the genealogy report."

"Your computer is the only place I can think of where anyone might access the information," O'Hare said, thinking of himself as a spider in the middle of the web, monitoring one of the strands.

"You're the one who made sure my computer was safe. Or least, your people in the Vatican. Are you saying it wasn't safe enough?"

"I'm going to check into it," O'Hare answered. She was easily fooled, had been from the beginning. "In the meantime, obviously Crockett knows just enough to be dangerous. If he was in your computer, then he knows plenty, but can't put the pieces together. My guess, he was trying to provoke you."

"This may surprise you," she answered, "but I have a lot of sympathy for him."

"He deserves sympathy," O'Hare said. "But this is much bigger than one individual. It's only a matter of days, then all of this is over."

"What if he finds someone to believe what he's learned? To make something of the pieces? We need Jaimie. What we don't need is to have her taken away from us."

O'Hare steepled his fingers. "I might have a solution then. You'll need to visit him in the morning. Early. And you'll have to make him believe that you need his help. Convince him to come out here by the end of tomorrow, and I'll take care of the rest."

"Any suggestions on how to convince him? Last two times, I've been cold." She thought of his thermostat remark and how much it had stung. "Very cold."

"Turn his sword against him," O'Hare said. "Tell him you just learned someone has been spying on you, to the point of getting access of your computer. Make him believe whoever has been doing this to him is now doing it to you. Give him just enough of the truth that he'll come back out here with you. Think you can do it? Sympathy for him or not, we've got to rein him in."

Chapter Forty-Three

Albino Luciani," Catfish said when Crockett walked into the Fishloft. "Heard of him?"

"Been a long day," Crockett answered. "And it's barely afternoon."

Crockett had not arrived as soon as possible. He'd walked the beach, barefoot, holding his shoes in one hand. Melancholy was a tough mood to shake. Worse, he was getting that feeling again. Like he was about to lose a child. A feeling nobody understood unless they'd been through it.

"Albino Luciani was elected pope. Took the name John Paul One. Wanted to bring Vatican finances to light. Thirty-three days into his papacy, he was found dead of an apparent heart attack. There are so many inconsistencies in the reports about his death and a rushed burial with no autopsy. Many believe he was poisoned."

"Sounds medieval."

"John Paul One died in September 1978."

"Oh," Crockett feigned interest. Catfish was jumping, had lots of energy. Crockett didn't.

"Among other things, John Paul One wanted to get rid of Vatican ties to a Masonic group called P2," Catfish said. "The grandmaster of P2 had been a Mussolini fascist, a liaison officer for the Nazis, and organizer of the rat-line that helped Nazi war criminals escape to Argentina."

Crockett stared at Catfish, beginning to catch some of the vibrations.

"You are going somewhere with this, right?"

"That's just the beginning. A year later, the judge investigating Vatican bank activities was murdered. Same with a journalist who had exposed the memberships and dealings of P2. A couple months later, a key witness in the bank investigation was, wait for it, murdered. Four other key witnesses were also killed, including bank executives. Poisoned. Thrown from windows. Hanged by rope. I am not making any of this up."

Crockett tried to say something, but Catfish was rolling. "Get this. Bank shareholders then sent a letter to John Paul II that exposed connections between the Vatican Bank, P2 and the Mafia. The letter is never acknowledged by anyone in the Vatican."

"Urban myth?" Crockett said.

"I spent all morning, reams of internet research, solid sources. We're not talking urban myth, we're talking documented. The bank scandal goes back a few decades, when the Vatican made deals with Hitler and Mussolini. Remember I said every country has its own spies, maybe even the Vatican? Has its own spy organization, called the Entity. People think Opus Dei is scary, but that's not where the power comes from."

Crockett well understood the implications, thinking of their previous conversation the day before when Catfish made him take the pre-paid. An organization just as good at computer hacking as physical intimidation. Again, the sense of surreal. This wasn't the stuff that an ordinary school teacher should be facing.

"Makes me sick," Catfish said, "Things seem the same today. Abuse allegations and a history of cover-up. Latest I read on this, the new Vatican abuse rules still provide no sanctions for bishops who cover up abusers. Bishops are still not required to report abuse to police. But the new rules do state that the attempted ordination of women is considered a grave crime, subject to the same procedures and punishments given for sex abuse."

"I'm not a believing guy," Crockett said. "but I don't want to forget that the Catholic church does a lot of good in the world. It's a sad thing then, that this one issue dominates the way people look at the church."

"They get no sympathy from me," Catfish said, shaking his head. "It's like living in a house and one room starts on fire. You drop everything to put the fire out. Vatican should handle this the same way. All out fight until the fire's gone. Then the rest of the house is safe. Think I'm exaggerating? Here's the weirdest and scariest piece I've found—there's Satanism in the Vatican."

"Come on," Crockett rolled his eyes. "The Vatican's an easy target, but that's got to be internet conspiracy stuff."

"Think so?" Catfish said. "Straight from the Vatican's chief exorcist. He says—"

"Back up. Chief exorcist? Like that's an official position?"

"Not sure. But that's how newspapers refer to him. And don't think I've missed the relevance of it to your situation. There's spyware planted on Mackenzie's computer via a Vatican IP. Mackenzie has taken Jaimie to an exorcist. Yesterday I said we were in deep waters. Let me tell you, now it's bottomless."

"And the chief exorcist? He says…"

"Got the article here." Catfish tapped some paper on his desk, and Crockett saw a photo of a bald man, late forties. "It's about what they call 'the smoke of Satan.' During the papal conclave—election—black smoke is released after an inconclusive vote, white smoke when a pope is elected. I've found the chief exorcist quoted directly as saying the smoke of Satan is in the holy rooms, that there are cardinals who don't believe in Jesus. This chief exorcist believes all the violence and pedophilia is part of Satan at work inside the Vatican."

Catfish put up his hand so Crockett wouldn't interrupt his roll. "A little earlier, before his death, another top Jesuit priest described witchcraft ceremonies right inside the Vatican. I don't like this. I don't like this at all."

"You're not making any of this up?"

"I'm not saying it's one hundred percent true. I am saying that it's all been documented. Thoroughly. Nothing's been proven either way. But to me, where there is smoke…" Tight ironic grin. "Maybe it does come from the fires of Satan."

"Don't go down that road," Crockett said. "Demons don't exist."

"Evil does. And there's plenty of evidence of it in the Vatican. I mean, talking about a top-down organization. Priests don't get away with pedophilia for years unless the Vatican lets it happen."

Plenty of links to Crockett's own situation, he realized. Exorcists. Spyware planted from the Vatican. And pedophilia. Even with the links, there was that one big question that Crockett visualized in his mind in all caps. WHY.

Crockett moved to the desk and picked up the article on the Chief Exorcist that Catfish had printed out. A man named Joseph O'Hare. Monkish looking, with a broad face and balding skull with fringes cut short. Crockett scanned the article. It was from a respected news source. Catfish had not been exaggerating.

"You don't think this kind of speculation about Satanism is pushing it?" Crockett said, tapping the article. It kept coming back to him. He was just a school teacher. Living in a small bungalow near the ocean. Crazy, to think he was someone mixed in with Vatican happenings.

"Just consider what's happened around here so far," Catfish said. "Arson. Attempted kidnapping of Jaimie. Your old lady friend is missing. Computer espionage. Heck yeah, I'm worried. Double-checked to make sure nothing in my cyber tracks points back to me."

"Good," Crockett said.

"I've been thinking," Catfish said. "I want you to take these glasses."

He handed the pair with a built-in video camera to Crockett and explained how to work them. "You never know when they'll come in handy."

Crockett took the glasses. Was he really in the gun sights of a spook organization that most of the rest of the world didn't know existed?

"Want to crash here at the end of your day?" Catfish said. "If I were you, I'd be freaked out getting back in my own bed."

"I'm okay," Crockett said. "What are they going to do next? Try to take me out?"

Chapter Forty-Four

In his bedroom, Crockett woke to the darkness of a shadow standing over him and the sensation of triangle pressed against his face. He could not help his quick intake of surprise, from which he sucked in something that tasted cloying sweet.

He realized the triangle was mask over his nose and mouth, the kind that paramedics used to administer oxygen. But it couldn't have been oxygen because he was growing fuzzy. He knew he had to breathe anything *but* the cloying sweetness. He held his breath and struggled with both hands to push away the wrists above him.

It was too late. The first lungful had been enough.

He first felt a tingling. Not unpleasant. Waves, growing in frequency. A twisting and spinning, but he couldn't decide whether his body was spinning or the world around him was spinning, and even as he was trying to decide, he couldn't follow his thoughts to any conclusion.

Was he standing?

Or still in bed?

Were the shadows moving around him, or was he moving through shadows?

He was in his own home, but the way the place was spinning, he felt as if it was a carnival haunted house. He felt a strange euphoria that told him he was immortal.

A dream. A pleasant dream he followed into depths of warm dark water in which he could somehow breathe. But his euphoria was interrupted by prodding.

The prodding ended and he rose from the depths of the warm, warm water. Then, there was a binding sharpness.

His next conscious thought was the awareness of a tight band stretching the skin on his throat.

His brain began to process what his five senses were delivering. The binding sharpness, pressing against the nerve endings of his skin. A dry mouth. The ticking of a clock. Seeing the tops of picture frames on the wall, across the living room, bathed in moonlight. The acrid smell of cigarette smoke.

Someone behind him. Silent.

That's when Crockett realized—without any way to judge how much time had passed—that he was on his bare feet on a chair, rope snug around his neck, hands bound behind his back.

He froze, returning to a world that was not euphorically blurred, but painfully real.

The person behind him, silent, had formed with Crockett an unspeakable intimacy, a violation that seemed almost physical to Crockett. He was entirely helpless, totally vulnerable to the person behind him.

This was a menace he'd never experienced, and he became paralyzed into silence, as if speaking the single question—*why?*—would acknowledge that he wasn't alone. And to acknowledge the other person would be acknowledging this terrifying intimacy. Better to pretend he had no awareness of the situation. Somehow, a subtle shift in his body must have signaled otherwise.

"Welcome back," the voice whispered.

He would have begged if he thought it would help. But it wouldn't. He was going to die. No one went to all of this effort unless they were serious.

No begging then. He would use the last moments of his life was well as he could. He pictured Mickey, catching a baseball. Naming one of the bearded lizards in the reptile exhibit at the zoo. Jumping up and throwing his arms around his neck. Crockett would die with the image of the only beautiful thing beautiful that remained in his life. The love he had for Mickey and the love that Mickey had for him.

There was a small scrape of the person's feet moving across the floor, and then the chair below him began to move.

Slowly. So Slowly. Inch by inch. As if the person was enjoying this. Still, in silence.

Useless as he knew the efforts would be, Crockett desperately tried to keep the weight of his body on his toes as the chair slid away and away and away. He couldn't help but think of Ashley, how hard she had fought in the last week of her life. It brought him to tears.

Then the chair was gone. The length of the rope had been measured so precisely that Crockett didn't drop. He merely started hanging, with all of his body weight on the rope at his throat, with a roar of blood filling his head. It was the sound of a monster wave crashing over him. The water pounded his body below the surf and tossed him like the insignificant piece of the universe that he was. The sound under the water by the pressure of the rope was a freight train in his ears.

Crockett flailed his feet, trying to run up a set of invisible stairs. The pain and roaring of sheer malevolent black closed in on him.

All of this in silence, with the unknown intruder waiting for him to strangle to death.

The roaring in his head began to calm and Crockett stopped kicking.

The malevolent black filled with pinpricks of light. *Ashley.* He clung to that one word until it started to disappear. He didn't believe in heaven, but maybe if he willed it enough, she would be on the other side, whatever it was. *Ashley. Ashley. Ashley.*

Then the sensation of gravity returned, the cool wood of the chair on the soles of his feet. A loosening of the pressure on his neck. Air returning into his hoarse throat as his lungs sucked for life. The pinpricks of light gone. The malevolent black receded.

He was standing again, on the chair, chest heaving. His hands were free.

The cigarette smoke was gone.

Chapter Forty-Five

Ten minutes past eight in the morning, Madelyne Mackenzie stepped out of a rented red Corvette, parked on the sidewalk in front of the address that Joseph O'Hare had given her for Crockett.

Small bungalow, neat trimmed lawn, neat painted trim.

She pulled own on her skirt, feeling extremely self-conscious, still thinking about his childish thermostat remark that had still managed to sting. She also was childishly thinking that now, he'd see what he'd never get. She had to look like she'd disguised herself, O'Hare suggested, dress as totally opposite from normal as possible, convince Crockett that she was a woman so terrified that she'd gone to great lengths to shake off any followers.

O'Hare had said it wouldn't be difficult, that he'd arranged for Crockett to get a good scare during the night, leave him a threatening note. He did not want to give details, stressing instead that it was crucial to get Crockett into the Corvette. She should tell him enough, tell him whatever it took but make sure he didn't have time to think things through. That would be another good thing about dressing like someone she was not. Wouldn't hurt if her altered appearance distracted him, took some focus off trying to think through what she told him.

So she walked up the sidewalk and pressed the doorbell.

Ready to be a distraction, but still tugging down the hem of her skirt.

A couple of hours already past sunrise, and Crockett, in boxer shorts and a Disney World t-shirt, was shivering on the chair, unable to get himself down from the rope around his neck. It wasn't a noose, but a double wrap, with the knot secured too high for him to reach with his free hands.

He could turn sideways just enough to better understand the situation. Above and behind his chair was the pull-down trap door that led into the attic of the small house. Where he'd stored the photo album of memories. Where cops had found the hard drive.

The night before, as usual, before getting into his lonely bed, Crockett had set his coffee pot timer for automatic brew. Now, as he looked toward the kitchen, the teasing aroma of coffee filled his small house. It reminded him of Julie; so close, but so far away.

Crockett looked up again. The pull-down was open. The looped rope from his neck went up to the top rung, where the other end had been knotted. The rung also served as a makeshift pulley, with the remainder of the rope running diagonally downward toward the front door, with the far end was tied to the inside doorknob.

Why had this happened? And why had the intruder left Crockett alive?

Crockett had spent the night listening to the sounds of the house, wondering again and again if each new sound was a warning that the intruder had returned to pull the chair away again.

But the intruder never came back, not to Crockett's knowledge. And now it was daytime. Crockett was shivering. The scent of coffee tortured him.

Of equal importance was Crockett's full bladder, which was increasingly dominating his attention.

He knew it was ridiculous that he simply didn't relieve himself where he was standing. Compared to the fact that someone had broken into his house while he was asleep, that he had been standing on a chair for hours, now acutely aware that losing his balance would kill him, compared to the fact that he had been accused by the legal system of pedophilia, compared to the fact that he was probably losing his son and his career, it should not matter that he just let go a stream of urine.

But it was his last semblance of control.

Maybe that's what the intruder had wanted to take from Crockett. The sense of control. *Why?*

Hadn't the 16th century astronomer Copernicus died from a burst bladder? No. Crockett went through his memory, trying to distract himself from the urge, aware of the irony that he was thinking about a bursting bladder to stop thinking about a burst bladder. Not Copernicus. It had been Tycho, the mathematician who worked with Copernicus. Tycho, who loved beer and parties, at a banquet where to leave the table before the host baron left the table was so unspeakably rude that Tycho held back to the point that his bladder burst internally, and died of infection a few days later, repeating deliriously *let me not seem to have lived in vain.*

Stupid, Crockett thought, the things a person remembered from college science classes. But maybe that should be every person's mantra. *Let me not seem to have lived in vain.*

The mental efforts were not much of a distraction. On the chair, he began to do a little pee dance. Seconds stretched like hours.

Why not, he asked himself, just let go?

That's when the doorbell rang.

Visitors were not a normal part of his life. The doorbell had recently become an ominous sound. He could see that the bolt was unlocked, no doubt the intruder had picked it while Crockett was sleeping. So maybe this time, someone was here to help him. No need for a doorbell if you're an intruder.

"Come in," Crockett said as loudly as he could, the air scraping his apparently bruised vocal cords. He remembered the pulley. "But open the door very, very slowly."

The door began to push inward, putting slack into the rope.

All Crockett needed was a foot or two of that slack. Once he had enough, he didn't wait to see who was coming inside, but reached up and unlooped the rope from his neck. Too desperate even to glance back at the door, he hopped off the chair and dashed into the bathroom. He wasn't sure there had never been a time in his life when anything ever felt better. Tears rolled down his face through his closed eyes and he told himself they were only because of the relief he felt not because he was angry and afraid and bewildered and alone and depressed and happy that he wasn't dead.

After he finished, he turned on the sink and looked up to see the handwritten note taped to the mirror.

IF YOU LEAVE THIS ALONE IT WILL BE OVER IN A WEEK AND YOU WILL BE CLEARED OF CHARGES. IF YOU KEEP LOOKING FOR ANSWERS, NEXT TIME YOU WON'T LIVE.

Past the note, he saw his reflection in the mirror.

His purple lumpy face now glistened with tears. There was an angry slash across his throat from the rope.

This was it. The second lowest point of his life. Ashley clutching his hand in those final moments. Lowest point, overwhelming sorrow. This point, becoming overwhelming anger.

He looked again at the note. Even if he could believe its promise that charges might be dropped, for the rest of his life, the pedophile reputation would still smear him. He had to beat this, on his terms. He needed more than some unknown marionette clearing the charges. He needed to expose whoever was doing these things to him and to prove not just his innocence, but someone else's guilt.

Madelyne Mackenzie. It was centered on her. Yesterday, he'd provoked her as much as could, hoping to stir up enough to know she was the hornet's nest. Hours later, he was attacked in his home. No doubt both were related. He'd be going back there today.

He wiped his face with a towel, and stepped outside of the bathroom, directly into the living room of his small bungalow—where a woman with blazing red hair gaped at his t-shirt and boxers.

She wore a neon-pink tube top that struggled to hold in its contents, a black mini-skirt, and to complete the street walker-style attire, fishnet stockings encasing legs worthy of attention.

Crockett moved his focus to the woman's face.

Dr. Madelyne Mackenzie.

Chapter Forty-Six

B y breaking into a studio apartment some ten blocks north and east of the Vatican walls, Raymond Leakey was doing something to manage his huge headache.

Previously, he had decided there was a degree of safety in remaining relatively ignorant of the vices of His Eminence Ethan Saxon. It had been enough for Leakey to be acting for O'Hare, bringing information to Saxon about O'Hare and the girl and the psychiatrist.

During those months, Leakey had been balancing a high wire act between Saxon and O'Hare, pretending to be a servant to O'Hare, and at the same time pretending to serve Saxon, assessing which side offered the best safety net when it was time to jump. O'Hare wanted one thing and Saxon another, but Leakey was determined to serve himself in the end.

Now, something about Saxon's desperation alarmed Leakey.

First the cardinal had tried to eliminate the girl. Then he was willing to kill the teacher's neighbor to ensure the teacher was in no position to be credible, and only because of the *possibility* the girl had talked. Now to want the psychiatrist killed?

Leakey had known about the cardinal's hideaway for a while—Saxon wasn't the first bishop or cardinal to have a place to stow a mistress or boyfriend—and now he had the motivation to take a closer look.

Leakey's instincts told him that the safety net was on O'Hare's side of the wire, but it seemed sensible to go farther and learn even more about Saxon before committing one way or another.

Upon entering the two bedroom apartment, Leakey noticed it was expensively furnished. No surprise there. Thick curtains hung from ceiling to floor covering the windows, putting the apartment in near darkness.

Leakey moved softly from room to room, scanning with a flashlight. It had been years since he'd engaged in operational work like this, but the instincts were hard to lose. He expected that it might take up to an hour to find a clue pointing toward Saxon's real vices, but the cardinal was so arrogant, he hadn't bothered to hide anything.

The evidence lie in an leather-bound trunk along the wall, in the second bedroom of the apartment.

The walls of that room were painted black, something that took Leakey a moment to realize with his flashlight. There were shelves with black candles, but no other furniture occupied the room except for the trunk.

It wasn't locked.

Leakey opened the lid. He wouldn't have been shocked to find the toys or masks that went with the hidden and twisted desires of men, but instead, he found a heavy polished silver chalice, like a communion cup.

For a moment, he wondered if Saxon's greatest sin had been to steal the chalice from a church. A closer look quickly changed Leakey's mind.

There was nothing holy about the chalice. It had stylized symbols and pornographic etchings. Its ornate handles were elaborately shaped with a Christ-figure on an inverted crucifix.

Latin words were engraved around the rim.

In nomine Magni Dei Nostri Satanas. Introibo ad altare Domini Inferi

Leakey set aside the chalice and pulled out a box he immediately recognized as a pyx, which in a church setting contained the Eucharist, the communion wafers.

This pyx matched the chalice in its unholy art. Same horrible lurid etchings, same Latin engraving.

And beneath these were dozens of Polaroids. Oddly old fashioned and yet graphic in a way that had an impact on Leakey. He had prided himself on being as cynical and world-weary as any of his colleagues.

In itself, the trappings of Satanism gave Leakey no sense of horror or fear. He didn't look around the room and shiver as if demons might attack him at any moment.

Leakey wasn't a believer in the supernatural. Any other setting, he would have found the décor of the room to be as laughable of a vice as discovering—which he had in the past—photos of the owner to be dressed like a baby and spanked by a mistress.

But today Leakey couldn't find the cynicism to laugh off the obscenities. Because the degradations in the Polaroids needed to be stopped and exposed.

Unless O'Hare's plan could be trusted, the man responsible for this would become the next pope.

A man utterly evil. And clearly insane.

Chapter Forty-Seven

D ang," Crockett said to Mackenzie. "Who knew a thermostat adjustment could make such a difference."

Holding a shopping bag, standing just inside the house, she was obviously working hard to keep her focus on his face. "I'd like you to put on pants before we talk."

"You need advice about the process if you expect to make much money. You see the pants should—"

"You wanted help, didn't you?" She snapped out her words, interrupting him. "I'm here to give it, but not until you're wearing pants. Otherwise, I walk."

In direct contrast to the way she was dressed, nothing about her gave any vibe of flirtatiousness.

"Pants. On. Now." She hefted her shopping bag. All business. "While you are doing that, I'm going to change too. That's the bathroom, right?"

"You're fine the way you are," Crockett said.

"I don't even think a drunk person would find you funny."

Then Crockett heard his favorite word in the world. One that normally filled him with joy, but now filled him with panic.

Daddy.

Mickey had pushed through the front door.

It was a frozen tableau. Crockett stood beside a chair, beneath a rope, in a T-shirt and boxers. Mackenzie squirmed in her scandalous outfit. Mickey gaped at them both.

Mickey spoke first. To Mackenzie, who was pulling at the hems of her mini-skirt.

"Hi," Mickey said. "I'm Mickey." He stuck his hand out as he introduced himself, the way that Crockett had taught him. He was waist-high to Mackenzie . His blond hair was cut short and the gap in his teeth accentuated his lisp that never failed to lift Crockett's spirits.

Mackenzie 's face softened as she smiled. It was the first smile Crockett had seen on her and it looked good.

"Mickey," Mackenzie said, gingerly bending to match his height and accept the handshake. "I'm Madelyne Mackenzie."

"Madelyne," Mickey repeated, to learn the name. Crockett had taught him that too.

Mickey pointed at the rope and the chair. "What's that, Daddy?"

Crockett wrestled briefly with the answer, then spoke. "A game."

"A game? Cool! How do you play?"

"Mickey…" Suddenly, Crockett's boxers didn't feel so comfortable. Pants seemed like a great idea. Because if Mickey was here, someone else was close behind. She had probably parked the car and let Mickey run ahead up the sidewalk. "How about I meet you outside, buddy?"

Too late.

Julie stepped into the house. Hair tied back, form-fitting blue sweater, black slacks, Starbucks in hand. This might have been the only time since their separation and divorce that Crockett wasn't overwhelmed by longing and regret and happiness to see her.

It became another frozen tableau. Crockett, Mackenzie and Julie. The fourth, Mickey, was oblivious of the tension.

"Hey Mom," he said. "Dad's got a friend over. I think she has cool pants. You can see right through those pants, can't ya? "

Julie stared at the rope, then shifted her gaze to Crockett. Then to Madelyne, back to Crockett and to the rope.

"Nice," Julie said. "Funny how you didn't mention your... friend... when I agreed to give you weekends with Mickey."

"It's not what you think," Crockett said.

"Just like the rope mark around your neck is not what I think?"

"Hey," Mickey said, brightly. "Mom's right. There's a mark, Dad. Is that part of the game you were going to explain to me? And your face. What happened to it?"

"I had had a change of heart," Julie said. "I realized that I shouldn't presume that you are guilty. I felt sorry for you. Thought maybe if you weren't busy, you could have a zoo day today with Mickey, but I should have listened to Dave."

She took Mickey's hand. "Let's go. Daddy's busy right now. Busy with his games."

"Julie... give me a minute to explain," Crockett said. "This is Dr. Madelyne Mackenzie. She's a child psychiatrist."

"Yes, I'm a doctor," Mackenzie extended a hand, straightening into a professional posture. "Nice to meet you."

"Quite," Julie answered, ignoring the hand. "House calls are how much an hour?"

"Come on," Crockett said. "She's helping a student of mine."

Julie shot Crockett a look of scornful pity that made him realize how ridiculous it sounded.

"The rope," Mackenzie interjected. "Look at his neck again. You don't get a burn like that from, ahh... games." She cleared her throat. "You get a burn like that from someone—"

Crockett cut Mackenzie off before she said too much in front of Mickey. "I want to tell you what happened, Julie—but later, over the phone. I'll call you. Alright?"

"Goodbye, Crockett," Julie said, pulling Mickey with her. "Enjoy your morning."

Chapter Forty-Eight

I've seen that knife before," Nanna said to Nathan. Although she continued to use her friendly grandmother voice that seemed to keep the disturbed young man serene, maintaining the tone took discipline. It was becoming exhausting, in fact.

"That knife came from my neighbor's house, didn't it?"

Nathan had just been talking to his invisible demon. He seemed aggravated that the demon was, as he put it, treating him like an idiot. The conversation had been disturbing to Nanna. The demon had apparently been instructing Nathan to wear rubber gloves when he carried the knife. Nathan said that he knew the importance of not getting fingerprints on the knife.

Nanna had been a big, big fan of the old television show *Murder, She Wrote.* Part of the appeal was the clean and wholesome approach to crime, an irony that wasn't lost on Nanna. Another reason was because of how often people commented that she looked so much like Angela Lansbury, although Nanna privately held she looked more like the sexy one on Golden Girls. Except Nanna wasn't so man-hungry.

Mainly though, Nanna loved *Murder, She Wrote* because it showed that an older woman could have spunk and class, and that's exactly how Nanna had decided she would die. Doing her best to survive, and with grace.

"Yeah it's a steak knife," Nathan said.

"I know. Crockett often grilled for me, so I recognize his cutlery. He's such a nice young man. Like you. But of course, Crockett doesn't cook nearly as well as you do."

Nathan gave a Tourette's type of flinch, and turned his head to the camper door, where his invisible demon stood guard.

"I don't know why I need to do this," Nathan said to the invisible demon. "Nobody has ever treated me like a real person... like Nanna does. We should let her go. She wouldn't tell anyone. She promised."

Nathan listened, then recoiled, then shook his head in disgust. "And she certainly doesn't deserve that kind of language."

Turning back to Nanna, he said, "I'm glad you can't hear him. He's had centuries and centuries to learn the foulest language."

She was still shackled on the cramped bed. It had become more and more difficult, her efforts to maintain appearance, keep herself neat. Nathan, at his demon's instructions, didn't even allow her to go to the tiny bathroom in the corner of the camper, but gave her a bedpan.

"I wouldn't be too hard on him," Nanna said. "I'm sure it hasn't always been easy on him."

From the beginning, the first meal Nathan had cooked, when he engaged in a monologue with the camper door, Nanna had guessed the delusion. She'd decided to treat it as real as possible, believing she might be the first person to treat Nathan normally and hoping he would respond to her like she was a harmless, nice old woman. It had worked so far.

"See?" Nathan said over his shoulder. "She's even nice to you!"

"Shouldn't you have a plastic sheet or something?" Nanna asked. She was gleaning from Nathan's conversation with Abez, that Nathan was slowly caving in to his demon's demands to kill her. She wanted to try to talk him out of it, but her instincts told her that she'd be better off being a friend than a frightened woman. She could subtly find a way to diminish Abez. For that, she had a guardian angel in mind.

"A plastic sheet?" he asked.

"To collect the blood. If any of it gets on a blanket, the police will find it and you'll be caught. You need plastic to protect the bed. I don't want to see you hurt, and I think your friend has forgotten how important it is not to leave evidence behind."

"Even now," Nathan said to his demon, "she's looking out for me. Can you say that about yourself?"

She'd seen the industrial roll he brought in the night before, orange Home Depot sticker on the side. She guessed he was going to use it anyway, so it wasn't like she was giving him an idea. Just faithfully working on reverse psychology. Wasn't much else at her disposal except her wits.

She had used the trick earlier in life when one of her daughters, Jenna, had been dating an obnoxious jerk, obvious to everyone but Jenna. Nanna had decided that trying to point this out would alienate Jenna and put her closer to the jerk. Instead, every time Jenna brought up the slightest complaint, Nanna had tried to make an excuse for him, until finally Jenna ended the relationship and questioned what her mother could have possibly seen in such a loser.

"Don't be so hard on him," Nanna soothed to Nathan. "Having one wing would be difficult. My guardian angel has two wings, and sometimes even he gets a little out of sorts."

"Guardian angel?" Nathan darted his eyes all over the camper.

"I think I'm the only one who sees him," Nanna said. "Remember I told you about him? When I was little, people thought I was crazy, but I wasn't going to turn my back on my friend. His name is Gabriel. He's one of the archangels."

Nathan spoke to his demon. "Heard of Gabriel?"

Then, "Archangel, is that a big deal?" Nathan paused. "You and Gabriel, who'd win in a fight?"

He turned back to Nanna. "My demon said he would win, but I'm not sure I believe him."

"Hey, Gabriel," Nanna said, rolling slightly so she was addressing her own imaginary entity at the head of the bed. "When I'm gone, can you protect Nathan? Just whenever his demon misses a thing or two."

To Nathan. "He says he will help you. But Gabriel can't make promises about being nice to your demon. They are mortal enemies, you know."

Nathan, who had been staring at the blade of the steak knife, turned back to the door to speak to Abez.

"Funny how you don't bring this up."

"No, no," Nanna said. "Don't be mean to Abez. Losing to the angels when the Red Sea drowned the Egyptians must have been hard on him. Right now, he's probably hesitant to admit that he's afraid what might happen when Gabriel makes a move after I'm gone."

Nathan gritted his teeth. "I never thought of that. Abez did lose once, didn't he?"

Nathan winced and spoke to the camper door. "Keep it down. Yes, yes. I know we need the knife."

He turned back to Nanna. "I'm so sorry about this but I need to get the plastic first. Then I'll do my best so it doesn't hurt, okay?"

Chapter Forty-Nine

I'm sorry for causing you that trouble."

Less than a minute after Julie left Mackenzie had walked into the bathroom in a miniskirt, carrying her shopping bag of clothes. She'd stepped out in an armor against any indication of femininity or youth—a loose-fitting drab olive jacket over a brown blouse, matching pants, flat-heeled shoes. The transition was a stunning reversal.

Crockett had been waiting for her in the living room. He was in jeans now, same Disney t-shirt, and holding his first cup of coffee. He knew that the caffeine charge didn't have a hope of improving his mood. Or outlook. He was too frustrated to even wonder why she'd shown up in the outfit, with a flashy corvette parked outside.

Crockett ignored Mackenzie's apology and walked through the living room, through the small kitchen and out the back door. He sat in one of the chairs on his deck. Closed his eyes. Took the first sip and tilted his face to the morning sun.

Only hours ago, he could have died. Even though his life had cratered even farther than he could have imagined thanks to Julie's arrival, he told himself to focus on the small pleasures. Prove somehow that being alive was a better alternative than what nearly happened. The warmth of sunlight felt good. Coffee rolling over his tongue felt better. The small things.

The screen door creaked. Mackenzie had followed him.

"I *am* sorry," she said. "I presume she was your wife. She's beautiful."

How did that comment help in any way? A tip of the hat to Crockett's good taste that he'd married a beautiful woman? Or that his longing to put his family back together was justified?

"Why are you here? " he asked.

"I can call her, from my office, and offer to meet. I'll explain."

"Why are you here?"

"Please. Let me apologize to her. If she really believes that the rope and the way I was dressed means something, and if it threatens you in a custody issue, then as a child psychiatrist—"

"Please stop talking. Unless you want to tell me why you are here." Crockett pressed his fingers to his eyes.

"I understand your frustration," she said. "You need time alone in your cave."

"What?" He snapped out the word.

"Men often deal with anger differently than women. They will go into a cave and stay inside until they are ready. They—"

Crockett stood, then hurled his coffee mug against the side of the house. He enjoyed the shattering sound.

"I'm out of my cave now," he said. "Why are you here?"

She looked so shocked and vulnerable that he quickly regretted losing his temper.

"I accept your apology," Crockett said more softly.

A male ruby-throat swooped in to one of Crockett's birdfeeders, with the buzzing of a loud bumble bee, a sound that never failed to fascinate him.

They both watched, wordlessly, until it swooped away again, accelerating almost straight up like a miniature fighter jet.

"Dr. Mackenzie…what's going on?" Crockett asked. "The corvette. Miniskirt. Change of clothes?"

"It was the easiest way of disguising myself that I could think of on short notice."

He studied her, thinking about the implications.

It wasn't the time to suggest that choosing a street-walker disguise had intriguing Freudian implications. Crockett was capable of knowing when some thoughts were better left unsaid. He would have admitted, however, that the disguise had been effective. Not many people seeing her in the outfit would have noticed her face, much less remembered it. For the hetero male, too much else to absorb. And in Julie's case, too much else to scorn.

"That begs another question," he said. "Why did you think you needed a disguise?"

"My question first. Why wouldn't you explain about the rope to your wife?".

"Ex-wife," Crockett said.

"Ex-wife. It's not difficult to guess that something happened last night. Did someone try to hurt you? Maybe it's the same person I was trying to escape."

"Wait," Crockett said. "I need a more coffee. You?"

She nodded. "I'd love some. Black."

When he returned, she was sitting. He handed her a mug, then took the other lawn chair.

"Last night…" she prompted.

"I didn't hang myself." He gave her a succinct, unemotional recap of what had happened.

Furrowed eyebrows. "Are you going to report what happened to the police?"

He snorted, thinking of his last encounter with the police and Pamela Yi in particular. "A guy is about to lose his career and family because a hard drive with horrific images was found in his attic. Do you think they are going to believe a conspiracy theory? Or the more sensical conclusion that the guy is suicidal? Or, that said guy fakes a suicide attempt to throw blame somewhere else."

"You could have at least told Julie."

"Not in front of my five-year-old son. He'd worry. Too much."

Madelyne nodded. "Laudable."

"Maybe I don't care if you think it's laudable." Even though it was a dig at one of her earlier comments, he gave her a smile to rob any insult. "You don't seem surprised that someone strung me up during the night."

"No. Not after what's been happening to me too"

Crockett could have told Mackenzie about the note on the mirror, but he didn't trust her.. A woman hiding something about Jaimie, and somehow in this mess. He didn't trust her at all.

"This has something do with Jaimie," Crockett pointed to his neck. "And you know something about it. Otherwise you would be surprised to hear that someone almost killed me. Did somebody try something last night on you too?"

Mackenzie didn't answer.

"Jaimie is the link between us," Crockett said. "And you're here because you're afraid? Of what?"

"It started with my condo," Mackenzie said. "Two days ago. Actually two nights ago. I got back after a long day, and I noticed things were different. Barely different. Like someone had searched, but was trying to be careful." She set her coffee down on the deck, untouched. "It would have been difficult to prove to a police officer but I knew. I'm almost obsessive compulsive about details."

Obsessive compulsive. Hm.

"And yesterday morning," she continued, "I learned my computer was loaded with spyware."

"Spyware." Crockett gave the courtesy repeat, making it seem automatic, although he had a tingling sensation that cat burglars might feel hiding in a closet when a homeowner arrives unexpectedly. Which layer had she found. The first? Or the second? Or both?

Crockett sipped more coffee, noticing she still hadn't touched hers.

"My computer had been driving me crazy for weeks," she said. "Running really slow and it has been crashing often. I thought it was me, because I'm not good with technology. I finally called an IT person to come to the office. It took him about a minute to tell me that my computer was so buggy that if it was an apartment, cockroaches would have been coming out of the drains, walls, and furniture." She shivered at the image.

"The IT guy told me the computer had a keylogging program. And another program inside the firewall that let someone roam around my computer at will."

"So someone could monitor your Victoria's Secret account?"

She glared at him. With not quite as much ice as she'd been able to muster on previous occasions.

"Sorry... I couldn't resist," he gave a sheepish grin. "Besides, you gave me a great idea for Mickey's next birthday. Your 'cool' pants. If only he could actually get my ex-wife to wear them, life would be complete."

Now she shook her head with resigned exasperation, not the previous icy disdain.

"Then," she said, "yesterday afternoon, after you left, I think someone was following me. First in a car. Then on foot, when I went to the market. He looked like the man you described as the fake social worker."

"So finally, you believe me?"

"With the computer bugged, it makes sense."

It begged the question as to why so much interest in Jaimie, but Crockett felt the rise of fury again. "Hang on. You believed me all along and did nothing to help me? You treated me like I was guilty."

She answered his look without flinching. "Jaimie was, and is, my first concern."

"Except now, when it looks like you're in danger. And now *you* are your first concern."

"I need to take care of myself so I can take care of Jaimie. I don't blame you for your anger."

"Too hypocritical," Crockett said. "It's the same argument I brought to you. Wanting to protect Jaimie, knowing it would protect me."

"I came here because I thought if he's after you and he's after me, well, it means we can at least trust each other."

She paused, as if wait for Crockett to agree.

"Makes sense," he said. That didn't mean he would trust her. Only that her logic had merit.

"Today, I needed to talk to you. I didn't want to call. Maybe phones are bugged too. So I went to the mall first thing this morning and bought this stuff. Found a place to change to disguise myself. Then went and rented the car. I don't think I was followed. I was thinking—okay, we can work together."

"You want to help me now?"

"Yes. But I'm not good asking for help, and I need your help too."

"Why would someone want to bug your computer?" Crockett didn't state the obvious. This, too, had to do with Jaimie. He just wanted to see how Mackenzie would answer.

"That's what I want you to help me find out."

He gave her an arched eyebrow. Silent question. She could do furrows. He could do arches.

She continued, "I don't know what to do about the computer. I don't know what to do about the guy following me. I'm scared. Correction. Way beyond scared. Did I mention I fight a combination of obsessive compulsion and paranoia? It means I'm not a trusting person to begin with. Thinking that a person or people have been spying on me, searching my condo, pawing through my clothes—I didn't sleep at all last night."

"Why don't you go to the police?"

"Sure. I'll do that when you go to them with a story about someone trying to hang you. Of all people, you can understand the paranoia to wonder if the police are in on this."

He grunted agreement.

"I decided," she said, "that if there is one person in the world who has more motivation than I do to find out what's going on, it's you. That's enough for me to trust."

"Why don't you hire a security service for protection?"

"It's too easy for whoever's following me to learn that I'm on to them. "

"If we are going to be in on this together," Crockett said, "Let's start with the exorcist?

She shook her head. "Let's not start there. I don't think you're ready for the answer."

"My neighbor next door is missing," Crockett said. "I'm about to lose my career and my family. I'm ready for the answer."

"You don't play the part of a bully that well. I'm not afraid of you."

"Wonderful. We're on the same side. Why take over her file? Why the priests? You should know that my only hope is to find out what's happening, and I'm not going to stop until I find out. Or get killed trying."

Mackenzie let out a long sigh. "Maybe. But I think it would be better if you came out to the Bright Lights Center today and talked to Jaimie about it."

"If that's what it's going to take, tell me when."

"Now," she said. "In the rental Corvette. You drive."

Chapter Fifty

The Vette, as he expected, had some juice to it, and he popped in and out of traffic, headed north on PCH, hills to his right, water left, the outline of Santa Catalina Island a smudge on the far horizon.

Not much conversation.

Crockett remembered taking Ashley out to Avalon on Santa Catalina. Best part for both of them was the glass-bottom boat tour.

They passed the Malibu state parks, passed the turn off to Pepperdine. Still not much conversation.

Thinking of Ashley always turned his thoughts to Julie.

More often than not, he felt like a panting puppy around Julie, bouncing around, hoping she'd throw something for him to fetch. He couldn't deny the sensation of an unrequited crush whenever he saw her, heard her, or looked at a photograph of her. During their marriage, she'd settled into an even friendship with him, with lukewarm romance, and plenty of nights she turned away from him, no matter how many candles he lit or how much he'd tried to please her during the day with a list of chores. Maybe that's why he always felt the pang. Because the balance of power had always been hers. She could live without him, but he couldn't live without her.

He felt a vibration in his back pocket. Crockett pulled out his phone. Caller ID indicated Amy Roberston. He answered. For the moment, he had a good cell signal along the highway.

"Crockett," he said.

"Not good, Crockett," she said. "Investigators went back to your house. They managed to finagle a search warrant and found a rag with blood on it under a bush in your backyard. They're saying the blood type matches your neighbor… Nanna."

"That will get them looking for her, right?" Crockett said. He clenched the cell phone so hard that the edges of it hurt his palm.

"It has them looking more seriously at you. The rag was wrapped around one of your steak knives. They know that because your prints are on it and it matched the set in your kitchen. Your bail's been revoked. It smells like a setup, so the best way to deal with it is to come to the office, and we'll go together to turn yourself in. That's what an innocent man would do."

Crockett swallowed hard. "Right." He was aware that Mackenzie on the passenger side, hearing all of his half of the conversation. "I'll get there as soon as I can."

"Where are you?"

Crockett lied. It was more important to get to Bright Lights to find out what Jaimie would tell him than to turn around and be back in jail that afternoon. "Palm Springs. Long story. Don't ask."

"That's two hours, unless traffic is good."

"Best I can do."

"I'll let them know and hold them off until then."

"Thanks." He shook his head at the futility of his charade. Nothing was turning his way so this trip to Bright Lights would go badly as well.

"Crockett?"

"Yes?"

"Don't do anything stupid here, okay? You're out on bail, there's been a warrant issued for you. There's a chance I can keep you out on extended bail, but only if you play this straight. I'm sorry it's happening like this, really. Let's still hope Nanna is found alive. She's your best alibi."

"Got it." He couldn't accept losing Nanna too. She had to be alive, despite the evidence to the contrary.

"Don't hang up," she said. "There's something else."

"Still here."

"Found out something you should know about Dr. Mackenzie. She is a member of a coven."

"I think I lost signal strength for a second," he said. "Can you repeat that?"

"Coven. You probably thought I said convent. No. Coven. Cee, Oh. Vee. Ee. En. As in a gathering of witches. It's a little-known-of coven, based out of Santa Barbara. I'll get Catfish working finding out more. But in the meantime, make sure you get here as fast as you can."

"Of course," Crockett said. "Be less than a couple of hours."

Chapter Fifty-One

Madelyne and Crockett leaned against a split rail fence at the Bright Lights Center. Farther down, Jaimie was talking to one of the horses, her face next to the horse's head and she rubbed the horse's nose. She had motioned for them to join her but Madelyne gestured for Jaimie to wait a moment longer.

"I need to set things up a bit before you talk to Jaimie," she said.

"Sure." He seemed distracted. She wondered what the cell phone call had been about, just before they'd turned off the PCH up into the hills.

"I am probably one of the few in my profession who take seriously the question of whether demons do exist, and if indeed some cases of instability or mental illness are because of demon possession. As a Catholic, I share this with you on a personal level. Professionally, I don't discuss it and if you take this elsewhere, I'll deny we had this conversation. In the eyes of other professionals, my stance would undoubtedly result in a stigmatism of sorts, and I don't want that to interfere with how I try to help the children in my care."

As Madelyne spoke, she found to her surprise that she wanted to touch Crockett's face. His bruises, the dark circles beneath eyes full of weary determination. A deep well of inescapable grief.

Crockett was much taller than Madelyne. All she could see on his face was a thousand-yard stare, focused on where the hills and sky met behind her. Almost like he wasn't listening to her, but thinking about something else.

Without meeting her eyes, he spoke. "Are you saying you think that demons exist? Literally? Like swivel the head and projectile vomit horror movie stuff?"

"Yes, I believe demons exist," she said. "No, I don't see it in a horror movie kind of way."

Crockett shifted his eyes to hers. It still was impossible to read what he was thinking.

"Witches and demons?" he finally asked.

"There are those who worship demons," she said. "So yes, I suppose some kinds of witches are part of it."

Crockett looked away again, resumed the thousand-yard stare.

"I'm not going to try to convince you of the existence of demons, okay? Consider what I'm saying from a theoretical point of view. Just like you're reading the paper that I'm writing on the subject, if I can ever put together enough empirical data to actually present it for peer review. I'll talk to you as if you have a theist world view. That you believe in the existence of God. And soul."

Crockett met her eyes again. "You won't be offended if I tell you that I don't. Believe in God. That I prefer the rational?"

"Yes, the rational. Then you're not that different from a lot of people who do believe in God. In their world, God and soul exist, but demons are part of the superstitions from the Middle Ages. They suggest that the demons Jesus cast out in the Gospels were just psychological afflictions, leaving them a rational faith with comfortable PowerPoint sermons to help them live better lives. Nothing mystical or frightening to confront."

"Nothing mystical or frightening for me either," Crockett shrugged. What I believe is what I can see or measure. No God. No soul. And no demons."

"In a way, I think it's that simple," she said. "Yes, for you, there is just one realm, the physical. If that's true, demons, as spiritual entities, do not exist. For me, there are two realms. Physical and spiritual. Two types of entities. Physical and spiritual."

"And, as you're going to argue in your peer-reviewed paper," Crockett said, eyes seeming to search hers now. "If there is another entity, with God and angels, it's difficult to deny that demons would exist. Much as some modern churches would prefer to ignore them."

She nodded. "If there are two realms, demons and angels are entities in one. Animals, plants in the other. As humans, we are the unique entity that exists or straddles both realms."

" If you are saying that demons can and will enter or possess humans, than demons too, straddle both worlds."

"At least you're listening," she said. "Demons only access the spiritual component of humans. Demons are not capable of acting, on their own, in the physical world."

"How about when they turn rooms into ice boxes during exorcisms? That's just in movies?" He arched his brows, underlining his sarcasm.

"You are verging on cavalier," she said. "But I will answer you seriously anyway. If you did any research on exorcisms, you will read accounts by priests where one person will feel the room turn cold, and at the same time, another other will feel it warm up. One will smell, yes, sulphur, and the other will smell something totally different. In a peer-reviewed paper that tries to piece together the reality of a spiritual entity from the other realm trying to possess a human's spiritual component, I would argue that the physicality of the room in this realm doesn't change, but the perception of the observer does. Perceptions altered by demonic presence. And psychology is rich with other situations that reflect this."

"Fair enough," Crockett said. "I grew up churched. I know the Gospel accounts. Are you going to tell me that all of the stories about demons are true? That there are no grounds to argue that some of those healed by Jesus had psychological afflictions?"

"You are getting to the crux of this. I think of it as a pendulum. In the time of Christ, up to the end of the Middle Ages, everything was blamed on demons. Today, everything, at least in the western world, is attributed to psychological afflictions. What if the truth is somewhere between those extremes? The Vatican's Chief Exorcist suggests that only one in five thousand suspected demon possessions are actually demon possessions. But that's still one real demon possession. And it makes a great playground for demons. In our society they can do as they please without fear. They are the ultimate stalkers, invisible because we ignore them."

"But demons don't exist," Crockett said.

"If they did, it would give a lot of people hope," she answered.

He frowned.

"If demons exist," she said, "then God exists. As does the spiritual realm that offers us the ultimate hope in the face of death."

"Now it sounds like you are trying to proselytize." She heard his voice go bitter.

"I hate phrases like 'hope in the face of death'. Death sucks away everything that matters. If you don't believe me, hold the hands of someone who is dying. So how about we get to the reason you invited me out here. Like telling me what it is about Jaimie that links us to threats against us. You took Jaimie to a priest because you thought she was demon-possessed, right?"

"I don't want to answer that." She gave him a direct look, suddenly very still and focused. She didn't want to betray this man but it couldn't be avoided. "Go over to Jaimie, and then she'll bring you to my office."

Chapter Fifty-Two

Jaimie stood at the fence, in the shade of a huge oak tree. She was in jeans and a light blue jersey that made her look smaller than she was.

"Mr. G," Jaimie said. She hugged him hard.

Crockett didn't push away from the hug. He couldn't help but think of Ashley.

"You're okay?" he asked..

"I'm okay," she said, stepping back, "Thanks for helping me the night of the fire. With all this stuff that's happened, I haven't had a chance to say that yet. I'm sorry about the trouble it caused you. I didn't mean it to happen."

Crockett refrained from rubbing his neck. Because of the circular bruise around his neck, before leaving the house, he'd slipped on a collared shirt that hid most of the damage. Nothing he'd been able to do about his face though.

"There's lots to talk about," Crockett said, thinking about witches and demons. The information that Dr. Mackenzie was part of a coven, her trying to convince him that demons existed, Jaimie's inexplicable involvement in all of it. "Dr. Mackenzie said we should meet her in her office."

"It's there," Jaimie said, pointing at the nearby building.

He had the horn-rimmed video glasses folded up in his back pocket. He pulled them out and slipped them on, ready to press the button to start recording.

"Let's go," Crockett said, turning to look squarely at her. "I'm looking forward to finding out what this is about."

———

Mackenzie was waiting for them on a couch in a room that looked like a library.

Jaime pulled him through the doorway, taking both his hands. He caught a glimpse of someone moving toward him and tried to make a defensive move, but Jaimie held tight to his hands.

The attackers arm came up from behind Crockett, around his neck.

Piercing pain followed. Centered in the widest part of his left buttock. The embrace held him for a couple seconds as he arched away from the pain, gagging him with that solid grip around the throat.

"Mr. G," Jaimie said. "I'm sorry. It had to be like this."

The grip was released, the pain ending as abruptly as it hit. Crockett whirled, back toward the doorway.

He saw a man, slightly shorter, standing, watching Crockett with a neutral expression, holding a hypodermic needle.

"Best you found a place to sit," the man said. "Soon."

Crockett made a half turn toward Mackenzie. She was rising, her face a strange mixture of concern and concentration.

She moved around the desk, rushing toward him.

He tried to put up his arms to defend himself, but there was too much disconnect between brain command and the obedience he expected from his arms.

His legs were going next. He felt himself begin to topple forward.

Just before obliteration, he smelled Mackenzie's perfume, felt the softness of her embrace as he fell into her head first.

There was only one word apt to describe her. What a witch, he began to tell himself, but couldn't verbalize or finish the thought.

All black after that.

Chapter Fifty-Three

A clicking noise woke Crockett.

He was on his back, beneath sheets, in natural light. He opened his eyes and saw that the sound came from the slow movement of a ceiling fan directly above him.

Without moving any part of his body, he licked his lips, very aware of the throbbing in his head. However hung over he had been the morning after the arson, this was a Richter scale worse.

Instead of sitting up, which he knew would be a disaster, he turned his head slowly sideways, moving his view from the ceiling to the end of the room. And saw a middle-aged man in a cassock who sat in a straight backed chair between Crockett and a door.

The man's head was bowed, his face obscured by shadow. He was reading a Bible, held in both hands above his lap. Crockett saw the top of the man's head and a monkish hair cut—fringes shot on a balding head the size of a bowling ball. In his lap was a short black tube, with two silver pins at one end, a weapon that Crockett recognized because he confiscated one from a student once.

A stun gun.

He continued to look around. He was in a hotel room. Not Motel 6 style, but something much older. The ceiling was tall, with ornate patterns in the white painted plaster. The chest of drawers was dark-colored wood, not cheap veneer. He was laying in a poster bed.

Crockett closed his eyes. Clueless to his location or to the reason he'd been abducted, he was obviously at an extreme disadvantage. At this point, the only advantage he could gain was in pretending that he was still unconscious, and even that probably wouldn't do him any good.

He wasn't a cop or spy, but didn't take much intelligence to identify step one. Assess the immediate situation as well as he could.

Silly as it seemed, he wondered first if he was dressed. So complete had his unconsciousness been, and so disoriented his awakening, it took a slight shifting of his arms against his body to determined he been stripped to his underwear.

He moved his legs slowly, didn't feel any sense of binding or manacles. Eyes still closed, he gave it more thought.

A priest, something familiar about the guy's face. A priest armed with a stun gun. Implicitly, there should seem to be no real threat of bodily harm from a priest. So far, it didn't seem like his captors wanted to harm him. Otherwise, of course, he wouldn't even be having these thoughts. He'd be dead, disposed during his unconsciousness. They just wanted him contained.

Why a stun gun, not a pistol?

Pistols killed, he decided. A stun gun only incapacitated.

Another thought struck him. Stun guns were silent.

Crockett thought is was unlikely that his abductors had sealed off an entire hotel floor. If there were other guests, shooting him would draw too much attention.

Should he shout for help?

No. Who would investigate? And if he started shouting, all the priest would need to do was take a few steps, jab Crockett with the stun gun. No more shouting.

The silence for Crockett was eerie, especially with his eyes closed. He had no idea if the priest had lifted his head from the Bible and was looking at him.

Weird, too, that it was a priest. Or maybe not so weird, considering all he'd learned in his investigations. He imagined Catfish rambling on about Vatican conspiracies. He'd love this situation.

Crockett wondered if the man was waiting for Crockett to wake, to begin a conversation.

He gave this possibility more thought, and decided he liked the conclusion. The stun gun would keep Crockett compliant and at arm's length. Lastly, by sitting between Crockett and the door, with that large space between the priests chair and Crockett's bed, it ensured Crockett would not escape.

Crockett gave it more thought, eyes closed.

The man in a cassock had a stun gun for a weapon. What did Crockett have? Only the fact that he was conscious without the man's awareness. And, perhaps, surprise.

Not the surprise of lunging out of bed and trying to overpower the man. That would be anticipated.

No. The surprise of the unanticipated.

Crockett tried to focus on what might be unanticipated. This was difficult. Each waking moment hammered to him how thirsty he was.

Anticipated: Opening his eyes, rolling over and asking where he was and what the guy was doing there.

Anticipated: Crockett jumping toward his guard.

Anything opposite, then, would be unanticipated.

Crockett rolled his head away from the direction of his guard. A waking man, especially in a strange situation, would immediate roll it back to survey his room. If his movement had caught the attention of the guard in a cassock, rolling his head back would be anticipated too.

So Crockett simply left his head turned sideways and opened his eyes, listening for movement behind him.

Nothing. Maybe the guard was watching. Maybe not. Either way, Crockett still had only one, pitiful weapon. Surprise.

Chapter Fifty-Four

Jaimie and Dr. Mackenzie sat in a stone courtyard of a big house, nestled between rolling hills. For Jaimie, the scenery felt similar to the familiar hills of southern California, but she could still feel how far away from her normal life she was.

"Whoever owns this has a lot of money," Jaimie didn't like letting people know when she was impressed, but there was no getting around it here. She'd passed big mansions in Hollywood and guessed this is what those mansions looked like on the inside.

"It's a summer residence," Dr. Mackenzie said. "For Cardinal Ricci. You'll meet him soon enough. How are you feeling?"

"Okay," Jaimie said. "Except about Mr. G. Why can't he be here with us?"

"It's better for Mr. G not to know why we are here," Dr. Mackenzie said. "He's in a hotel. Father O'Hare is going to explain a few things to him. But not everything."

"When this is over," Jaimie said. "Will Mr. G know what it was about?"

"Best if he didn't," Dr. Mackenzie said. "We both agree, don't we, that it's going to be something you need to keep to yourself."

For the next thirty seconds, still listening for the scrape of a chair that might indicate his guard had stood, Crockett played it out in his mind, tried to calculate his odds. The upside of his plan. The downside.

Odds, maybe fifty-fifty. The latch on the closed sliding door was in the upward position. Chances were that meant the door was open. With the element of surprise, he should be able to get there before the guard and stun gun.

The downside of an unsuccessful attempt didn't seem horrible. Stun gun, not pistol. They were only trying to contain him, not hurt him. If he didn't make it to the chair with his clothes in time, at worst, he'd be stun gunned, maybe bound and gagged to stop him from trying something else.

The upside was it was unpredictable. From his limited view, he saw that natural light was coming in through opened curtains at a sliding door. He saw the balcony behind the glass sliding doors, a matched set of chairs and table on the balcony, another good indication this was a hotel on the upscale side. He didn't see branches, so his best guess said his room was at least three stories about the ground. Crockett also saw his clothes folded neatly on a chair in the corner, near the sliding door.

He had no idea what was beyond the balcony. On the other hand, he did know what was inside the room. Somebody in a cassock armed with a stun gun.

Crockett went with the odds.

Hoping his guard was still immersed in reading, Crockett flipped out of the sheets, toward the balcony. He didn't look back.

Two steps, he was there, pulling on the door, grateful it wasn't locked. As it slid open, he grabbed the chair with his clothes and moved it onto the balcony. Then he pulled the door shut.

Only then did he glance inward.

Stun gun in hand, the man inside was rushing toward the balcony.

Crockett managed to slide the glass door shut before the guard made it. Now Crockett was in a good position, he thought.

It didn't matter that he had no way of locking the door. He put his full weight on the edge of the sliding door, at the center. The man inside could only pull futilely on the handle. Not enough leverage.

This was delicious irony. They were only separated by a quarter inch of clear glass. Their faces were barely a foot apart, with his guard's face clearly stricken by anger and frustration. A pistol could have obliterated the barrier, but the stun gun was useless.

Next step.

Shoulder holding the sliding door closed, Crockett reached with his outward hand for the chair he'd pulled outside. He maneuvered it to put one of the square legs at the base of the closed glass door, and quickly shifted the weight from his shoulder to both hands on the chair. Now he was pushing the door shut with the entire chair.

Inside, the man in the cassock had dropped the stun gun and was trying to pull the door open with both hands.

James Bond would have pulled the door open, reached around, punched the man in the face, grabbed the stun gun, but Crockett was no 007. The man on the other side had considerable bulk. Even after a good night's sleep, Crockett had doubts he'd be able to win a fight. Weakened by whatever drug had been pumped into his body, Crockett had no chance.

Instead, he tilted the chair back, keeping the leg in place, and wedging the back of the door against the opposite edge of the casement.

Exactly how he'd visualized it thirty seconds earlier. The chair was a wedge, making it impossible to open the sliding door from inside. Short of the breaking the glass, cassock man couldn't get at Crockett.

Which meant Crockett had purchased some time. And a chance to learn more. At worst, if there was nothing further he could do to help his situation, he'd have to sheepishly open the door and accept the consequences of his failed attempt.

From the bed, he had hoped for more, like a minute or two to stand there and shout for help. Maybe other hotel guests had open balcony windows and would come out and give him a chance to explain he'd been abducted.

In bed, he even considered throwing the balcony table and chairs over the railing to attract attention.

Inside, the man in the cassock was speaking into a walkie-talkie. Calling reinforcements. Okay, that would cut down on the time that Crockett had out on the balcony.

Crockett scooped up his jeans and slid one leg, then the other into his pants. As he hopped to dress himself, he glanced over the balcony. Six, maybe seven stories high. Overlooking a fenced pool, with an array of lounge chairs, and beyond the fence, tile roof homes, and beyond the homes, a valley with cultivated green fields. It didn't look like California.

Crockett's best guess was that this was a small hotel, but he'd have to lean over the balcony and look both ways to assess that.

Crockett hated heights. He already felt nauseous as it was.

He threw on his shirt.

Then, idiotic as it seemed, he screamed as loud as he could. "Help! Kidnapped! Send police to this room!"

Maybe a dozen people down below. Three, maybe four elderly women in bathing suits. Husbands to match. A young couple with kids. Two girls swimming. He saw their heads turn upward.

"Send help!"

Crockett glanced inside. The man in the cassock had clearly heard him. He saw the man's face tighten with determination, then he retreated.

"Police!" Crockett shouted. "Police!"

People below simply stared. No movement that Crockett could see. Nobody lifting a cell phone to their heads.

Another glance inside. He saw that cassock man had grabbed his chair from the doorway. Didn't take rocket science to figure out what was coming next.

"Come on people!" Crockett screamed. "Do something!"

Now Cassock man was back at the glass door, raising his chair. About to slam it into the window.

Crockett scrambled to stand on the balcony railing. He cursed about his hatred of heights.

"Clear the pool!" he screamed. "Now!"

He launched himself forward.

Chapter Fifty-Five

Jumping from the balcony had not been one of the options that Crockett had considered from the safety of his bed. But because he acted without thinking, the adrenalin and urgency took away any conscious deliberations that would have paralyzed him.

He found himself flailing through the air, trying to peddle an invisible bicycle. Had he been going head first, the impact probably would have snapped his neck.

Instead, the terror-inflicted bicycling action save him from serious injury, as his feet broke through the surface tension of the water in two simultaneous spots. His clothes prevented the water from smacking bare skin and the worst of the damage he suffered was banging his feet against the bottom of the pool. He'd been prepared for this, trying to roll sideways at impact.

In a burst of bubbles, he tried to orient himself, then pushed off the bottom of the pool to break surface against and gasp for air.

Briefly, he dog paddled, looking upward.

He saw the priest staring down. Crockett grinned, purely out of exhilaration of survival.

The priest disappeared from view, and reminded Crockett that he was far from safe.

He splashed to the edge of the pool and clambered up. The two girls who'd been swimming were still paddling, well clear of where he'd landed.

Their faces still registered shock.

As did the faces of the elderly couples.

"Police," Crockett said. "Get police! Don't any of you speak English!"

He was met with silence, until one elderly man spoke in heavily accented English.

"Drunk American! Have you no shame or public decency? Go home. Stay there. And tell your friends not to visit."

It was a clear message that he would have to do all of this himself. But not in bare feet.

He saw a pair of sandals beside one of the men. He jumped out of the pool, dripping water, and grabbed the sandals.

"Pay you later," Crockett said, hoping the man didn't chase after him.

The man waved him away, apparently, scared of a madman.

Crockett ran toward the gate that led outside the pool area. His jeans and shirt dripped water.

He didn't know where he was going, just that it was best to be gone.

Chapter Fifty-Six

Crockett sprinted from the back of the hotel, going down an alley to a main road that paralleled the beach of a small lake, his best guess only about a couple miles across, small enough to see it was circular, surrounded by hills. A volcanic crater lake?

He saw Old World piers and Old World wooden fishing boats. Light traffic. Cars like Renaults. Couple of Fiats. But no big Chevys or Fords. The surreal feeling that surrounded him since opening the door to Jaimie settled on him once again when he saw the street sign in front of him.

Via Spiaggia del Lago.

He was in Europe. Crockett knew he should have felt something. People don't just get parachuted into foreign countries without some kind of reaction. But most, if not all, of his emotional currency was spent. He'd been swept into this flood of events and, exhausted, was simply trying to keep his head above water.

Italy? Spain?

No. Italy.

Crockett recalled that in ancient times, where ever three roads came together, notices would be posted everywhere, because this was where the highest amount of traffic would see the postings. The word trivia came from the Latin words for "three" and "road".

With all the links from Jaimie and Madelyne Mackenzie to the Catholic church, he had to be in Italy.

He didn't have much time to consider why he was there. His first priority was to put distance between himself and the hotel.

Only trouble was, it didn't look like any of the side streets led anywhere. This lake was in such a steep bowl, it was obvious that the main road followed the shore line and circled the lake, with the side streets ending barely hundreds of yards up the hills.

He squinted ahead at a larger sign. SP140 Roma, with an arrow pointing at an exit. Another arrow pointed straight ahead. *Castel Gondolfo.*

Roma. Yes, he was in Italy. And it was obvious by the rise and broadness of SP 140 that the road would take him out of this lake bowl.

He took a couple steps, then told himself that's what his pursuers would expect him to do.

So Crockett moved off the road and found a thick set of bushes to hide in.

He checked the ground for a colony of bugs or excess debris, and then he stretched out, glad for the warmth of the sun.

Give it a couple hours, he thought. Then it would be safer to try to thumb a ride away from the lake.

He was on his back, staring at the leaves above him, when he remembered what was significant about Castel Gondolfo. Catfish had mentioned it somewhere in passing, during all that talk about the Catholic church.

Castel Gondolfo was the pope's summer residence.

Chapter Fifty-Seven

In Crockett's understanding of the world, most women had a reason to be wary of strange men. And the more attractive the woman, the higher the level of wariness. Men always wanted something. Crockett knew his face still bore bruises, and that would only add to the level of suspicion, especially because he was a man without money and a man who could only speak English in a country of Italians.

Yet, there were two simple words which could instantly diminish the wariness altogether.

At the counter of the internet cafe he'd hitched a ride to, after establishing that the young, attractive woman behind the counter spoke English, he began the story that he'd prepared with those two words.

"My wife," he started, smiling appropriately apologetic, "went for a drive with our rental car before I could get my wallet and phone from the trunk. It's the best place for valuables they say." He touched his face and gave a dramatic wince. "Especially after what happened in Rome last week. Some men tried to steal my wallet then, and I made the mistake of saying 'no.' I kept my wallet, but paid the price. Gypsies, the police said. They told me next time… not to risk my life. I told them I wasn't protecting my wallet, but my wife."

He watched the girl relax. A man who immediately establishes he is married is likely not on the prowl. And a tourist who fought off gypsies, especially to protect his wife, didn't he deserve some sympathy?

She shook her head in dismay at his predicament. "Your wife is a fortunate woman to have someone like you. My boyfriend…"

She let her voice trail as she shrugged.

Crockett kept his hands below the level of the counter. He didn't have a ring on his left hand. Even if it was morally wrong to deceive a college-aged girl so callously, he wasn't going to spend any time second-guessing himself or regretting it.

"I'd like to send an e-mail to her smart phone to return with my wallet," Crockett continued. "Could I leave my watch as a deposit for coffee and lunch and some time on a computer?"

He put his watch on the counter.

She barely glanced at it. "Soup? Sandwich? I'll bring them to your table."

She pointed at an open table with computer screen and keyboard and slipped him a piece of paper with the necessary login information.

"Thank you," Crockett said. He smiled and pushed the watch toward her. She pushed it back at him. "Some places in Italy are friendlier than others."

No wonder people lied, Crockett thought. The rewards were great.

Crockett gulped his coffee. It had been served in a small bone-white cup. Espresso. Not big steaming cups like at Denny's where the refills were fast and frequent.

He didn't dare immediately go back for more. Instead, he rubbed his eyes, waiting for the caffeine to kick in.

On an intellectual level, he recognized he was halfway across the world, without money or identification. In a cafe with college kids with backpacks.

Fighting jet lag and drug residue, he worried if any second an avenging priest might burst through the door. Not to mention he was wanted for arrest in the United States and had broken all bail and bond conditions—involuntary or not—that made him a fugitive and it would be unwise to turn to the local authorities for help.

On an emotional level, however, it was simply a new time bubble, a new reality. And a person could only live in the present. Crockett was beginning to feel like the dazed survivor of a car wreck, limping down the highway in search of help. A walking wounded on autopilot.

Maybe it was like this for, say, soldiers new to combat. Ripped away from home and all the comforts of routine and familiar surroundings, looking through gun sights to fire at other soldiers who were buzzing bullets over their heads. You just accepted what it was, and did the best you could.

A new reality. One you endured to the best of your ability until you could go back to the old reality.

But could Crockett even return to his old reality? Chances were it was as gone as the marriage he knew he'd never recover.

He logged onto his server, noticing that his fingers trembled on the keyboard.

As much as he wanted to compartmentalize it philosophically, here was evidence that wasn't adjusting as well as he wanted to this new reality. It took was one image in his mind to steady himself. Mickey.

He straightened his shoulders then began reading through his new emails. There was one from Catfish entitled Prelim on Genealogy Request—WITCHES!!! In another window he checked the hotmail account he'd set up and saw an e-mail from Dr. McFarlane, with the subject heading Magnet and Gene Code Update.

Good.

He'd get to those as soon as he fired bits of data halfway across the world, asking for help .

Email number one to Fish, cc: Amy.

Fish, got a challenge for you. Find a way to wire me some money. You're going to have to scan my photo to go with it, because I don't have any identification. Let's go with $1000, USD. I'm in an internet cafe in Marino, Italy, so you'll need to figure out the nearest location for where I can pick it up. Walking distance. As soon as you've figure out the logistics, call the cafe and ask for me by name. I'll explain what I can over the phone and you can tell me how to get the money. Once I'm in a hotel, I'll call you back and we can plan what's next.

All that he could do next was read his other emails, and wait for a phone call.

And eat.

He had finished his soup and read and reread the emails from Catfish and the geneticist, and was halfway through his sandwich when she walked in.

Dr. Madelyne Mackenzie.

Chapter Fifty-Eight

N ice place," Crockett addressed a man with thick graying hair. "I really appreciate the invitation."

"Sarcasm," the man answered. "A poor cousin to irony."

So the guy spoke English. And well.

After Mackenzie arrived at the internet cafe, she had given Crockett a simple choice. If he wanted to find out what was happening, he needed to come with her. She'd led him out to a small black Fiat, where they sat in the back as passengers. Both the driver and Mackenzie kept silent. The drive had been less than ten minutes from the internet cafe, up into the hills, past vineyards and small homes that looked centuries old. They'd reached a walled estate, then driven through an electronic gate opened by a remote control in the car, down a tree-lined lane, to a large villa surrounded by garden.

Mackenzie had then escorted him into this shadowed courtyard, leaving him alone with this gray-haired man who had been waiting with his hands behind his back. He was elegantly dressed, in tan trousers and a white shirt, and had the calm self-satisfied demeanor of one born into wealth.

Crockett knew he was powerless to fight any of this process. They'd found him once, they would likely find him again. They'd taken him to Italy without his knowledge.

But he wasn't going to show any of his fear, and he'd preferred focusing on his curiosity instead. In short, what was going on? Six days ago, his life had been routine. Six days ago, he'd only wanted to get as drunk as possible to ease his way through an anniversary night of his daughter's death. How did a school teacher end up in a villa near the Pope's summer residence? More to the point, why?

"Really, this is a nice place," Crockett said, keeping up his unfazed act. "But sorry, I can't think of anything ironic to say about being kidnapped. "

"The irony," his host said, "is your lack of gratitude, given that you were taken here as means of protecting you."

"I'd suggest that a lack of consent on my part is a good reason to explain my lack of gratitude."

"That lack of consent is also something that should earn your gratitude. Your consent would have had negative implications on your conditions of bail. As it is, you did not voluntarily leave the United States."

The man had a point. Crockett shut his mouth and looked around. In the center of the courtyard was a small table protected by an open umbrella. An envelope had been placed on the table. Beside the envelope was a pitcher of water with sliced lemon in it. Some glasses. Crockett was thirsty, but didn't want to show any sign of weakness by asking for water.

"How about you tell me who you are and why I'm here?" Crockett said.

"I'm Cardinal Ricci." Slight bow.

Cardinal.

"Accept this first, please." The gray-haired man moved to the table and picked up the envelope. When he passed it over, Crockett caught the faint scent of cologne.

Crockett opened the envelope. It held an American Airlines ticket. He scanned the details. First-class seat from Rome's Leonardo da Vinci airport to Chicago O'Hare, then LAX.

"You are not a prisoner," the man said. "You can walk away. The men behind you will escort you to the airport. I can arrange for someone from the American Embassy to meet you there. You don't have your passport, but as a returning fugitive, you'll be allowed on the airplane, and authorities will be waiting for you in Chicago when you clear immigration. There is, as we both know, you'll be met with a warrant for your arrest."

"And if I stay," Crockett said, "I'll be guarded by a priest with a stun gun?"

"We were hoping to keep you in the hotel long enough to explain the situation," the gray-haired man said. "It would have been safer and more discreet. As it is now, the chances are much greater that our plans will be discovered."

"Who is 'we'?"

"You only get the answers if you stay," the gray-haired man said. "If you decide to stay, I'll need that ticket back. At least for a few days until the situation is resolved."

Crockett considered his options. He could come up with three. Either stay, get on the airplane, or try to escape again.

Getting on the airplane meant certain arrest, with nothing learned about any of this that might help him avoid going to prison.

A successful escape wouldn't help him much, as he still had no money and no identification, no place to go, and they'd probably find him as easily as they did after his first escape.

And staying meant he might learn what was going on. More importantly, if he learned what was going on, he'd have a chance at recovering his former life. Quiet daily routines, with weekends of hope and joy with Mickey.

He handed the ticket back to the gray-haired man.

"Thank you," the man said. He made a fluttering waving motion with his fingers, and the uniformed men retreated from the courtyard.

The man motioned toward the table and they sat.

"Please," the man said. "Help yourself. I'm guessing the affects of the drugs it took to put you on our jet have left you thirsty."

The man was charming, but Crockett wasn't in the mood to be charmed. He refused the offer of water.

"Who is 'we'?" Crockett asked. "And what is the situation that needs to be resolved?"

"Have some water. Make yourself comfortable. My villa is yours for the stay. We've moved all your personal possessions into a guest room. Think of it as a complimentary vacation. You'll find plenty of books, but no internet. Part of the conditions are that your presence here remains unknown. When the situation is over, we will fly you back to California. All the charges against you will have been dropped. Your life will be what it was before Jaimie showed up at your house."

Crockett thought of the note on his mirror, promising the same thing. Pretty strong odds, that this was connected.

Cardinal.

"I'm supposed to believe that?"

"Your alternative is to get on a commercial flight and take your chances when you land."

"No," Crockett said. "The alternative is that you tell me what's going on, as you promised."

"You are not in a position to make requests."

"I know that Dr. Mackenzie sent out a sample of Jaimie's blood for DNA analysis. And that she also ordered a genealogy report."

"You've already informed her of that. Rather melodramatically from what I understand."

Now Crockett knew that this man who exuded such European arrogance was working with Madelyne Mackenzie.

"Not curious to know how I found out?" Crockett asked.

The man sighed, in a manner that implied Americans were be such simple children. "Spyware. It was so very difficult to guess that you had hacked into her computer. Hacking into someone's computer is a crime, but we made a decision not to begin any prosecution for it. It's your good fortune that it's more important to keep you comfortably in hibernation for a short while than it is to address that blatant invasion of privacy."

This was beginning to feel like a poker game to Crockett and it seemed smart to hold on to what he knew. Like that he wasn't the only one who had been prowling Mackenzie's cyberspace.

"What if you and Dr. Mackenzie have been looking in the wrong family tree?" Crockett said. "What if it turns out Jaimie's great-great-great grandmother was burned to death for the crime of witchcraft?"

The arrogance was replaced by a stillness. A predatory stillness.

Crockett had him, and knew it.

"I'll be glad to tell you about Jaimie's real mother," Crockett said. "I want to know what's happening here, why you're so interested in Jamie and how you are going to get us both home and back to normal lives."

Chapter Fifty-Nine

In the dim late afternoon light, in a king-sized bed in a room darkened by closed blinds, a slight creak of the door woke Crockett from his nap.

Earlier, the cardinal had refused to discuss Jaimie with him, saying there would be time for that later. He'd left Crockett alone, advising him to rest. Easy advice too take, given the combination of massive jet lag and a hangover from whatever drug had been used on him.

He was on his side, facing the door. He opened his eyes slightly. He didn't feel a sense of danger. There seemed to be no violent intentions against him. They just wanted him contained.

Mackenzie had entered the room, was walking softly toward him. He kept his eyes nearly shut.

When she reached him and was about to touch his shoulder, he opened his eyes more fully. She wore a loose blue dress, and her hair was pinned up in a tight bun. Once again, she looked ready for a senior's discount at the Goodwill.

"Hello," Crockett said.

It startled her, which of course, is what he wanted. She withdrew her hand as if a wasp had stung it.

"Get ready," she said, stepping back. "You need to get dressed and ready to go. Cardinal Ricci has sent us a car to take us to Rome. He'll give you some answers when we get there. Crockett reached for the horn-rimmed glasses on his night stand, then slipped them on.

"Fine. More mystery and deception. Maybe this time I'll wake up in Brazil," Crockett said. "But maybe you could at least clear up one thing. Can you tell me why you belong to a coven of witches?"

In the courtyard, Mackenzie stood in front of Crocket, staring at a far wall. She spoke softly, "Hail Satan. Hail Satan. Hail Satan."

Crockett watched her carefully, wondering where this was going. He found it curious that she hadn't even asked him how he knew about the coven before leading him out to the courtyard.

She finally focused on him. "One of my patients is a woman from a foster home background who was abused as part of a Satanic ritual when she was only five years old. She told me that both her and another boy living in the house, one who was four at the time, believed they were hearing the 'men in black robes' say the phrase, 'Hales Ate In.' Then, long after, she finally realized she had misunderstood. Instead, the robed individuals were saying 'Hail Satan'."

"Hail Satan?"

"Black Mass. Satanism rituals."

"Thought that kind of Satanism stuff was urban myth."

"Tell that to the woman who was abused as child," she answered.

"Or maybe she just believed she was abused as a child."

"It happens that way too," Mackenzie admitted. A cloud passed in front of the sun, seemingly cooling the temperature by a few degrees. "But in this case, one of the Satanists was a Catholic priest, the one in charge of both the rituals and the abuse. I'm talking about witchcraft, in it's truest evil sense.

Not the feel good Wicca new age stuff. Actual worship of the devil. *The* devil. I'll spare you the graphic details, but imagine the girl's helplessness. In the dark, in a circle of candles, listening to incantations, shadowy figures like gargoyles. She was only five years old."

Crockett hated stories like this. He loathed them. All of it was abstract, unless you were a parent, then every story you heard brought it home. Every story made you think, what if it happened to your little girl?

"People do evil things," he said.

"See, there's our divide. You are defining evil as the bad things that people do. I'm defining it as a force. A real thing, apart from people. I've come to the point where I believe some of the horrors that people do are a result of this evil. An evil that more often than not nudges people instead of threatens. Caresses instead of commands. Always probing, always looking for cracks in psyche, like tendrils of a vine, hoping to find a place to reside. Yes, the devil. And demons that obey him, preying upon humans."

"You're saying humans don't have a choice. The devil just chooses victims?"

"I'm saying the devil is constantly looking for people who are open to his seduction, often those who have been abused and whose despair makes them more vulnerable. But humans have the choice to resist, and then the devil will go seek his prey elsewhere. This woman made a choice to refuse to let what happened to her open the door to inviting a demon inside. Instead she's spent her life fighting the attempts of demons to get through the cracks that were caused by the abuse. If she didn't believe they were real, she would have succumbed."

"I've been told by another psychiatrist that exorcism a placebo," he said. "Self-fulfilling prophecy. That so-called demon possession is just mani-festations of other mental illnesses. Maybe a woman like that believed in demons, so she believed in exorcism, and allowed herself to be cured."

"Or the alternative," she countered. "Demons are real. Born into a family of love, our psyches are intact, no cracks for evil to enter. But the abused are susceptible, and in turn, demonically-influenced, they abuse a new generation. A vicious circle of evil spawning new victims, open to infiltration of more evil. Abused boys grow into adults who abuse boys—and they join and hide within this institution, knowing it will be safe to abuse the next generation."

She shifted her eyes away, then back to Crockett. "An institution, like, say, the Catholic church. And here's what's frustrating, not only to me but to millions in the church. It's an institution that does so much good all across the world. It's like a beautiful mansion, with one horrible, dark closet. But the closet draws all the attention, and the fact that the church is beautiful too often gets lost because of it."

The cloud passed and it was bright again.

Crockett shook his head. "Let me get this straight. There's a dark closet of witchcraft in the Catholic church. Witchcraft that explains the pedophilia and all the cover-ups. Generations of witches inside the church."

"You've got the circle wrong. Witchcraft is a symptom. The cause is simple. Demons."

"I'll give you this," he said. "This worldview that you present is well constructed. I mean, once you accept a certain premise—that demons exist—everything falls into place. Demons reside in humans who abuse other humans which opens cracks in the psyche of those humans that makes them susceptible to demon possession and once they are possessed they in turn abuse other humans. And these demons have found a safe haven in the hierarchy of the Catholic church. But that doesn't explain why you are a witch."

"I joined a coven and began attending Black Masses to hunt the priest who had abused this child."

"This is crazy. You were willing to engage with that kind of abusive circle until you catch the priest in the same abusive act?

"Not for a moment would I engage in abuse," Mackenzie said. "Most of this stuff is only damaging in a spiritual sense. Very few Black Masses involve real abuse or human sacrifice. You don't just waltz in and get accepted in a secret circle of hard-core Satanists. I've been on the fringes, with the dabblers, trying to get close enough to the core to catch this priest at a ceremony. I've always had my cell phone with me, ready to make a call that would bring in cops to arrest them at the first signs of real abuse, even if the priest wasn't there."

"Why not just confront the priest. Expose his Satanism to his congregation?"

"Without proof? No."

Crockett wanted, no needed, to be able to trust Mackenzie. If he couldn't now, then he couldn't trust whatever happened next or where ever she might lead him. "I'm still trying to accept your motivation. Getting this involved, isn't that blurring the lines between psychiatrist and patient? Why not have your client make the allegations? Priests all over the world have been brought to justice decades after molesting children."

"With the charges ignored or dismissed as fabrications until more than one accuser comes forward. My client was the only one who saw this man's mask slip. I mean a literal mask, not metaphorical. And the sad reality is that the church has a history of trying to cover-up the abuse. If ever a situation demanded proof, this was it."

"That was your motivation," Crockett said. "Finding proof to help a client? I'm not trying to be a jerk, but sounds thin."

"Definitely sounds thin," Mackenzie said, her smile grim. "There's a

little more to it than that. It's been months since I first made contact with
Father O'Hare, and he's the one who suggested we try to trap that priest at
a Black Mass."

All roads lead to Rome, Crockett thought. *More specifically to Father
O'Hare in Rome.* "And his reason?"

"Although a quarter-century had passed since my patient endured the
Satanic ritual," Mackenzie said, "she identified the man she remembered
as a priest when she saw his photograph in the *Los Angeles Times.* He had
become a cardinal."

"Cardinal." Crockett felt stupid echoing the word, but couldn't help
himself at the audacity of the accusation.

"Cardinal," she confirmed. "O'Hare believes the Satan has managed to
infiltrate the Vatican. And he's desperate to stop it."

Chapter Sixty

The car turned onto a narrow cobblestone street. Trees dominated one side, a high stone wall on the other. Crockett had no idea where they where; the drive through the countryside into the heart of the city had taken nearly an hour, long enough for dusk to become night. Long enough to totally disorient Crockett.

"We can trust these guys, right?" Crockett whispered it to Mackenzie from the back of a massive black BMW. These guys referred to the driver and passenger in the front seat of the car at the front of the villa, which threw long shadows at the end of the afternoon.

"Cardinal Ricci sent these Swiss Guards," she said. "The equivalent of Vatican police. He described what they would look like and the car they'd be driving. If that isn't enough, there's the fact that no one else knows we're here."

The driver parked along the stone wall. Above it, was the outline of a tall square building.

"Where are we?" Crockett asked Mackenzie.

She half turned. "Not sure. But this is where we are meeting Jaimie."

"Mr. Swiss Army," Crockett said. "Where are we?"

"Swiss Guard," Mackenzie corrected him.

The driver turned. "Church of Domitilla."

Crockett nudged Mackenzie. "Good. A church. Now I feel much safer. Nothing bad has ever, ever happened in a church. Especially a Catholic church."

Jaimie sat in the back of a fancy black car, while the driver wove in and out of traffic on crazy roads that left her totally lost. All she knew was that she was somewhere in Rome.

Alone.

This had not been part of anything promised to her by Father O'Hare or Dr. Mackenzie when she agreed to help them hunt Evil.

She was trying to be brave, mainly because all her life she didn't have a choice except to be brave. If she stopped trying, then she would be allowing herself to worry about all the things she was scared of. She really didn't want to go there.

More difficult, though, than the usual kind of brave was being brave in a city halfway across the world from home, in a car with a driver she didn't know, taking her to a place that he wouldn't tell her about.

It was more difficult to be brave after what had just happened. Evil was in Rome. She'd been warned that she would have to face it, but she'd been promised she wouldn't be alone.

Jaimie was tired of being alone.

To comfort herself, Jaimie closed her eyes and remembered the night that she'd gone to Mr. G for help. She pictured herself in the kitchen with Nanna, with the mug of hot chocolate, and how safe she had felt with that nice woman treating her just like she belonged in that home.

Not in the house.

But in the home.

As Jaimie swayed with the movement of the car, she held tight to the memory, telling herself she would visit Nanna again.

Chapter Sixty-One

You're the guard from the hotel room." These were the first words spoken by Crockett Grey.

O'Hare had been waiting at the church, in a room with plain furniture, but crowded with oil paintings centuries old. Exactly on time, as promised by Cardinal Ricci, Mackenzie had delivered the man.

"Not much of a guard," O'Hare said, allowing a rueful tone into his voice. "I have to admit, it was impressive how you bolted.

It was O'Hare first chance real chance to take measure of Crockett Grey, awake. He liked what he saw. Quiet watchfulness. Surely the man had to be exhausted, but wasn't showing it. And most surely, the man had to be bewildered. Less than a week ago, his life was that of a school teacher at the beginning of the summer break. Now he was in Rome, thrown into events far beyond his comprehension.

Although Crockett didn't know it, this would be an important meeting. O'Hare saw some use for the man, especially with the pope growing weaker and weaker. Soon, all would come to a head. O'Hare had been patiently been manipulating people and events for months. At the pope's death, it would all come together. Or all fall apart. Crockett, O'Hare had decided, might be the difference between success and failure.

"Apparently you know a great deal about our search for Jaimie's DNA and ancestry," O'Hare began. "And, as Cardinal Ricci informed me from your discussion with him at the villa, you know something about Jaimie that we don't. Who her true mother is."

"I'd like to know more," Crockett said. He was wearing horn-rimmed glasses that must have been a little too heavy, because for the second time since entering the room, he pushed the frames back up on his nose. "Where is Jaimie? I thought we were meeting her here"

"She'll be joining us soon," O'Hare said. "She came voluntarily. To help us."

"Why does the Vatican's Chief Exorcist need her help to stop Satanism in Rome?"

"You told him who I was?" O'Hare asked Mackenzie.

She shook her head, negative.

That Crockett knew who O'Hare was gave another indication of Crockett's potential danger and correspondingly potential usefulness.

O'Hare smiled as if he was relaxed, but thinking he'd have to play this man carefully. Give him just enough to give him the illusion of seeing the whole picture, but never enough to know the truth.

"It began about six months ago, with a phone call from Dr. Mackenzie here, arranged through a priest in Los Angeles that she knew," O'Hare said. "Because of my position and decades of experience, Dr. Mackenzie wanted to consult with me about Jaimie. Dr. Mackenzie told me that Jaimie described feelings of darkness she couldn't articulate very well. Under hypnosis, she began to say things that suggested demonic influence. Yes, Dr. Mackenzie?"

Mackenzie paced slowly. "I had a chance to spent many hours with Jaimie. It took a while for her to open up, but after hearing what she said in session about feeling like evil was hunting her, I thought Father O'Hare was an expert I should consult. From the beginning, I had Jaimie's full permission to learn what we could in regards to the demons. I informed her of what the implications were if Father O'Hare was correct. It seemed to lift a tremendous burden off her shoulders."

"No offense," Crockett said. "But that's probably one the upsides of demon possession. The burden is off your shoulders. You've got the best excuse in the world. You can blame the devil."

"You are absolutely correct," O'Hare said. "Time and again, parishioners want and hope to be able to cast the blame elsewhere. Much better a demon than mental illness, from their point of view. That's why we are so careful to conclude it's a legitimate demonic possession before we begin an exorcism. Jaimie is unique. I wanted to confirm my suspicions through Dr. Mackenzie's discreet research before bringing her to the attention of the Vatican."

"Suspicions. That she is demon possessed? You run DNA tests and genealogy reports on anyone you think is demon possessed?"

"I understand your impatience," O'Hare said, "but let me give you more background first."

"Impatience?" Crockett said. "I doubt you understand at all. You might think we're having a polite clinical conversation, but from my point of view, even if you think there's a danger of Satanism in the Vatican, there'd better be a strong reason I was drugged and thrown onto an airplane and taken halfway across the world. I'm a guy whose life had been turned upside down and I'm in danger of losing contact with my son unless this gets cleared up. I didn't ask to be involved."

"Of course there's a strong reason," O'Hare said. Although he felt in full control, he allowed a trace of impatience into his voice. "The election of the next pope depends on the girl. Do you want me to leave it at that?"

Crockett gave him a level gaze for a few seconds, and then a faint smile.

"Father, you do know how to set a hook. Go ahead, reel me in."

O'Hare didn't think of Crockett as a fish on a hook, but someone snared in his web. Someone O'Hare needed to wrap completely at the end of a strand.

"Six months ago," O'Hare said, "our current pope was getting closer and closer to the end of his papacy. That made it all the more urgent to learn what we could about Jaimie. Yes, we needed DNA analysis and genealogy. Without that, I would have nothing to convince any, let alone many of the cardinals that Jaimie was important to the Vatican. Demons, you see, are dismissed by a large, large percentage of the church, including bishops and cardinals."

"You needed her to prove that demons exist?"

"More than that," O'Hare said. "Much more than that."

Madelyne spoke again. "Father, I believe the rest of this is much better coming from Jaimie than ourselves. Crockett needs to know we've been completely open with her."

"Of course," he answered. "Mr. Grey, I hope you'll be content to wait just a few more minutes."

Crockett was still not content to sit back with his eyes closed.

"Father," he said, "what exactly is at stake here?"

Madelyne kept pacing slowly.

"Don't think for a moment I'm suggesting that the true importance of The Roman Catholic church is strictly in secular terms," O'Hare said, "but one way of grasping its impact is to understand that it is the oldest organized institution in human history. Almost two thousand years now, and with a billion adherents. In power and influence, the Church rivals nearly any nation. Its leader, the pope, carries the same political power, if not more, than the president of the United States—with one profound difference. Our billion adherents are taught that the pope, as a direct representative of God, is infallible. When he speaks, it is God speaking."

"Put in those terms," Crockett said. "He's a dictator, and to question him puts you in danger of going to hell."

O'Hare chuckled. "I understand your cynicism. It's shared by too much of the world. But you should understand that the pope simply cannot function as a dictator. Trust me, the machinery of the Vatican ensures that. Even the most revolutionary popes are incapable of imposing their will unless they are willing to work with the machine."

"Or willing to be killed," Crockett said. "Remember John Paul the first? Thirty-three days only as pope. Symbolic perhaps?"

O'Hare was liking this man more and more. Intelligent and capable. "There are those," O'Hare said carefully, "who favor conspiracy theories and wonder if John Paul was stopped before he could upset the apple cart, but that's outside of the scope of this discussion. Let's just say that as an earthly institution, the Church is very top down driven. If a pope understands the politics of the Vatican, he wields as much power as any man on the globe. World leaders come to him and ask for help. He lifts a finger, it makes world news. A policy change or fresh thought on theology can be like an earthquake. Millions and millions are affected by any new decree. That's why the Sacred College of Cardinals might wrestle for days to elect a new pope."

"Sacred College of Cardinals?"

"There are one hundred twenty cardinals world-wide.. The new pope will be one of those cardinals, elected by the Sacred College themselves. But it's never as democratic as it might sound. Out of those one hundred and twenty, there are generally only a few seen as credible for the papacy. Right now, as you probably know from newspapers, there are three top contenders for the papacy. One is an American, your Cardinal Saxon from the Los

Angeles dioceses. The other two have been political rivals for years here in Rome. You met His Eminence Eduardo Ricci, the Cardinal Vicar of Rome, this afternoon at his villa.. His rival, Eminence Leonardo Vivaldo, is the Cardinal Secretary of State. Permit me to explain what's not so obvious in the headlines."

Crockett nodded.

"First," O'Hare said, "there's never been a situation like this in church history, with the pope in an extended coma. During medieval times, medical technology didn't exist to prolong a man's life like this. Therefore, our church fathers didn't need nor could they foresee provisions that would solve the dilemma."

"Dilemma?"

"There is no special legislation to specify who rules this institution while the pope is comatose. You see, during the ten or so days between the death of a pope and the election of a new pope, the camerlengo is authorized to make any necessary decisions to run the daily affairs of the Holy See, but neither he nor the other cardinals are allowed to make appointments or innovations to the government of the Church."

"Except this pope is not dead." Crockett said.

"Nor really alive," O'Hare answered. "The seat of the Holy See is vacant, but not vacant."

"A power vacuum."

"Precisely. The explanation is dull but necessary for you to understand what's at stake. It's has led to a power struggle based on precedent applied elsewhere. In general, in any diocese, if a bishop was incapacitated, the auxiliary bishop will automatically run the affairs of the diocese. The pope is the bishop of Rome, and as his auxiliary bishop, Cardinal Vicario Eduardo Ricci argues that with the pope alive and incapacitated, it his role to continue to run the Holy See. In direct opposition, Leonardo Vivaldo, the Cardinal Secretary of State, argued that as the Holy See's de facto prime minister, he has the authority to preside over the Vatican. As I said, because the situation is unprecedented, so are both arguments. It does not help that both men have been notorious as political rivals for the previous three decades. Many cardinals believe it will be allow the third contender to be pope, instead of risking a pope with clearly defined enemies and allies. "

"So the cardinal from Los Angeles benefits."

"Yes," O'Hare said. "Such is politics. But there is yet another factor, one that must never reach the public eye. The Los Angeles cardinal is unsuitable to be pope, and it would damage the church for decades if he were to be elected. Jaimie is the only way to stop him because—"

Before O'Hare could offer more, the door opened. Another ubiquitous man in a gray suit escorted Jaimie inside, then wordlessly shut the door.

Chapter Sixty-Two

Jaimie, in jeans and a sweatshirt, ran to Mackenzie, and threw herself into Mackenzie's arms.

"I'm sorry, Mr. G," she said looking at Crockett while still in Mackenzie's embrace. "So sorry that you're here. Dr. Mackenzie said it was the best thing for you. That taking you here would save your life. That's why I did it."

"If that's why, I'm glad you did," Crockett said.

Mackenzie stroked Jaimie's hair, her eyes closed. The woman really cared about Jaimie.

O'Hare stood, so Crockett followed suit. O'Hare waited until the embrace ended.

"Miss Piper," O'Hare said. "Was not Cardinal Ricci supposed to be with you?"

"We were in a creepy old building," she said, "before we could get to the pope, he spent a long time talking to some men. They spoke in Italian. I couldn't understand, but they all seemed mad. Then he sent me here alone with the driver and said he would come back as fast as he could. Maybe it was because of that other meeting. Some other old guy. A friend of Cardinal Ricci's. He smelled funny. Weird funny. Probably just the old person smell. I wasn't really afraid, at first, but then when the cardinal took my bracelet away..."

Had Crockett heard correctly? Jaimie was supposed to have met the pope?. *The* pope.

It was insane. But here he was, in conversation with the Chief Exorcist of Rome, and feeling like he had still not really learned much about why all this was happening.

Jaimie wrapped her arms around herself. "Everything went dark. Dark, dark. Like I was in a black room, a million miles across. All alone, with cold wind blowing across me. I felt so tiny. And like hunters were coming for me in the darkness. I said what Father O'Hare taught me to say, and somehow it felt a little better, but I knew Ricci's friend would have killed me if I was alone with him."

"We're with you," Mackenzie murmured to Jaimie. "Tell us what happened."

Jaimie shivered. "Cardinal Ricci asked this man if he would bless me. First Cardinal Ricci said he needed to take away my bracelet. I gave it to him and then he stepped away. That's when I felt Evil.. Then the old man jumped on me and tried to kick me. Cardinal Ricci had to grab him and pull him away and take me out of there."

"Where?" O'Hare asked.

"I don't know," Jaimie said. "Remember, I said a really old building? To get to it, we passed these guys in striped clown outfits. Like guarding it. Really…clown outfits. I wanted to laugh, but everyone looked so serious. Especially when another man—I think he was a cardinal too—stopped us on the way out and talked to Cardinal Ricci. I couldn't tell what they were saying because it was Italian, but when they were finished, Cardinal Ricci said it I would be safe if I went with the driver. You told me I could trust Cardinal Ricci, so I did and the driver brought me here."

Mackenzie hugged her again.

Long hug. Enough time for Crockett to pull O'Hare to the side and speak in a low voice. "The old man had to be a priest if he could offer a blessing, right? Why did he go crazy when he decided Jaimie is possessed by a demon?"

O'Hare looked like a man trying to hold himself together, the look of someone on a commercial flight hearing the pilot announce the jet had run out of fuel.

"Mr. Grey," O'Hare said. "Striped clown outfits? That would be the Swiss Guard, in uniform, which meant this took place within Vatican City. It makes sense, as Cardinal Ricci had intended to take Jaimie to meet one of the other cardinals. To test him."

"The old man she met was another cardinal?" Crockett asked.

"I'm almost certain."

"A cardinal who attacked Jaimie because she is possessed—" Crockett couldn't keep the skepticism out of his voice. "What kind of a test is *that*?"

"Cardinal Ricci wanted Jaimie to meet this cardinal because we've always wondered if this cardinal hosts one of the devil's servants."

"Repeat that," Crockett asked. "In a way that might even come close to making sense."

"Mr. Grey…we've never believed that Jaimie was possessed by a demon," Father O'Hare explained. "Rather that she can sense demons in other people. And that demons, in turn, detect her awareness of them."

Chapter Sixty-Three

C rockett was trying to gasp the implications of O'Hare's claim about Jaimie when the door opened again and two men entered. The same men from the BMW he and Mackenzie had rode in.

The driver tossed zip-tie plastic handcuffs into the center of the room. He spoke briefly in Italian to O'Hare. O'Hare replied, nodding.

O'Hare switched to English and spoke to Mackenzie. "He says you need to handcuff me. Then Crockett."

"What?" Mackenzie said. "You told me it would be safe in Rome."

"He says we are safe," O'Hare said. "If we do as told. They'll need you and Jaimie in handcuffs too."

"If they know about Jaimie," Mackenzie said. "We can't trust them. If we put on these cuffs, we don't have a chance."

One of the men barked to silence them.

As a teacher, each year Crockett was been part of safety-first training for kids. The moment of resistance, they were taught again and again, was at the beginning of an attack. Yell, scream, run if anyone tried to move you into a car. Once you were in a car, escape was almost impossible.

It was no different here. Once they were handcuffed, they would be immobilized. Yet all of this was so utterly insane for Crockett that he felt like he was on the water, on his surfboard again, dealing with a shark attack. Then, like now, it was about reacting at a primal level to an intellectual assessment. And most of all, it was about reacting.

While the driver focused on the conversation between Mackenzie and O'Hare, Crockett dove forward. The distance was short between him and the men in the grey suits. He was hoping to knock one of the men through the doorway, hoping for help from O'Hare.

He was expecting to feel the impact of the top of his skull against the first man's chest. Instead, there was nothing but air. Both men stepped aside, but one tripped him. He landed hard, falling through the doorway, and as he was trying to recover, he felt a knee in his back. Then the unbelievable sensation of a million fish hooks pulling at his skin, and the simultaneous affect of a wire tightened around his forehead and down and around his armpits, savagely jerking his chin down in convulsions toward his chest, his arms flopping and legs cramping.

By the time he realized he'd been hit by a stun gun, it was over, but his muscles were still vibrating, and he couldn't even manage to groan as he was dragged back into the room. He hoped he had not wet his pants.

On his side, limp and too exhausted to roll over, he heard the instructions in Italian again, Crockett heard O'Hare speak in English, but couldn't make sense of that either until Mackenzie knelt beside him. He smelled her perfume and felt her hands take his wrists and heard the ratcheting of the plastic zip ties and felt his hands drawn together.

Whatever was happening, it was clear these were enemies of O'Hare and Mackenzie. Which, by default, probably made them his enemies too.

More barking in Italian, followed by a translation from O'Hare. "They said to cuff his hands behind his back. Not in front."

"Tell them too bad," Mackenzie said. "He's hurt badly enough already. If they want him cuffed otherwise, they can do it themselves."

She helped Crockett sit up and pulled him to the wall and leaned him against it. She ran her hands softly across his face and whispered to him. "I'm so sorry. So very sorry."

One of the guards pulled her away.

His vision was clearing. Beyond her, Crockett saw O'Hare putting Jaimie in handcuffs. Then saw O'Hare turn around so that Mackenzie could cuff him. Then, finally, one of the gray suits cuffed Mackenzie . The four of them now, in some room in the bowels of an ancient church, with only one door out, guarded by the man with a stun gun.

Crockett was panting, trying to still his muscles, when another man stepped inside the room to survey them. He was tall, dressed in elegant brown, slacks and a thin cashmere sweater, with short cropped dark hair.

Mackenzie moaned slightly and pushed herself away, back up against the wall.

The nicely dressed man smiled at Mackenzie. "You are such a fool. I know everything you've done. Including your pathetic attempts to snare me by posing as a witch." Then a sneer. "I liked you much better when you were a child."

Mackenzie bowed her head.

Then he walked up to Jaimie's shoulder and touched her. Jaimie stared at him defiantly.

The man stepped back and spoke to the gray suits. One walked to the tall elegant man and, from behind, maneuvered him into a bear hug. Even with his arms bound the older man was able to remove a band from his wrist, and handed it to the second man, who stepped outside of the room.

Later, Crockett would attribute the unbelievable moments that followed to a post-stun hallucination, because they were just too unbelievable for reality.

As the door closed, it seemed to Crockett like the tall elegant man transformed, going from human to some kind of hairless werewolf. The man's face became a rictus of bared teeth and hatred, and he tried to shake himself free of the bear hug by lunging forward. His bodyguard strained, and he growled unearthly utterances and spit and hissed at Jaimie.

"Show no fear, Jaimie!" O'Hare said. "You know what to say! Say it now!"

Still handcuffed, Jaimie took a step toward the frothing man and spoke clearly, but with her voice shaking.

Padre nostro, che sei nei cieli, sia santifico il tuo nome...

The man howled, still in the grip of the man behind him.

Father O'Hare joined in the chanting with Jaimie.

The howling grew louder, and the man's face contorted even more violently. Crockett had no doubt the man was about to tear himself loose, but the second gray-suit had returned to the room with the cardinal's bracelet, and stepped into the center, then slapped the bracelet on the cardinal's wrist.

Immediately, the older man grew quiet. Dignified. He stopped fighting the guard who held him.

O'Hare stopped chanting, then Jaimie.

The older man spoke sharply to the two guards. They nodded and bowed their heads, and he stepped backwards, out of the room.

One of the two guards spoke directly to O'Hare, paused then nodded.

"He's asked me to translate," O'Hare said. "He told me if we don't follow instructions they will shoot Jaimie. They've promised we will be kept here for a couple of days, then released."

"Here? In the church of Domitilla?" Crockett asked the man. He was keenly aware of the weight of his horn-rimmed glasses. For what felt like the hundredth time, he pushed them up his nose again. How long would the hidden video camera record?

" Domitilla was built at the entrance to the cemetery of thousands upon thousands of long dead Christians," O'Hare answered. "They are going to take us, into the necropolis below. Where there are miles and miles of catacombs, four levels deep."

Chapter Sixty-Four

From behind, one of their captors held Jamie's by the hair. The other held the pistol in one hand and a flashlight in the other. O'Hare and Mackenzie and Crockett walked ahead of them, obeying commands at every turn through a series of tunnels that grew narrower as they descended stairs cut into the stone, finally reaching a door.

Signs above it gave warning in different languages. German. French. Italian. English. Spanish. Clearly meant for tourists.

DO NOT GO PAST THIS POINT WITHOUT A GUIDE. MANY TUNNELS ARE NOT MAPPED.

The man with the pistol spoke in rapid Italian.

"The door is open," O'Hare translated. "He wants us to slowly go through it, one at a time.."

No choice but to obey.

Deeper into the tunnels, now beyond the sanitized tourist area, the flashlight beam from behind Crockett bounced light off the volcanic rock of the narrow tunnels. The creep factor was high for him. Not only did he feel the tension of an insane man at his back with a pistol and the worry of what the man intended to do to them, coffin-sized ledges had been cut into the walls and had been filled with shrouds covering bones, the light occasionally showing hair still attached to a skull. The ledges were arranged like bunk beds, sometimes two or three high, so that every few steps took them past the remains of a couple long-dead Christians on each side.

At every turn, they were commanded them to stop, and Crockett would hear a mysterious scratch.

They advanced deeper and deeper.

The perfect place to cover up a murder, to leave the dead among a labyrinth of the dead.

The darkness was beyond anything Mackenzie could have imagined. It was like a presence, squeezing her awareness with a cold physicality. It didn't help, knowing that within arm's length were the bones of men and women whose bodies had lain into the stone chambers for undisturbed centuries.

From the beginning, months earlier, O'Hare had promised her nothing would go wrong. O'Hare promised he had the backing and help of Cardinal Ricci, one of the most powerful cardinals in Rome. The priest promised that everything Mackenzie and Jaimie shared with O'Hare would remain secret. And most of all, O'Hare had promised that Mackenzie would be safe from the one man she'd been terrified of since childhood.

But Cardinal Ricci had sent Jaimie away with the drivers. O'Hare had failed.

Because the two men had left them there, commanding them not to move, the flashlight beam getting smaller and smaller, until it had flicked off, isolating the four of them. Alone. In the depths of the labyrinth.

Chapter Sixty-Five

W e'll be okay," Mackenzie told Jaimie. "Just lean into me. "
With all of them standing on the rock floor of the tunnel, the
sound of Mackenzie's voice told Crockett she was barely a foot away, but he
wouldn't even be able to see his own hand if he reached for her. The darkness
was so horrible for Crockett that he lifted his manacled hands and pressed a
knuckle into a closed eye, just for the sensation of light it gave him.

"He's not ever going to send someone to get us," Jaimie answered Mackenzie. "I think pretending we'll be okay will just make this worse."

"Jaimie…"

Jaimie didn't let Mackenzie continue. "He left us in handcuffs. No water. Nothing. If he really meant that someone would come back after a new
pope is elected, we'd have water at least. Right, Father O'Hare? And this is
the perfect place to leave bodies. We won't ever be found, even if some tried
looking for us."

"I prefer to hope for the best," O'Hare said. "But if you'll pardon the
pun, yes, things do look dark."

Crockett had to know. "Jaimie, what was that scratching sound every
time we turned? "

" It was chalk. He traced our way here. If we had a light, we could find
our way back the way he did."

"Anybody have anything sharp?" Crockett said. "Let's at least get out of
the handcuffs."

"Maybe rub one set against the other," Mackenzie suggested. "Let the plastic heat up?"

"Mr. G, your hands are in front of you," Jaimie said." Dr. Mackenzie, you have a pin in your hair right? Can you let Mr. G pull it out? Mr. G, can you hurry? I have to pee really bad."

"I'm right here," Crockett tried to locate Mackenzie by sound. "I'll move closer."

He reached forward. His fingers brushed against something solid but yielding.

"That's me," Mackenzie said sharply. "My head is a little higher."

"Sorry," Crockett said. His fingers found the pin in Mackenzie's hair. Slowly, gently, he withdrew the pin, the type with a small plastic ball on top. "Got it."

"How about helping Dr. Mackenzie first," Jaimie said. It was weird for Crockett, the disembodied voice coming from the cool black of the air around him. "What you need to do is push the pin between the plastic teeth of the tab and the backward teeth that hold the ziplock tab in place. Then you can pull the tab loose."

"Mackenzie?"

"I'm turning," she said. "My back should be toward you now."

Crockett held the pin in his right hand. He reached forward with his left hand.

He found Madelyne's wrists with his left hand. He tried to visualize Jaimie's instructions, seeing the pin slip into the small gap between the tab and the ziplock teeth. At a slow and deliberate pace, he found the gap and pushed the pin into it. The tab slid upward as he pulled. He made sure to keep a finger on the top of the pin's plastic ball, so he wouldn't lose it.

"You should be able to slide your hand out now," he told Mackenzie.

It took him fifteen minutes to free Mackenzie and Jaimie and O'Hare from the plastic handcuffs, moving cautiously so that he wouldn't drop the pin. When he finished, Jaimie unlocked his handcuffs.

"Cool trick," he told Jaimie, "Where'd you learn it?"

"Mr. G., it's routine," she said. "All kids who've spent time in juvie know about this. Think we don't learn about stuff like this in foster homes?"

Chapter Sixty-Six

J aimie and Mackenzie had moved farther down the tunnel, so that Jaimie could have privacy as she took care of her urgent business.

"Jaimie is right," Crockett said to O'Hare while she was out of earshot. "That guy is not sending anyone back for us. "

"I'm afraid your assessment is accurate, Mr. Grey."

"I'm thinking that by the time people are jammed together in a necropolis, first name basis is appropriate."

"Certainly, Mr. Grey." Crockett heard the humor in O'Hare's voice.

"So, how bad is the situation?" Crockett said, sobering again. "I mean in terms of trying to get out of these catacombs?"

"As bad as you can imagine," O'Hare answered. "Ten miles of tunnels. Even guides have been lost for days in the catacombs. This is a labyrinth, and we're somewhere off the mapped area. You heard what he did, using chalk marks to find his way back. If we had a light, maybe we'd have a chance of getting back to the door. But without a light, we'd just be wandering uselessly. Or if we had a compass, it would stop us from going in circles. Maybe in an hour or two, we'd find one of the doors that seal off the unmapped areas. But no light or no compass, it's not promising."

"So since I'm about to die," Crockett said, "at least satisfy my curiosity. What did I see back there? The whole werewolf routine? And what's going on that this guy is willing to murder four people by dumping them in the catacombs?"

"Mr. Grey, I've performed hundreds upon hundreds of exorcisms. Most were successful. Some were not. Without fail, demons hide inside the host for as long as possible. It takes hours and hours of prayer and confrontation to get a demon to acknowledge it's there. And again, without fail, once the demon knows it has been exposed, it reacts as violently as possible. That's why an exorcism demands a team. What you saw was a confirmation of what I told you earlier. Unless she is wearing her bracelet, Jaimie can sense demons in other people. When it happens, the demons react no differently than when their presence is exposed during an exorcism."

"What if a person like me doesn't believe in demons?"

"Frankly, it doesn't matter what you believe." O'Hare sounded matter-of-fact. "But do you have another explanation for what you saw?"

"The guy is insane. He believes he's possessed, and he believed Jaimie could detect the demon inside him, so he reacted as if that were reality. Some people are good at hiding their insanity. And someone like that would be easily susceptible to believing that demons exist. They would be just as susceptible to believing that the words you chanted are like kryptonite."

"Kryptonite?"

"If someone was insane enough to believe he was Superman, then he'd have to believe that rock painted like kryptonite would stop him. Jaimie is his kryptonite."

"Your skepticism defines the problem here. I wished I could convince more cardinals of the existence of demons… because demons prey on humans, Mr. Grey. We know it, but don't acknowledge it. Vampire legends, for example, are a reflection of our race's subconscious awareness that we have been stalked for as long as we have been humans. To fight a danger, first you need to be aware of it."

"Mackenzie said you were desperate to fight Satanism in the Vatican."

Crockett thought better to belabor his skepticism. "The guy back there, he was a cardinal, wasn't he?"

"Yes. His Eminence Ethan Saxon. Los Angeles diocese. Remember our discussion? He's the man favored most to become the next pope."

Chapter Sixty-Seven

C rockett felt a chill.

"The next pope," Crockett said, "Could be the insane guy who had us locked down here?"

"It's worse than that. Here's a term I doubt you've heard before," O'Hare said, his voice calm from the utter black that surrounded Crockett. "Cardinal Saxon is perfectly possessed."

"You are correct. I have not heard that term before."

"Most people associate demon possession with what they learned through Hollywood. Weird deep voices and all the other special effects. And there's truth in those assumptions. I do see that during exorcisms. Those who to a priest or who are taken to a priest for exorcisms are literally fighting their demons. It's this struggle—host against parasite—that hints to the outer world of a demon's existence within that person. There are some, however, who are totally at peace with the demon inside. Nothing outwardly betrays the existence of the demon. A perfect possession. And nobody ever knows, unless it's someone like Jaimie."

"Not saying I buy into this," Crockett said. "You are telling me that Cardinal Saxon, likely to become pope, is perfectly possessed. He's happy to host a demon."

"Yes."

"With Jaimie the only one who would know?"

"Well, her or someone like Jaimie," O'Hare said.

"Like the old man that Cardinal Ricci brought her to see a few hours ago. To test to see if that cardinal too is demon-possessed?"

"The perfectly-possessed are a dangerous force that has faced the Vatican for centuries. The trouble is that in our modern times, most people don't believe they exist. Even those in the top hierarchy of the church don't even give a thought to their existence. And that makes it all the more dangerous."

"With Jaimie in a position to stop this?"

"I believe," O'Hare said, "that's exactly why we've been left to die in the catacombs."

"But you don't think we'll die, do you, Father O'Hare?" Crockett said. "Because I don't think it's an accident that you had us meet here at the Church of Domitilla."

After a beat, O'Hare said, "That's a bold statement,"

"Not really." Crockett had been giving it some thought. "If you had those suspicions about Saxon, could you have made it any easier for him to get us all in one place, the perfect place to get rid of us?"

Crockett had been giving something else some thought. The email he'd received from the geneticist and had read earlier in the day—although it seemed like a week had passed since Mackenzie had shown up in the internet cafe.

"Hammerhead sharks," Crockett continued. He assumed the silence around him meant that he had O'Hare's full attention. Still, the sense of isolation was so complete that he didn't even know if stretching his arm would touch one of them.

"Hammerhead sharks?" Jaimie asked, approaching unseen.

"Jaimie," Crockett said. "How much have Mr. O'Hare and Dr. Mackenzie told you about all of this?"

"About me and knowing about demons?"

"Yeah."

"A lot," she said. "It's made me feel way better, knowing why I feel the darkness and all that."

"And you know it might be because of genetics?"

"That I'm wired this way? In my DNA? Yes." Jaimie said.

"Dr. Mackenzie and I are aware of the genetic aberration," O'Hare said. "We were happy to tell Jaimie."

The email from McFarlane, the one he'd scanned in the internet cafe offered the comparison results. Jamie shared a gene code sequence found in hammerhead sharks. Most sharks have an eye on each side of their heads. Facing forward, one eye sees to the left, the other eye to the right. But the hammerhead doesn't have this problem. It's eyes can look forward, because the head is t-shaped and the eyes are set apart. Great advantage for depth perception. But with its mouth so far below its eyes, when it moves directly above its prey, say shrimps in the sand, the hammerhead's eyes can't see its food. It would have to back up to see the shrimp, but then, of course, its mouth is too far away. Through experimentation, scientists discovered that the shark relies on electro-magnetic currents, which are found in every living creature. Hammerheads have twenty-thousand times the sensitivity of other sharks. It's a slight anomaly in genetic programming.

Like in Jaimie. Who didn't need the currents to find food.

Poor child, thought Crockett. With Mackenzie and O'Hare convincing her that when she detected hostility or aggression, she was actually detecting demons, they had accomplished what Dr. Moller had warned was a danger. Through auto-suggestion, particularly hypnotherapy, they had altered her perception of what the ability meant, and brought her to the point of blaming demons for what she felt around her.

Was the magnetic bracelet a placebo, or did it really work?

Crockett had no opinion on that, but was prepared to believe it did have a true physical effect on her. After all, if you draped a magnet around a hammerhead's throat, it probably wouldn't find a shrimp.

Just as significantly, if people who believed they were demon-possessed now believed Jaimie could detect the demon by taking off the bracelet, they too would fall for the auto-suggestion affect. This was not the time to argue that in front of Jaimie.

Crockett spoke. "Father O'Hare, you knew all along, thanks to Mackenzie I presume, that the cardinal from Los Angeles is a Satanist. I can't believe, knowing that, you would have been stupid enough to put us in an isolated room in an isolated church, at night, where he could trap us. I think instead, you put Jaimie in the room, hoping he would come and expose himself and his insanity."

"The man is possessed by a demon."

"While you won't be able to convince me of that," Crockett said, noticing O'Hare hadn't really answered his question, "you'd have foreseen that these catacombs are a tempting place and very convenient for an insane man to hide the people who might expose him as a Satanist. So, let me ask you a blunt question, Father O'Hare—what steps did you take to make sure we could get out of here?"

"If you know about the electromagnetism, then surely you know about the rest of it. How animals migrate because they sense the magnetic field of the earth?"

Crockett sat silently for a moment, trying to get his head around O'Hare's suggestion. It was utterly crazy. But either all of it was false, or all of it was true.

"She's a compass."

"Yes, a compass," O'Hare said. "If you ever wanted proof of Jaimie's abilities, you're about to get it. It may take a while, but I'm confident she'll be able to keep us from wandering in circles as we track our way backward."

Chapter Sixty-Eight

C ardinal Ricci stepped into the courtyard of his villa where Crockett
and O'Hare had been waiting for him to arrive from Rome,
finishing a light breakfast of cut up fruit and croissants.

Both rose from chairs and faced the Cardinal.

"The doctor and the girl?" Cardinal Ricci asked, rushing forward to
embrace O'Hare. "Safe? Here in the villa?"

Crockett stood to the side, wanting this to be done.

"Safe," O'Hare said in answer to Ricci, stepping back from the embrace.
"I believe both are still sleeping. As you can imagine, it was a long night."

Long night?

Understatement. All of it was an eerie memory that Crockett expected
would be fresh for him for the rest of his life. The escape had been as spooky
as the rest of it. Moving through the complete darkness of the catacombs
with all of them linking by holding hands—Jaimie at front, then Mackenzie, Crockett and O'Hare. At every turn, the four of them stopped and
Jaimie decided which direction felt north, and then O'Hare made the decision which way to turn based on it. Slowly feeling their way out, based on
the certainty that they were not wandering in circles. It only had only taken
them an hour, but it had felt like days. The mental strain of wondering
whether they'd reach safety had worn him out far more than the slow shuf-
fling in the dark.

Yes, it was a long night.

O'Hare had found a cab to take all of them to the villa, and Crockett had slept poorly, not knowing if the sensation of holding together a shattered body was a result of aftereffects of the Taser shock, or his struggle to accept all that he had witnessed.

Demons were not real, he'd told himself again and again, staring in upward in the dark. Yet how else to explain the catacombs? How else to explain Jaimie and how the cardinal had reacted to her?

Demons were not real. But what if they were? To accept that, for Crockett would almost be like being struck with blindness on the road to Damascus; not easy for a person to make a total shift from seeing the world as purely physical to one filled with spirits that stalked humans.

Overwhelming as it was—he'd witnessed a cardinal contender for the papacy turn into a savage beast—it was still secondary to the things he wanted most.

Home. Mickey. No charges hanging over his head.

O'Hare had promised him it would happen. But, as O'Hare had explained over breakfast, Cardinal Ricci needed some assurances from Crockett before Ricci could put the wheels into motion that would clear him.

Cardinal Ricci gestured for all three of them to sit at the table. O'Hare cleared it of dishes, then Cardinal Ricci took a chair and sat back, appearing relaxed.

Crockett and O'Hare joined him, and the three of them formed a triangle at the small circular table.

"Do you fully understand what happened last night?" Cardinal Ricci asked Crockett.

"I doubt it," Crockett said. It was a sincere statement. "Hell isn't something I want to believe is real, let alone the fact that demons live among us."

He'd been running through the either-or possibilities during his hours of sleeplessness. Either the cardinal from the Los Angeles diocese was perfectly possessed and Jaimie had the genetic ability to sense the man's demon. Or the cardinal was insane, and because he believed Jaimie had the ability to sense demons, he had reacted accordingly.

"My question was too ambiguous," the cardinal said. "Nobody likes to be reminded that the gates of hell are open. What I meant is if you understood the need for Cardinal Saxon to know about Jaimie? Has Father O'Hare explained to you that we needed for him to take the bait?"

"He has guessed at some of it your Eminence," Father O'Hare, "I thought it best for the complete explanation to come from you."

The cardinal gave a slight bow of his head and spoke again. "I will tell it as simply as I can. As you know, months ago, Dr. Mackenzie contacted Father O'Hare to ask if his decades of experience as an exorcist had ever brought him in contact with someone who could detect demons. This eventually led to Dr. Mackenzie's disclosure of what she knew about Cardinal Saxon from a patient who had been abused by the man as a child. Father O'Hare came to me with this information. Because of Cardinal Saxon's high-profile, it would have been disastrous for the Vatican to be forced to prove his innocence or guilt in court. After a lot of consideration, we devised a trap of sorts. It involved planting spyware so that Saxon would believe the information brought to him by a middle-man in Entity, who continuously reported back to O'Hare. I'm sorry if this seems complicated."

"Not complicated," Crockett said. Politics and betrayals, he could accept far more easily than demons. "I didn't think it was an accident that O'Hare allowed Saxon to find us last night."

"You understand, then, if Saxon was an innocent man, he would have never reacted the way he did to learning about Jaimie. It put us in a position to take action so that he would never become pope. This is not a scandal that the world needs to discover. Not with a papal conclave ahead of us any day."

Crockett blinked a few times. He wanted to be slow and measured in his response. "What about justice?"

O'Hare leaned forward to answer, but Cardinal Ricci waved him into silence.

"Justice?" Cardinal Ricci said.

"There's already been cover-up of church abuse, going back decades. This, too, you want hidden from the world? A cardinal who abused children as part of Satanism rituals?"

"Please understand. Actions were taken to stop him as soon as possible. The cover-up is not of ongoing abuse. The stakes are so high here that the Vatican should not have to pay for his sins too."

Again, Crockett tried to stay slow and measured. "Tell me something. Why was I dragged into this? Because somehow, through Jaimie, it looked like I'd interfere?"

"It was a mistaken assumption," O'Hare said quickly. "Based on Jaimie's time alone with you. The decision—not by me or Cardinal Ricci—was to immediately discredit you to prevent you from speaking publicly about Jaimie's situation."

"To keep this covered up," Crockett said. "This is the same reason you hired Amy Robinson, your pet lawyer to do that. She knew I was at that internet cafe, and wow, what a coincidence, ten minutes later Mackenzie shows up with a couple of Swiss Army Knives waiting in a car to drag me to the villa."

"I made the decision to hire her so that you had the best legal help possible," O'Hare said. "You would have been cleared sooner than later. When you disappeared from the hotel near the lake… of course I used her help to find you."

"Someone broke into my house and strung me up to the point of unconsciousness to get me to quit trying to find out why I was wrong accused," Crockett said. "That was for the greater good too?"

"Think of the hundreds of millions of people who desperately need the church," Cardinal Ricci said. "There was no intention for you to die. Only to buy time."

"I will confess," O'Hare injected. "We needed you so scared that when Dr. Mackenzie came to you for help, you would agree to go to Bright Lights. I won't ask for forgiveness, but only for understanding."

Anger had begun to displace Crockett's weariness. "From an outsider perspective, I still understand that the Catholic church is overwhelmingly a godly institution. I understand the unfairness that its reputation suffers because of the small minority of its terrible priests. But can't you see the real obscenity here? It goes far beyond the abuse that has hurt the Vatican, but the efforts to cover it up. It makes you part of that abuse."

"If that's the case," Cardinal Ricci said. "That is a burden I accept. For the sake of the church."

"Because you want to be pope?" Crockett asked. "With Saxon out of the way, it's now down to you and the other cardinal right?"

"Please," Father O'Hare said. "Let's keep this conversation civil and resolve what we need to resolve."

"Mr. Grey," Cardinal Ricci said. "Tomorrow, you'll be on a private jet to Los Angeles. The authorities won't even know that you've left the country. All charges will have been dropped by the time you step off the airplane. "

'Not good enough," Crockett said.

"There will be a financial settlement as well," Cardinal Ricci said.

"You're going to pay me to keep my mouth shut?"

Crockett wasn't ready to tell them yet about the glasses he'd worn the previous night. He'd been able to video three hours of what happened in the catacombs until the internal memory ran out, but he hadn't been able to access a computer or the internet yet to download the data and email it to himself and Catfish. Until then, it was his back-up leverage. He hoped.

"Paying you is better than the alternative," Cardinal Ricci said.

"I don't like this," O'Hare said to Cardinal Ricci, standing. "I predicted this reaction."

"What choice do we have but a legitimate threat?" the cardinal answered to O'Hare, who began to pace.

Cardinal Ricci turned his attention back to Crockett. "Mr. Grey, Cardinal Ethan Saxon died in his sleep last night. The press release has indicated it as a suicide, brought on by clinical depression."

Crockett couldn't help but gape, but had no chance to respond.

"Furthermore," Cardinal Ricci continued, "Given your responses, it seems crucial at this point that you meet with a friend of ours in Rome. Your answer to him will determine whether you get onto that jet tomorrow."

Chapter Sixty-Nine

O'Hare and Crockett were on a hotel balcony in central Rome, twenty stories above ground, less than two hours after the meeting with Ricci.

It was clear that Crockett was a prisoner. He and O'Hare had been escorted by three men from the Swiss Guard, who now waited outside the doorway of the hotel room.

The air on the balcony was humid and still and hot. A third man stood partially in the shadows. He had a thin face and a comb-over, just beginning to show the shine of scalp.

That's how men ended up looking so ridiculous, Crockett thought. Early on, before too much hair is gone, the sideways combing ends up doing as hoped, adding fullness in appearance. But as the hair grew sparser, so did the entrenchment of the habit, until came the pitiful few strands glued to the scalp, from one ear over across to the other.

It wasn't the time, however, for Crockett to offer any advice.

"Mr. Grey," O'Hare said. "Meet Raymond Leakey."

Crockett thought of asking for some kind of identification, but immediately realized the futility of it. As if spies carried identification. It ruined the whole spy thing. And even if Entity people had official badges, if Leakey wasn't part of Entity and this was a scam, he'd certainly be prepared with fake identification.

The man in the shadows stepped forward. He leaned on the balcony and looked down at the traffic. He turned his head and with half-lidded eyes said to Crockett, "Long ways down."

Crockett hated heights. He took a chair and sat, crossing his legs to bluff that he was relaxed.

It wasn't difficult to realize that Leakey had begun with a threat.

O'Hare sat beside Crockett and spoke to Leakey. "Move away from the balcony. We're here to talk. Not play games."

"None of this is a game," Leakey said, but he moved away from the balcony, back into the shade. Still standing, not sitting.

"First," O'Hare said. "It's important at this point for Crockett to get a clear understanding of what's been happening and who is responsible."

O'Hare nodded at Crockett to begin.

"Back in Los Angeles," Crockett said. "I was framed. Someone put a hard drive with child porn in my attic. Planted false complaints about me in my work record. Kidnapped an old woman next door. This is something Entity could do if directed?"

"Entity. C.I.A. Mossad. Name a spy agency. All of them are capable of this."

"Entity, operating in the United States," Crockett said.

"C.I.A. operates in other countries. Boundaries don't mean much."

"Entity ever involved with assassinations?" Crockett said.

"If you are talking about John Paul One," Leakey said, "I'd give it a rest. Same with the Mafia banking deaths. That's conspiracy stuff, decades old."

Leakey gave a short laugh. "But seriously? If someone unknown, say you, was a big enough threat, it's easier to avoid that if possible. Murders and accidental deaths when other police forces can get involved draw attention. No sense in creating such a risk if there's another way."

"Too risky, huh? What about maybe it being morally wrong?"

"Don't be an idiot. This is the real world. Catholic church is a bigger power than most countries, but Entity doesn't like attention and there are other ways of taking care of a problem. Bigger troubles to distract people. You maybe being a case in point. The stuff that happened was supposed to take you off the table."

"Who wanted me off the table?" Crockett asked.

"Nice try. Next question."

"No," O'Hare said sharply enough for Leakey to snap his head to face him.

"No?" Leakey said.

"Saxon is dead," O'Hare said. "I want Crockett to hear from you what brought Crockett into this."

Leakey went to the balcony and looked down again, then wandered back to the shade. A restless man. A man who maybe needed a cigarette.

"I made a quick and bad judgment call," Leakey said. "The girl had stayed the night. You had a complaint on your record. I thought it would be a distraction to build on that. Didn't work out like I wanted. It's why I'm on this balcony, letting a priest order me around. Next question."

"Did you arrange for something to happen to my neighbor. An old woman."

"No. Saxon had a man we didn't know about. He's the one who started the fire, then took the old woman. Saxon said something in passing that let us start tracking him. It took a while to find her, but she's alive. She's stuck in a trailer park. Saxon's man cut her with a knife to draw some blood and helped her immediately bandage it. As you and I speak, we're dealing with the situation there. She'll be fine. Him? Not so fine. It's going to take you off the hook with the cops too, now that they have her testimony about her captor and about the girl's presence during the night in question."

Crockett felt immense relief. This was so unbelievable and despite all the deception and insanity of recent days, he clung to this one piece of hopeful news.

"Thank you for the information," Crockett said.

"No need. It's payback. You did the Vatican a big favor, backing up O'Hare's audio with your little spy camera. It was exactly what was needed to authorize last night's actions. But I wouldn't put too much hope in using it down the road."

Crockett's relief dissolved. His surprise must have been obvious, because Leakey laughed.

"You really believed a pair of eyeglasses like that would fool us? Come on. We just let you play with them to see what you had in mind. Last night, while you were showering, O'Hare made a switch on you."

O'Hare gave an apologetic shrug. "Didn't have much choice. It did prove helpful though."

"Bottom line," Leakey said, "you ended up helping us take out Saxon. The guy would have destroyed everything."

"Taking out Saxon?"

"Did I say that? What I meant was Saxon took himself out. It's very helpful that the Vatican police are investigating this. Unlike in Santa Monica, we control the police here. That guarantees a verdict of suicide. Same thing if you jumped off this balcony right now."

"No games," O'Hare warned Leakey.

"Just saying," Leakey replied from the shade. "Especially because someone needs to tell Crockett here why I've been allowed to take this meeting. It's because I was told to let you know what happened to Saxon so that you'll have a full grasp of how serious this is, enough grasp to convince you never to talk about this. Outside Vatican City, where we don't control the police, what happens is there's a conversation or two and word gets out on the street. Mafia's got connections in Los Angeles. Keep that in mind if you want to stay safe. Or if you want your son to stay safe. Mickey, right? Likes naming animals at the zoo, gets to kindergarten every day at 8:45?"

Crockett stood so quickly his chair fell over. He lunged for Leakey, but O'Hare managed to get in the way, standing too with impressive quickness for a man of his bulk.

"Don't bother making a dramatic threat," Leakey said as Crockett glared at him over O'Hare's shoulder. "I'm just laying out the facts. When you get off the plane in Santa Monica, don't bother opening your mouth about any of this. No one's going to believe you anyway. And bad things will happen to people around you."

Chapter Seventy

Nobody gave any notice to a tattooed-man with dark greasy hair grown into a mullet behind the wheel of a battered air-conditioning repair van as it rolled through the trailer park. The van, with smoked glass windows, provided him necessary anonymity where ever he was sent.

He had a rifle on the floor between the bucket seats.

He parked a short distance from Nathan Wilbur's trailer. The dogs at the end of the chains began to bark, straining to get closer.

Nobody came out from the trailer, but he expected that. It was why he'd chosen to arrive at this time.

The barking dogs didn't draw attention.

He'd expected that too.

The man with the mullet reached across and rolled down the passenger window.

He lifted the rifle, rested it on the ledge of the window, and with only a few inches of barrel and aimed at the closest of the dogs.

When he pulled the trigger, the *pfft* of the rifle was lost in the background of the barking. The dart struck the first dog squarely in the hind end, and it arched its back sideways in a violent attempt to bite the source of pain.

In seconds, it was dead. The tiny dart had not been loaded with tranquilizers. The man had used the air rifle simply for the convenience of relative silence.

The other dog went down the same way.

Quiet. Efficient. Deadly.

No way any one could have noticed. The man with the mullet haircut set the rifle down between the bucket seats again.

He reached into the glove compartment and pulled out a pistol and a silencer. He screwed the silencer onto the barrel of the pistol, and waited for Nathan Wilbur to arrive.

The man with the mullet hair was good at waiting too.

When all of this was done, he'd trash the wig, wash off his temporary tattoos and the suntan cream that had made his skin so dark. He'd become invisible again.

Crockett and O'Hare reached a sidewalk cafe and ordered espresso and croissants. Crockett looked past O'Hare, at the spires of St. Peter's, continuing the silence they'd shared since leaving Leakey at the hotel.

O'Hare guessed that Crockett was trying to play it cool and cavalier. The man had not only been thrown onto a jet that took him to Italy, he'd been kidnapped at a cardinal's instructions and left for dead in a catacomb. Then learned that the very same cardinal had been assassinated by the same Vatican organization which had set up Crockett to be jailed back in Los Angeles. A lot to absorb, including the supernatural aspects of a perfectly-possessed cardinal.

But Crockett was doing an amazing job of hiding whatever emotion and confusion the man felt at this point, playing it this way from leaving the hotel meeting with Leakey, both pretending that they weren't being shadowed by men from the Swiss Guard.

Maybe, O'Hare thought, Crockett was one of those rare soldiers, first thrown into combat, who could act and think clearly as shells began bombardment. Or maybe he was so shell-shocked he was incapable of feeling or showing fear.

"Feel good about yourself?" Crockett finally said. "You took your vows so you could be part of death threats and all of the rest of this?"

"Don't feel good at all," O'Hare said. "This is bigger than me. I don't have a choice."

"Lots of Nazis said that too." Crockett suddenly flared with the anger he must have obviously been trying to contain all during their stroll. "It's one thing to threaten me, but Mickey? He's just a kid. Why should you care though. I guess the age of the victims didn't matter to the guards at Auschwitz either. Remember that little thing the Catholic church ignored a while back?"

"I understand why you are lashing out at me," O'Hare said evenly.

"No. You have no understanding at all. I've been framed for pedophilia, kidnapped, hung from a rope believing I would die, taken halfway across the world, abandoned in a catacombs and just listened to a man calmly tell me that my son is in danger at any time in the future. And that's only part of it."

Crockett leaned forward. "My single biggest priority is to be the best father I can be to my one remaining child. Nothing, I repeat, nothing is more important to me than that."

He didn't stop speaking as a middle-aged waiter set down the tiny cups and large pastries between them.

"There was a time once, on the water, when I had a choice between paddling to safety or going back for someone who'd been attacked by a shark. Later, when I thought about why I'd gone back it was because I didn't want to live with myself knowing I'd been a coward. I don't see it any differently now. Part of being a great father is being a man the son can respect, but he's not going to be able to respect me if I can't respect myself. Think that's going to happen if I let myself be bullied into silence? If I swim to safety? This was a cardinal. Into Satanism. Who'd abused kids, probably for decades. Burying this is unthinkable."

"Mr. Grey—"

"You shut your mouth and listen. I haven't heard anything from you about what's going to happen to Dr. Mackenzie and Jaimie. You've arranged an apparent suicide to take care of a cardinal. How do I know you won't take care of them like the pawns they were to you when—"

"I did not arrange Saxon's death. It was done by—"

"I said shut your mouth. Are there any real guarantees of Jaimie's safety?"

Crockett was speaking so vehemently that one of the Swiss Guard escorts started to drift toward them.

O'Hare waved away the Swiss Guard as he answered Crockett's question. "She is of great value to the church."

"Listen to yourself. I didn't hear you say she's a scared and lonely twelve-year old-girl. Or that it's unthinkable that she would be taken care of with the same discretion of a convenient suicide."

"Mr. Grey—"

"Priest or not, I swear, O'Hare, I will punch you in the mouth if you interrupt again. Here's what I've decided. I'm promising right now that you don't need to use Mickey as a threat over me in the future, because I'm not waiting that long. When I arrive in Los Angeles—or even before if your Swiss Guard goons let me find a phone booth—I'm taking my story to the *L.A.*

Times. Reporters there know how to dig deep. They'll find something, probably find plenty. I'm making you this promise right now because you can decide before I get on the plane whether I need to be pushed off a balcony or whatever method you and your Entity buddies decide is the right action to demonstrate that Jesus loves all of us. But don't think it will end there. There's a computer geek back in Santa Monica who will have plenty of questions if I don't make it back. And you can bet that killing him won't end it, because he'll have squirreled away all he knows as backup and someone else will end up taking over and asking questions. And other people are going to wonder about Jaimie and Mackenzie, and in the end, even if I'm dead, my son will eventually know I was unjustly accused and died trying to clear myself and expose something really wrong and evil. Attempting to cover this up is going to be a nuclear bomb that you'll wish you never detonated."

O'Hare pushed his chair away from the table, deciding he wanted to be out of Crockett's reach in case speaking again would be considered an interruption.

"Finished?" O'Hare said mildly. "Because I have no intention of interrupting if you are not. I really don't want you to punch me in the mouth."

Crockett took a deep breath. He looked spent. "Not much more I want to say to you."

"Wait here then," O'Hare said. "I need to make a phone call."

O'Hare returned ten minutes later and sat. He sipped the espresso, which Crockett knew had to be cold and becoming acidic.

He spoke to Crockett without any preamble. "It has been decided that I can make you an offer of sorts."

"I thought I was pretty clear about not accepting payment for silence."

Crockett's rush of anger had washed away, but he was resolute. If they killed him, Mickey would be safe.

"This offer does not involve compensation," O'Hare said. "Instead, you will learn the truth. All of it. Then you judge for yourself if silence is the better or worse of your choices."

Crockett gave it some thought, wondering what deception this offer might involve. How much worse could it be than a Satanist cardinal, killed before he could become pope?

"Sounds too simple," Crockett said.

"It's not," O'Hare said. "There are things no man should bear the burden of knowing. My advice is to decide you are better off trusting that the matter needs to be buried."

"You know my response to that."

"Then there is only one thing I need from you before we continue. The name of Jaimie's real mother."

"I've learned you guys don't play nice. There's nothing to stop you from pushing me off a balcony once I tell you."

"We can go in circles all day," O'Hare said. "There's nothing to stop you from lying to me about the name. You're all the way in. Or you're not."

"Start then, by telling me why it's so important."

"Satanic ceremonies have taken place within the Vatican. They must be stopped from happening again."

"Not just Saxon?" Crockett said.

"You're all the way in. Or you're not. Tell me the mother's name, and you'll get the truth."

"You'll never convince me that demons exist." But that was a lie. Crockett no longer had that certainty.

O'Hare took a bite of his pastry, and cleared his mouth before speaking again. "If, as you strongly feel, demons don't exist, it doesn't make any difference to how Jaimie sees the world with this heightened sensitivity to electro-magnetism. Poor child. Imagine her life if it had never been explained to her. Feeling that Evil was hunting her, as she describes it, whenever she's around mentally disturbed people. It's very likely that sooner or later, it would literally drive her crazy. Think she's the only person to have this genetic anomaly?"

"You didn't discover this through by Mackenzie's genealogy research. You were tracing a family tree that didn't belong to Jaimie's biological mother. "

"A fact of which I'm keenly aware," O'Hare said. "You're holding the knowledge of her real mother as leverage, and it's something I desperately need. She's the proof I need to take to the College of Cardinals before the next pope is elected. Her family tree will confirm it."

"Why do you need that proof? Saxon is gone."

"Last chance," O'Hare said. "We can leave this table and go back to the villa with your promise that Saxon's death will always been seen as a suicide. Or you can tell me who Jaimie's mother was, and follow me to the Vatican archives and learn about the canary list. Because the truth starts there."

Chapter Seventy-One

I t wasn't until he saw the metal shelving and ponderous brown spines of bindings with handwritten markings, that Crockett fully comprehended the vastness of the Secret Vatican Archives.

The aisles of the shelving were barely wide enough for two people, and seemed to stretch for a hundred yards in front of him. Crossway aisles intersected every two steps. Six high, the stacks of ancient documents, packed in those equally ancient bindings.

"Unreal," Crockett said to O'Hare. He reached and pressed the palm of his right hand against the cool metal of the shelf nearest him. Yeah, it was real.

O'Hare needed both hands to pull a book off the shelf beside Crockett. It was twice the thickness of a New York City phone book.

"Papal correspondence, seventeen ninety two," O'Hare said, letting Crockett heft the volume. "Interested in a year's worth of light reading?"

Crockett handed it back. The question didn't need any other answer than that.

The hush of the archives and the overwhelming amount of documents and the sense of history of being inside the heart of the Vatican filled Crocket with reverence, a sensation he didn't feel often. It was like the centuries pressed upon him, and he finally understood how fleeting a man's life was.

There were 35,000 volumes of cataloguing, with material dating from the eight century. Hearing this from O'Hare as they'd first entered the archives, Crockett thought O'Hare had made a mistake and meant 35,000 volumes. Now he understood. *Thirty-five thousand volumes of just the cataloguing.*

"I'm told this gallery holds over thirteen thousand linear yards of documents," O'Hare said. "Best estimate so far is that the Vatican Secret Archives total fifty-two miles of shelving."

"Easy to keep a secret hidden in here," Crockett said.

"Ah," O'Hare said. "That comment alone shows the difficulty a layman like you would have in searching for answers in here. That word, secret, in the title is not meant in the modern sense. Instead, it refers to the fact that these archives are the Pope's own, not belonging to the Curia."

"Curia?"

"The Curia is the central governing body of the entire Catholic church. Here, all of this belongs to the Pope. Documents in Arabic, Greek, Hebrew, Latin, Italian, French. You get the picture."

"The vastness seems almost supernatural," Crockett said. He pressed his palm against the shelving again.

"In a sense, I would argue it is," O'Hare said. "Writing sets us apart for every other creature on earth, a gift given to us by the creator. What you see is time frozen, centuries of knowledge, of correspondence, state papers and papal account books. We have the privilege of being able to dip in and out of time, just as does our Creator."

"You succeeded in impressing me with the Archives, as you promised," Crockett said. "What does this have to do with Saxon?"

"We will join Jaimie in an hour, when she is scheduled to meet with another cardinal. Until then, we become tourists, wandering St. Peter's Square. There I can speak to you freely about what was found down one of these endless aisles."

With the immense columns of the Basilica behind them, O'Hare began his explanation. Their shadows fell in front of them as they walked.

"It reached me by accident," O'Hare said. "A researcher stumbled across it in the archives, and because it dealt with demons and exorcisms, he thought it was curious enough to bring it to me. I immediately dismissed it as medieval quaintness to the researcher, and thus effectively eliminated the danger of any public attention to it. But over the last few years, I did my own research and found more and more within the archives to support this. But there's a metaphor involved here. Canaries in a coal mine."

"Early warning system."

"Exactly," O'Hare said. "Canaries are far more fragile than humans. In the old coal mines, they would die before humans did, giving warning to coal miners. The miners knew to stay away until the air is clear. Only here, we need warning about the perfectly-possessed, the infiltrating of the Vatican."

O'Hare held up a forefinger, lecturing in a classic sense. "However, calling it the canary list is an anachronism. The list was in existence long before the coal mines of the Industrial age. As the first chief exorcist in centuries to rediscover the list, I gave it the name that I believe is so apt."

"I can see how something could be lost for centuries in those archives."

"Actually not lost, but deliberately erased. Until it disappeared, the canary list guided exorcists who helped guard the Holy See against demonic infiltration. Men in my position would cultivate relationships with bishops to ensure that girls like Jaimie would enter convents, and then arrange for the sisters to be transferred to Rome. The reasons would be kept confidential—the bishops themselves would not even know. It was crucial that the list remain unknown, so that candidates for cardinals would be screened for demon possession, without their knowledge. Simple enough to bring one of the sisters into his presence and gage the reaction. Candidates for cardinal who were discovered to be perfectly possessed would be publicly diagnosed as having any one of many different maladies, and be classified as not suitable for appointment."

"But it only proves what I would argue," Crockett answered. "That demons are simply a superstition from the middles ages. Something like this from the fifteenth century is a natural extension of that."

"Pope Leo X, from 1513-1521. Pope Clement VII, 1523-1524. Are you aware of the nature of their papacies?"

"If you needed to explain to me what the Curia was, you already know the answer."

"Evil men. Literally. If you go through a documented description of their behavior as popes, not a difficult conclusion that each man was perfectly possessed. Under Leo X, even according to the Catholic encylcopedia which certainly does not try to cast the popes in a bad light, Christianity assumed a pagan character. He died too quickly to receive last rites. Make of that what you will."

"Superstition," Crockett said.

"Or not. It was shortly after Leo X began his papacy that the canary list disappeared. All my research shows that Leo X was responsible, that he wanted the canary list destroyed and all references to it obliterated, so that future generations would never know it existed. Only the vastness of the archives protected the vestiges that came to my attention. I've discovered six families trees with women who were on this list. Jaimie's family will be seven.

If Leo X had had his way, Jaimie would never have been born. He wanted all descendants of women on the canary list destroyed. When he took possession of the list, the Holy Inquisition also began targeting inquisitions to hunt down the women of the families on this list, essentially in effort to wipe this genetic anomaly from human existence, lumping these women in with other so-called witches who also died at the hands of torture."

"You have the other six families. Why Jaimie?"

"The papal election is going to be within days. I don't have time to get another canary but her. And she's the one who can convince the College of Cardinals of the danger they face.

Chapter Seventy-Two

S tupid dogs, Nathan thought as he lifted a bag of groceries from the trunk of his Taurus. Not much good asleep. Maybe he'd have to replace them.

He sure wasn't going to go over and kick them awake. They'd grown more and more vicious over time, so bad that Nathan stayed out of range and just threw them their food. Nathan attributed the viciousness to Abez, who regularly liked to walk up to the dogs and taunt them, something that provided Nathan with a degree of entertainment.

His mind turned to cooking.

Oil-poached swordfish, he'd decided, with white corn, guanciale and chive oil. Nanna would like that. He was happy that the cut on Nanna's arm was healing so quickly. She had a good appetite, and was very appreciative of Nathan's culinary skills.

Abez, not so much.

Abez was still in the back seat. Sulking.

Things had changed a lot since Nathan had refused to kill the old woman. Abez didn't quarrel so much, but remained an ominous negative presence. Even when Nathan had removed the chains on the old woman—except for one ankle—to let her move more, Abez hadn't only given a token protest.

Too bad for Abez, Nathan smirked. It probably was because of Nanna's angel Gabriel, that Abez didn't push Nathan around so much anymore.

Nathan turned away from the trunk, and there was some guy in front of him. Taller, almost Hispanic-looking, with a mullet. He wore a wife-beater tee shirt, and his arms and shoulders were blue with tattoos.

The man was holding out what looked like a computer hard drive in one hand, and cash and a baggie with weed in the other. A big baggie with weed.

"Peddle it somewhere else," Nathan said.

Not speaking a word, the man tossed the hard drive and cash and the baggie in Nathan's open trunk.

"Wrong guy to mess with," Nathan began, but shut his mouth when the mullatino guy reached behind his back and pulled out a pistol that he must have had tucked in his belt.

Nathan struggled with a stupid decision, thinking that if he dropped the bag of groceries to make a defensive move, it would probably break the bottles of chive oil and olive oil, and spoil the taste of an excellent cut of swordfish.

He didn't struggle with that stupid decision for long.

Mullatino guy pulled the trigger twice, and the shock wave of pain knocked Nathan into the Taurus. He fell, twisting onto his back with the precious swordfish cradled in his arms.

It didn't matter. The first bullet had smashed the bottle of olive oil.

Didn't matter, the second bullet tore through Nathan's lung, narrowly missing his heart.

In seconds, Nathan was unconscious, groceries spilled out from the bag and his limp arms. He didn't hear the man close the trunk. He didn't hear the man call 911 from a cell phone.

He didn't hear Nanna thanking the police when they helped her out of the trailer within minutes of their arrival.

And he certainly didn't hear those same cops going through his trunk, concluding that it must have been a drug deal gone back and suggesting that maybe someone in forensics needed to look at the hard drive.

Chapter Seventy-Three

D eep inside Vatican City, Crockett looked across a large, bare desk at one of the two remaining men favored to be the next pope, Cardinal Secretary of State Leonardo Vivaldo. Getting there had involved moving through three layers of security, each checkpoint manned by the ubiquitous Swiss Guard.

O'Hare's small briefcase had gone through screening without incidence, and he held it on his lap, sitting on a chair beside Crockett.

Physically, Crockett was feeling less jet lag and more himself every passing hour, even recovered from the Taser shot. Physically, it took no effort to sit in this office with O'Hare and Vivaldo.

Mentally, it felt like he he'd been plunked behind a steering wheel in the middle of a Formula One race, able only to react to what he saw directly in front of him. O'Hare had convinced Crockett that a skeptic like him, able to testify to the events of the previous days, would have a better chance of making their case than O'Hare alone, who would be perceived as having a previous bias.

So here Crockett was, in that metaphorical race car, sliding through another turn, everything at the sides blurred.

Crockett focused on Vivaldo, who was heavy-set, with jowls the hue and texture of cherries left too long in the sun. Bulldog in appearance, and, as O'Hare had already described to Crockett, Vivaldo was a bulldog in tenacity, personality, and social niceties. O'Hare said that Vivaldo's theology favored the Old Testament God—leaning toward judgment and harsh righteousness, as opposed to the Son who was the foundation of the New Testament.

"In five minutes, at your previous insistence, I am to meet with Cardinal Ricci and the girl," Vivaldo said. "If this doesn't go well, Father O'Hare, you've cost yourself."

"Cardinal Vivaldo," O'Hare said, "I'm well aware of the machinations of the Vatican, and equally aware of your standing in the Sacred College of Cardinals. Yet I'm far less concerned about the politics of my career than I am about the Holy Catholic Church. It should tell you something about the seriousness of this situation that certain men have agreed to call in favors to ensure you would meet me first, then the girl and Cardinal Ricci."

"Nothing was said about another observer."

"His name is Crockett Grey. He was there in the catacombs last night when Saxon tried to kill the girl."

Vivaldo examined Crockett owlishly.

"All the more reason," Vivaldo concluded, "that he does not remain here. Saxon was clearly insane. Perhaps an autopsy will show a tumor or sorts, affecting his sense of reality. It would do his memory—and the Vatican—an extreme disservice to air any of Saxon's beliefs to the world."

"We have tried to unsuccessfully convince Mr. Grey of the same thing," O'Hare said. "But because he is determined to disagree, it has come down to a three choices. He sees and hears everything in our discussion with the girl. Or he tries to take the real reason behind Cardinal Saxon's death to the public. Or we have to kill him to silence him. If you send him out now, you are sending him to his death."

Vivaldo's eyes bulged briefly. "I will not be bullied, Father."

O'Hare said. "Letting you choose of the three is not bullying. I believe you are aware enough of the Saxon situation to understand what's at stake."

"Alright then," Vivaldo said. "Start. Why do I need to see the girl?"

O'Hare answered by pulling a file folder from the briefcase and handing it across the desk to Vivaldo.

Vivaldo pulled a pair of reading glasses out of a drawer and unfolded them, put them on his face and glanced at the top paper.

Vivaldo took a closer look. "*Serinus canaria?*"

"Notes on particular family trees whose women over the centuries have served exorcists in the Holy See," O'Hare said. "I've called it the canary list. If you are going to be the next Pope, you'll need to know its contents. "

Crockett knew the contents and waited for Vivaldo's reaction. When he finished reading, he lifted his head and reacted with a single word.

"Ridiculous." It came out as a guttural snort.

O'Hare started to protest, but Vivaldo cut him off.

"You are suggesting that in the Sacred College of Cardinals there is a secret ring of men who are possessed by demons. That these men are Satan worshippers, perfectly possessed, in harmony with their demons. And that they will try to ensure that the next papal enclave results in one of them raised to the Papacy. That there is danger that the next pope will be demon possessed? And you suggest that a twelve-year-old girl with the genetic ability to detect electro-magnetism is needed as some sort of divination whether cardinals are demon-possessed?"

Whether or not a spiritual force existed that Crockett needed to accept as reality, he recognized a chilling elegance to electing a new pope who was perfectly possessed, giving evil a chokehold at the top of the power circle. A power circle in an institution with far too high a percentage of men who had abused children with impunity for decades. Crockett remembered what

Mackenzie had told him. Demons look for a crack in the psyche, often finding it in the abused, who then in turn grew to adults who abused others. A
perfect circle. But perfectly possessed? A pope? *The future pope?*

"Ridiculous," Vivaldo said again, growing visibly anger. "This strains
any sort of credulity whatsoever. Do you have any idea of how the world
would mock the Vatican if the office of the Holy See was seen to depend on
the whims and vagaries of a girl like this?"

"Saxon is not the only one. I have no intention of making it something
the world gains knowledge of."

Vivaldo was visibly angry. "I understand that from your point of view,
demons are a reality. You are known as the Chief Exorcist of the Vatican,
and you have a bias toward seeing the devil in as many places as possible. Yet
you are well aware that His Holiness, and the pope before him, both give no
emphasis to their existence. In the modern church, demons are a relic. You
are also aware that from my point of view, the only reason that exorcism is
publicly supported is because of the delicacies of denying demonic existence
in light of ancient church teachings, and the liturgies of exorcism that have
been in place for centuries."

"Tell me," O'Hare said calmly but forcefully. "Can you think of anything that would motivate me to come forward in private like this, knowing
how it might sound to you, someone who has publicly scoffed at the notion
of the existence of demons? What do I have to gain?"

"I'm not a fool," Vivaldo said. "It's not you who might gain, but someone else. An ambitious cardinal, hoping that I'd react in such a way as to cast
doubts on my suitability as candidate for the papacy. I would be a laughing
stock to support you regarding this matter in any way. It wouldn't surprise
me if this is a plot that Ricci devised to remove a legitimate rival from the
upcoming enclave. Believe me, the moment you step out of this office, you
may consider your future within the church effectively ended."

"Before you send us out," O'Hare said. He pulled a single sheet out of his briefcase. "I suggest you read this too."

"More nonsense about demons?" Vivaldo snorted.

"No," O'Hare said. "A letter from Cardinal Ricci, addressed to you in your official capacity as cardinal secretary of state, requesting that the Sacred College of Cardinals remove him from consideration as a candidate for the Papacy because of recently uncovered health issues. Fictional health issues. Meet with Cardinal Ricci and the American girl and her doctor, and the letter is yours to submit to the College, effectively removing Ricci as your rival."

A long silence blanketed the room as each man tried to judge the other.

Finally, Vivaldo spoke. "I will meet with them."

Chapter Seventy-Four

Holding Dr. Mackenzie's hand, Jaimie stepped into Vivaldo's office. They were followed by Cardinal Ricci. Jamie wore a neat yellow dress, and because of it, appeared like the girl she would have been if that car accident had not killed the upper middle-class parents who had believed she was their baby. She looked like an innocent girl, wrapped up in love and unaware of the evils of the world.

Crockett wished that Jaimie did have that innocence, but he knew nothing would bring it back.

Mackenzie's appearance too, was softer. Perhaps because she wore a light blue sweater that contrasted with black designer slacks, a sign that she'd gone shopping for upscale Italian clothing.

"Eminence," O'Hare said. "I do have an embarrassing request."

From his briefcase, O'Hare pulled out a hand-held security wand, like the ones used at airports for screening.

It beeped several times as he powered it.

"Security screening? How far to you expect to push me?"

"It's part of the process," O'Hare said. "The quickest explanation I can give you is that any type of magnet alters what Jaimie can sense."

"What does that have to do with anything?"

"I need to be assured you don't have a magnet in your possession."

"Of course I don't have a magnet on me!" Vivaldo said. "What is going on?"

"We need to ensure you are not one of the perfectly possessed," O'Hare said.

Vivaldo glared at Ricci. "You seriously expect me to dignify this? I see through this sham. You'll leak word that I allowed myself to be tested for demon possession. That alone will ensure all my credibility in the College of Cardinals is destroyed. You become the next pope."

"You have my letter of resignation," Ricci said." Our rivalry is secondary to what's at stake. I'd rather see you with St. Peter's ring, if that's what it's going to take to make sure the Holy See is protected:"

"Noble," Vivaldo said, with just enough ambiguity to make it impossible to decide if he was being sarcastic.

Vivaldo pursed his lips in silent frustration, but rose slowly and stepped out from behind his desk. He spread his arms as O'Hare, waved the wand around him. It beeped several times, but only for his rings and watch.

"Thank you, Eminence," O'Hare said.

"Now what," Vivaldo snapped. "The girl touches me? Walks around and does incantations?"

"We're finished," O'Hare said. "At least with Jaimie."

Vivaldo frowned. "Finished?"

"Trust me," O'Hare said. "If you were among those who worship our enemy, you would have already reacted to her presence. And, given you have no magnet and she wasn't wearing hers, she would have known of the demon's presence the instant she walked through the doorway."

O'Hare gave a placating smile. "Even the worst of your own critics—and of course, one would be hard pressed to find a single one—would find nothing of your actions in the last few minutes to criticize during a Papal enclave. You allowed a girl to step into your office, and you gave her a blessing. For Eminence, despite her unusual ability and despite her importance to the church, she is a girl, a child of God."

"I should not have forgotten," Vivaldo said. "Child, step forward and let me pray over you."

Jaimie gave him a sweet smile, and knelt in front of the man.

Crockett marveled that such a ferocious presence as Vivaldo could be transformed into a beautiful benevolence as he placed a palm on Jaimie's head. Like God had allowed his presence into the room, and Crockett felt a peace of his own.

When Vivaldo finished his quiet prayer, he looked at Ricci. "I have done enough?"

"Perhaps we should have a degree of privacy again," Ricci answered. "Dr. Mackenzie will take the girl. If you need confirmation on any of Dr. Mackenzie's findings, she'll come back, but in the meantime we've arranged for them to take a private tour of the Sistine Chapel. Father O'Hare and Mr. Grey will remain. "

"I do not take kindly to orders."

"Please," Ricci said. "It is a request. Remember that I have essentially submitted myself to you by withdrawing from any consideration for the papacy."

Dr. Mackenzie smiled at Crockett from across the room. He enjoyed the lift it gave him.

After Mackenzie and Jaimie left, all softness left Vivaldo's square face. "Ricci, if you honor your promise to leave me this letter, you've given up the Papacy for your ridiculous belief in the existence of demons."

"No," Ricci said, "there's more. We need to ensure every the girl meets with every cardinal."

"At the risk of being repetitive, if I proposed this become a condition of entering the conclave before a papal election, I would be put in a straitjacket."

O'Hare was prepared for the cardinal's objection. "In the days after the pope's death and before the enclave, between you and I, we will ensure that

every cardinal visits either of us. In addition to current security, there will be
new security measures in place that apply to everybody, like airport screening. No one will question a security wand in the hand of a Swiss Guard. We
will have Jaimie in our offices, as if she is seeking a blessing. This way, before
the election, we will discover who serves God and who serves Satan. We will
never have to fear the election of a pope who is possessed by the Evil One."

"Cardinal Ricci," Vivaldo said. "Your fears are invalid."

"The Holy See must be cleansed. Surely the letter on your desk shows
you how much I believe this to be true."

"Superstition," Vivaldo repeated. "I will not be tarred with it."

O'Hare said, "The women in the families belonging to the canary list
are almost extinct. Jaimie is close to the last of the canaries. Quite by accident, Mr. Grey established that for us, and it took me less than fifteen
minutes in the archives to link Jaimie's family tree to this ancient list. As Mr.
Grey will testify, he is a skeptic. I would argue that this too, is evidence that
must be considered seriously, for he has no motive for trying to convince
you what I'm trying to convince you, which is that we must begin again
the ancient tradition of screening prospective cardinals for demons. And
we must maintain the secrecy of the list. As future pope, you will have the
power to do both."

Cardinal Ricci leaned forward and addressed Vivaldo with urgency.
"You may not believe that demons exist or that for centuries they have tried
to infiltrate the church, but to ignore the possibility puts the fate of this
entire church at risk. My personal ambitions pale in comparison to that. I
withdraw, not asking you to believe, but to simply act as if you believe. All
I'm asking is that you ensure that each cardinal passes the test, so that in the
future, the church is not controlled by a man who worships Satan."

"I refuse to gain a papacy through deception," Vivaldo said. "You, of all people, know me better than that. Acting as if I believe in demons simply to ensure your resignation is not something I can do, no matter how important you believe it is."

Ricci spoke, almost sadly. "This pope, before his election to the Papacy, was head of the Congregation for the Doctrine of Faith. As you know, his biggest public controversy is his responsibility over several decades in that position for the alleged cover-up of child abuse at the hands of priests."

"Let us stress the word *alleged*," Vivaldo said.

"Allegations with enough credibility to be splashed across the pages of every major news media source in the world," Ricci said. "My brother, there is one last thing you need to see."

Chapter Seventy-Five

The final item in O'Hare's briefcase was a laptop pulled from a leather sleeve. He addressed Crockett. "Do you recall our conversation in the Vatican archives when I warned you there was no turning back?"

Crockett nodded.

O'Hare touched the keyboard and the laptop screen came to life. The four men stood at the edge of the desk and looked down to see the pope, comatose on a hospital bed. Jaimie stood near the man, his famous features marred by the clear plastic tubes running from his nostrils and IV tubes ran from his wrist, but the big ring was clearly identifiable.

"She's going to put her bracelet into a bag lined with lead," O'Hare said. "The type of material that shields X-ray machines. Watch."

Ricci added, "Until I saw this footage, I wasn't fully convinced that I needed to offer you my letter, Vivaldo. I beg you to stop it from happening again."

"Now?" Jamie asked, facing the camera. The hum of medical equipment filled the background.

"Now." It was O'Hare's voice. He held the camera steady, the screen shot tight on her face, her freckles obvious.

"I've never been so scared in my life," Jaimie said.

"God is with us. Take off your bracelet," O'Hare said. "Drop it into the bag."

Jaimie did as directed, and immediately her face showed terror. "All alone. Dark. Dark. With cold wind blowing across me. I felt so tiny. And like hunters are coming for me in the darkness."

"It's okay," O'Hare said. "We are protected by Christ."

Howling suddenly filled the camera's audio sensors. The picture frame wobbled and flickered Jaimie, and then O'Hare moved the focus on the comatose pope. The face had gone from the plastic look of the dead to a rictus of pain and rage.

"Padre nostro," O'Hare said. *"Che sei nei cieli, sia santifico il tuo nome."*

The man in the bed, the man with the most famous face in the world, the man who had been in a coma for weeks, opened his eyelids and revealed intense black dots for pupils, against the whites of his eyes.

"Who dares interfere with The Prince," the man croaked from the hospital bed.

"Padre nostro, che sei nei cieli, sia santifico il tuo nome." O'Hare moved forward, and from a small round container, sprinkled water on the man in the bed.

With Jaimie crouched and huddled, the man arched his back and began to scream as if liquid fire was burning through his hospital gown.

"Dear, dear Lord," Vivaldo trembled,, all the color drained from his face. "The pope. It's already happened."

Chapter Seventy-Six

I t's almost finished, Jaimie," Father O'Hare said, sitting down beside Jaimie in the courtyard. "Two days more is all we need."

"Sure," she said, putting down her e-book reader.

She liked it in the villa. Father O'Hare and Dr. Mackenzie stayed with her the whole time, leaving no chance for Evil to hunt her here. It was easy, spending hours in the courtyard, reading books. Dr. Mackenzie had presented her with the e-book reader and showed Jaimie how to load up on plenty of new titles.

"We'll need to take you into Rome during the day. Back to Vatican City. You know, to see if there are others."

"Sure," Jaimie repeated.

She felt stronger, more sure of herself. There was an explanation for the darkness that had always plagued her and she knew she wasn't crazy. She also knew that it was possible to defeat Evil, so she wasn't as scared of it hunting her anymore.

Father O'Hare said. "In California, they found the guy who started your house on fire Nobody thinks anymore that you did it."

"What about Mr. G?" she asked. "Will it be okay for him?"

"The police know that same man who started the fire tried to make it look like Mr. G had some secrets too. Mr. G is clear and good to go home."

"Got my horse yet?" Jaimie asked.

"Still working on it," Father O'Hare said.

"Not a big deal," Jaimie said. "The place I'm planning on spending a lot of time at doesn't have much room for a horse. At Nanna's house."

Mackenzie sat with Crockett in the elegant garden behind the Pope's residence, enjoying the afternoon sunshine, songbirds hidden among the flowering bushes. It was surreal, considering what they had survived together.

"I want to ask you a difficult question," Crockett said."

"Then ask."

He stared at the garden wall. Miles away, down in the valley of the Tiber, Rome bustled, but here time was frozen. "You told me that you counseled a patient who'd been abused in a Satanic ritual as a child in a foster home. Lawsuits, all that. You said you were trying to find Saxon to stop him. You were that little girl, weren't you?"

All the images came back to her. The shaking little boy, his descriptions of the rituals, her attempt to defend him, and then her own horrors during the abuse that followed later.

Hales ate in. Hales ate in.

"Yes, it was me." She nodded slowly.

"Saxon's dead. Is that enough for you?"

"What do you mean?" she asked.

"He's dead and no one knows what he was guilty of. Do you need to see more justice than that?"

"Like more horrible headlines about the Vatican?" She shook her head. "No. It's not like anyone in the church tried to hide was he was doing. Only what he did. They stopped him. And they're tracking down others like him. Even though there are some things you never get past… all along I just wanted to make sure it didn't happen to other little girls."

She saw him flinch, as if she'd physically jabbed him, and she caught the hurt, trapped animal look in his eyes. Even when his shoulders began to shake, she couldn't comprehend that he was beginning to weep, until the sobs became audible.

It took him a while to compose himself. The entire time, Mackenzie held both his hands in hers, but didn't say anything.

Some things you never get past.

Tears were still streaming down his cheeks, but he managed to speak clearly.

"I want to tell you something. I haven't told anyone else. Not even Julie, because it hurts too much. The last words that Ashley said to me were, "Daddy, it's okay. I get to go to heaven. I'll see you there. Right, Daddy?"

She didn't remove her hands from his.

"I lied to her," Crockett said. "I told her yes, that Daddy will see her in heaven. That's what a daddy's supposed to say when his little girl is slipping away."

Some things you never get past.

"Where I'm going with this," Crockett said, "is that I need to thank you. For the first time, I'm thinking that maybe I didn't lie to my little girl. It's hard not to believe in demons at this point. It gets me thinking about what you said. If demons exist, it also means there is God. Maybe dying is not the end of it. Maybe I'll get to see my little girl again."

Chapter Seventy-Seven

F ather O'Hare ducked his head as he stepped through the doorway
of the private jet. He saw Crockett on a couch, holding a copy of
USA Today.

Crockett glanced at his watch.

"Hard habit to break," O'Hare said. "Get used to flying commercial,
you think everything is on a schedule. I just need five minutes with you."

There was another couch at the back of the jet. No scrimping here.

O'Hare sat, and then pointed at Crockett's newspaper. "Enjoying the
headline?"

The pope's death dominated the front page, but the particular headline
that O'Hare referred to was the one about Cardinal Ricci's announcement
that health reasons precluded him from any consideration of the papacy.

"I don't know what you're talking about," Crockett said. "I'm just an
American tourist. A free man. Happy to go home and see my kid and enjoy
my summer. Nothing more, nothing less."

"Excellent. Excellent." O'Hare really hoped this was true. Crockett had
made his decision to keep silent. But O'Hare's wasn't certain himself if Entity had intended to honor the offer, or if the organization was running a
bluff, with the intent to remove Crockett if he had decided to go the *L.A.
Times.* Either way, O'Hare wanted to add some insurance.

"I'm here," O'Hare gave a significant pause, "because I owe you the truth. I want to set your mind at ease about demons. In that video, Jaimie was not with the pope."

Crockett frowned, an expression of total bewilderment that O'Hare found encouraging

"It wasn't difficult to set up the scene. A hospital room, and actor made up to look like the pope. Phenomenal, actually, the latex mask. Made from an impression of the face of the real pope. It was taken, of course, while the pope was in his coma. That exorcism was elaborately acted out. Think of it as a Hollywood scene, done in one take. Not difficult at all to accomplish."

Crockett's frown deepened.

"Perhaps, though, you should hear my story from the beginning," O'Hare said. "Which started, sadly enough, with a slow and gradual erosion of my own faith. It came to the point that I no longer wanted to be a priest. Exorcisms? As Vivaldo said, superstition. The rituals are merely placebos for those who want to blame their ills on a third party. The sad thing, Mr. Grey, is once you no longer embrace the faith—well, you still need a business. The only business I knew was Vatican business. Some men leave the cloth because they can no longer embrace celibacy. I don't have those needs. I'm content with the life of a man of the cloth, just not the beliefs of a man of the cloth. Are you with me so far?"

"Yes. No. This is a lot to track. All I wanted to do was sit and read the paper until I could watch Italy disappear below me."

"How best to secure a good position within the church? The answer was plain. Ensure that the new pope favored me. Six months ago, it was impossible to chose a winner. What helped was that first phone call from Dr. Madelyne Mackenzie, wondering if I, as Chief Exorcist, knew of anyone with the ability to detect demons. I'm glad I resisted my first temptation to dismiss her. As I learned more about her own background, I also learned about Cardinal Saxon. I brought what I knew not to Ricci first, but to Vivaldo, who was both disturbed and happy to have this information about one of his rivals. Disturbed, of course, to discover a cardinal like this among us, and disturbed at the possibility that this man—a Satanist in his deluded beliefs—might actually become pope. You can understand, Mr. Grey, how important it was to find a way to bury this problem completely. Vivaldo and I coldly planned a way to take advantage of Saxon's delusions. Dr. Mackenzie had given us the seeds of an idea. Indeed, what if a girl could detect demons? Thus began an elaborate con job that drew three people together. Saxon, Mackenzie and the girl. Vivaldo authorized Entity to do as I needed, including having Richard Leakey pretend to work with Saxon. You saw the results. It was important to get rid of Saxon, and we succeeded in that. Having a Satanist as the next pope could have destroyed the church."

"But—"

"Mr. Grey, that was the original intent, but it evolved. Yes, the primary purpose was to remove Saxon. But we—Vivaldo and I—saw that it this con job might also serve a secondary purpose. If we could make Saxon believe that there was a canary list, then perhaps too, we could convince Cardinal Ricci. Once we realized this, we first only intended to use it to discredit Ricci in the eyes of the Sacred Cardinal of Colleges. If Ricci sounded the alarm about a so-called list, Vivaldo would benefit greatly. But then we recognized the plan could actually go one step further, in convincing Ricci that the danger was so great, only his noble self-sacrifice would save the church from a demon-possessed pope."

"Hang on," Crockett said. "Just so I'm clear on this. You and Vivaldo were working together?"

"Masterful, wasn't it? You saw how Vivaldo pretended outrage, accusing Ricci of trying to make him look a fool by reacting to the danger of demons.

How could Ricci ever suspect that Vivaldo was the one setting up a game, using the threat of demons to convince Ricci to give up the papacy? The more skeptical Vivaldo appeared of demons, the more that Ricci would try to prove it. When all along, Vivaldo's goal was to utterly convince Ricci the danger was real. All of this has been carefully manipulated, and your role proved very helpful in disguising that it was simply a scam. A great con job, designed for only one person. Cardinal Vicar Eduardo Ricci."

"A con job."

"Think back, Mr. Grey. Every step was rigged. Hypnosis sessions with Jaimie to convince her that her own problems were demon problems. Forged documents planted all through the Vatican archives. When you became a accidental casualty, someone Saxon wanted out of the way, I began to work that to our advantage. Tell me… how much help did you get from our attorney, Amy Robinson, as you began to uncovered the genetic reports and genealogy searches? Wouldn't you say she pointed you in the right direction to uncover the so-called evidence that Ricci would end up believing was real? Didn't she point you to the hacker who uncovered this convenient information?"

O'Hare watched Crockett's face, seeing that Crockett's mind must be whirling, seeing the puzzle pieces all tossed into the air again. O'Hare wasn't going to give him much time to think.

"And finding someone like Dr. Mackenzie, easily swayed to misdiagnose a child like Jaimie?" O'Hare continued. "Poor children. Both of them, each unaware they were pawns in a complicated chess game."

"I'm trying to make sense of this," Crockett said.

"Then consider this. The expense and complication of running a scam like this is nothing compared to gaining the papacy. Ricci has no idea, of course, who I truly serve in these politics. Nor any idea of my reward. I will become Cardinal O'Hare within months of the election of Vivaldo as pope. What a wonderful retirement." O'Hare crossed his arms and smiled wryly. "I'll not end my days as a rum-soaked priest."

"Will Jaimie and Dr. Mackenzie ever find out?"

"I doubt they'd believe you if you told them what you've just learned from me."

"So Jaimie and Dr. Mackenzie were not part of this con job?"

"Never. For it to fool Ricci, they had to believe it as much as Ricci did."

"I won't keep secrets from Dr. Mackenzie. I'll tell her about this conversation."

"Will you? She's at peace now, believing she's conquered her demons. Saxon is dead. Do you want to take that away from her? Someday, she'll have a chance to publish a paper. It won't have details about the Vatican or the canary list, but it will link family trees with genetic sensitivity to electromagnetism and witchcraft. I think the paper will be quite believable, don't you?"

Crockett kept his stare fully on O'Hare, again his emotions obvious to O'Hare.

"Don't be too disappointed, Mr. Grey," O'Hare said. "Much less has been done by other men to gain much less. Getting the ring of the papacy is far greater than becoming American president. Vivaldo will be declared infallible. He has the job for the rest of his life, with a billion people in his power."

"When we were lost in the catacombs," Crockett said, "Jaimie used her sense of magnetism to find our way out."

O'Hare shook his head, smiling. "Lost? Hardly. While the apparent threat of our deaths helped convinced Ricci this was a serious situation, we were never in danger. The three of you were told we had been taken into an unexplored area, but I'd been there many, many times to prepare for this. In the dark, always. I knew where we were. I guided Jaimie with subtle pressure until she found the door."

"Jamie's mother's birth records? You had the wrong genealogy until I gave you her real mother's name."

O'Hare chuckled. "Mr. Grey, it was almost enough to restore my faith in the existence of God! A good con job becomes a great con job when there are a few difficulties for the conned to overcome. If, at first, Jaimie's genealogy had shown witches in her family tree, it would have been too perfect, too smooth, like someone had set it up. If you only understood how much work went into this. Almost from the beginning, Vivaldo and I were aware of the discrepancy in the hospital records. He and I agreed it would work better, at first, if the genealogy didn't fit the profile we wanted to prove. And how the report would ring perfectly true to Ricci if it was a later discovery showing how the genealogy fit. When it was you who exposed it for us, it was a wonderful bonus. Why else would I have let you be so involved in every moment of the last week? Once Ricci heard from you, not from me, about Jaimie's real family tree, all of his remaining doubts disappeared. I owe you a huge debt of gratitude."

"Do you?" Crockett glanced at the headlines again. "I'm not so sure."

"You can be sure."

Crockett didn't say anything for a while. O'Hare gave him time to stew.

"Father O'Hare," Crockett finally said. "You know I'm a skeptic by nature. So I'm wondering where the real lie lives. You're telling me this was a con job. But that might be the smartest way to stop me from ever suggesting, beyond Vatican walls, that the papacy was held for the last few decades by a demon-possessed man."

O'Hare laughed again. "It would make for a terrific best-seller. Dan Brown tried convincing the world that Jesus married and had children."

"Careful, Father," Crockett said. "Don't oversell this. We both know that given the decades of sexual abuse and systematic cover-up by the pope during his time with the Congregation for the Doctrine of Faith, that more than a few influential people might give the accusation serious consideration. It would be interesting if Dr. Mackenzie extended the scope of her paper to give scientific and historical credibility to all of this, backed up by documents from the Vatican Archives. After all, the genetics and genealogy convinced Ricci."

"She wants to publish, true," O'Hare said. "But Dr. Mackenzie wants to protect the church even more."

Crockett gave a grim smile. "Maybe that's your real motivation for visiting me this morning. Protecting the church. I'm one of the few who knows the truth behind the headlines. I've already told you I have no intention of ever speaking about this. Maybe you want more than my promise. If you can get me to believe that what I witnessed, revealing a demonic presence in the pope, was part of a Machiavellian con job, then you've succeeded. You've buried secrets about centuries of witchcraft in the Vatican and a long, lost canary list. In essence, presenting it to me as a scam would be an elegant way to hide the real truth behind your lie."

O'Hare stood. Although there was no hint of untidiness to his appearance, he dusted off his cassock.

"Come on, Mr. Grey," O'Hare said. "Surely you don't believe in demons."

Afterword

—❦—

"When one speaks of 'the smoke of Satan' in the holy
rooms, it is all true—including these latest stories of
violence and pedophilia... Cardinals who do not believe
in Jesus, and bishops who are linked to the Demon."
—THE VATICAN'S CHIEF EXORCIST, FATHER GABRIELE AMORTH
AUTHOR OF *MEMOIRS OF AN EXORCIST,*
AS QUOTED IN *THE LONDON TIMES*

"The prince of darkness has had and continues to have
his surrogates in the court of St. Peter in Rome."
— THE LATE JESUIT PRIEST MALACHI MARTIN
EXORCIST AND BEST-SELLING AUTHOR OF *HOSTAGE TO THE DEVIL,*
EX-SECRETARY OF CARDINAL AUGUSTINE BEA,
FORMER PROFESSOR, THE VATICAN'S PONTIFICAL BIBLICAL INSTITUTE